'As a detective, I very often deal with the bizarre. Sometimes involving murder. Always involving mystery. Deep down though, I'm a Pragmatist, bent on finding practical solutions to claims of perculiar activity.
Even when I fail, I think I come pretty damn close . . .

. . . I'll let you be the judge.'

Cameron Josey

Book 4

Holiday Horror

James William Davis
©

James William Davis

Holiday Horror ©
Written by James William Davis

Published by James William Davis
davisible@yahoo.com.au

Copyright 2021, James William Davis
International Standard Book Number
ISBN 978-0-646-84269-1
©

National Library of Australia Cataloguing-in Publication entry
Author: Davis, James W.

Holiday Horror/ James William Davis.

Draft: W Holiday Horror Draft -01 M-Word W.doc
Cover: 022 B4 Cover Version 8 Submit 200623

©

Cover Design and Layout by James William Davis.

In this fictional book, names, characters, businesses, organisations, places and
events are either the product of the author's imagination or are used
fictitiously. Any resemblance to actual persons, living or dead, events or
locales is entirely coincidental.

Born in 1944, James Davis first branched into writing during his time in the film and television industry. Story telling became a driving force in his working life, albeit with a camera or an editing device.

Now he likes to hone his craft using the written word—that essential step prior to all other forms of expression.

James William Davis

List of Books
by
James William Davis

THE IMMORTALITY CONNECTION

MIND SET

ZEROZONE

HOLIDAY HORROR

GHOST WRITER

OVERKILL

WITHOUT SOPHIE

See more at
davisible.com

Living in a small town west of Sydney, next door neighbours find themselves trapped on the holiday from hell.

When Detective Josey attempts to solve the mystery of what transpired at Arthur Sheridan's country cabin, he becomes a target himself, along with his family.

To save his wife and daughter from certain death, it becomes a fight against time, and a twist the detective never saw coming.

To avert the inevitable, Josey's success in finding them is in no way guaranteed; or even to consider snatching them from the hands of a Psychopath – close to achievable.

James William Davis

James William Davis

CHAPTER ONE
The Crime

Condobolin had never even heard of a crime like this one—

Now, it was theirs . . .

The story of what *really* happened in this tiny New South Wales town was born out of two affirmations from next-door neighbours. Long-time residents and well known to the entire community, Arthur Sheridan and Lester Perkins had lived side by side for over thirty years; and in that time neither man had ever been involved in any sort of crime - until now.

Sheridan, a motor mechanic, operated a small oily shop in his back yard; a long way from the house. If not for the small sign on the front fence, it would be impossible to appreciate his ramshackle shop even existed.

Whenever Arthur would wander out to the mail box in his overalls, neighbours often thought he seemed at complete odds with the pristine property; the gardens on the allotment were his wife's doing, and maintenance on the house was totally credited to contractors.

By any measure he was rough and ready, even on the odd occasion that he'd take his wife Arlene out for an evening meal at the local Chinese. His long dark hair was questionably as laden with shop soil as his oil clogged fingernails. It didn't bare thinking about.

People quietly considered he might take a little more care of himself, especially in the presence of his wife, who often turned heads. No one was prepared to criticise him to his face, because although he was short in stature, he was known to possess a very short temper, possibly because of it.

There were people who knew *exactly* what it was that made him the way he was, something apart from his being vertically challenged; something that brought the sudden outbursts to the surface.

His neighbour, Lester Perkins on the other hand, being the Sergeant of the local cop shop, always appeared calm and collected; well-dressed both on and off duty. His high profile status made him feel there was a need to project the image of a man in control; someone that always led by example. In contrast to his neat dress sense, he had all the earmarks of a weathered boxer. At a foot and a half above Arthur, he came close to filling most doorjambs with his powerful shoulders. If you had to guess which of these two men were in trouble with the law, you'd probably choose the mechanic, but you'd be wrong. For most people in the town, it was hard to believe their well respected sergeant was the one who was now under the spotlight from his own people at the station, who until now were a bunch of young rookies totally reliant on him for day to day guidance, but help was at hand, or was it?

Young Andrew Perkins entered the town's busy hotel, searching the faces of the patrons for the very man who might be able to save his brother. Although sitting with his back turned he wasn't hard to pick, he was the only person in the place sitting-alone. 'Detective Josey,' he announced as he walked up from behind.

Josey turned from his meal; he hadn't seen the kid since he was in school back in Sydney, around fifteen years ago, but he managed to recognise him quickly. 'Andy; hello.'

He was a tallish young man, surprisingly well dressed for dinner time in a country town. He looked a bit like his brother in the sense he was solidly built.

'This's a hit-and-run,' Andy assured him gesturing to the other seat at the small table, 'I don't want to interrupt your meal.'

'Please - sit,' Josey offered knowingly as Andrew took up the chair opposite; his impromptu arrival clearly deliberate. A few patrons were looking their way, evidently their interest aimed at Andy.

But Josey was getting looks too, out-of-towners stood out like sore thumbs. A few might imagine he was dressing down to fit in, but in fact Josey was dressed the way he always did; casual slacks, jeans, open neck shirt and on this occasion with a baseball cap perched on his knee.

'Your brother's in a bit of strife it seems,' he suggested eloquently.

Andrew briefly glared at a few of the rubbernecks, and came back onto Josey and spoke in a low voice. 'Have you been to see him?'

'Briefly; He was in a bit of a state; surprised I was in town but cottoned on to my being in Condobolin was no coincidence.'

A curious expression came to the young man's face. 'What'd he say?'

'Well, you know, we had a five minute chat prior to my booking into the motel; and you're right; he's crooked on you for calling me. But I wouldn't get too worried; he's in pretty unfamiliar territory at the moment.'

'So, you'll investigate?'

'Not as such; at this stage, I'm prepared to listen to his story.' Josey didn't want to burst Andy's bubble by suggesting it was too early to make promises, or admit help might not even be possible. 'How's he been holding up?'

He scoffed, 'he's been better.' Andrew slumped in his seat as the gravity of his brother's situation surfaced. 'Like you say, his world is falling apart.' He took another glaring glance at the gawking rubbernecks. 'Since this whole thing blew up, people have jumped on the muckraking wagon, a little too enthusiastically if you ask me.'

Josey guessed the kid was being ostracised along with his brother and recognised the anguish. 'You soon find out who your friends are when you're in trouble.'

'Aren't that the truth,' he mumbled dropping his eyes to the table.

'Andy, how much has he told you?'

'Not a lot, in truth I think he's deliberately shutting me out.'

Josey surmised the sergeant's obstinance toward his brother might be all about saving face, but asked, 'Do you know why?'

'I had to speak with his men to find out anything at all,' Andy grumbled; 'blokes my age - all good guys, but fairly tight lipped. But they agree he's been falsely accused; *attempted murder* is a total stretch. It's the Police District Office in Orange that's considering the charge, not the local boys.'

'*Considering?*'

'Yeah, they don't have sufficient evidence to actually charge him. If you were to ask them they'd say his lost his mind. I have no idea what that means; he won't talk to me. That's why I called you; I figured you might get it out of him.'

'You said his own coppers are on his side, weren't they able to fill you in?'

'They've been gagged by the District Office.'

Josey nodded glumly. 'Look, I'll see if I can organise for you to sit in on our chat, I'm guessing you wouldn't mind.'

Andrew lent across the table with his elbows spread. 'That would help me a lot – he'll listen to you; you guys go back a way.'

'That's true, but until today I hadn't laid eyes on your brother in years.'

Young Andy shuffled in his seat, conscious of all the looks he was getting. 'Um, look you're having your dinner; I'll just split and talk to you later.' He handed him a card.

'You're a Lawyer now,' Josey said reading; instantly understanding why the help of a private detective was so important. 'Are you intending to defend him?'

'If it comes to that; I'm hoping it won't.'

Josey thought defending one's own brother sounded like real pressure for a fresh young lawyer; *Dispassionate Council* is often impaired when emotion comes into the picture.

'Just holler and I'll be there, Mr Josey.'

'If we're to be working together you better start calling me *Cam*.'

He stood purposefully and offered a hand shake. His grip was strong, the type you get from a person who is immeasurably grateful. 'Thank you for doing this.'

'Not a problem, Andy; I'm glad you're giving me the chance to help.'

The worried young man left on a nod without making eye contact with any of the other patrons.

Josey's first port of call was to revisit the three young coppers at the local police station, from whom he hoped he would pick up a few more clues about what had happened to their chief. Andy was right, they had clearly been gagged, given they were answerable to the Orange Police. He also discovered all three were happy not to be the ones in Josey's shoes.

'Better you than me,' young Rob Mathews told him with a smirk.

Josey understood what he meant.

'I hear you're a friend,' Mathews expressed kindly. 'He could do with one of those right now.' Getting no response from the private eye, he added, 'You do know we're sworn off talking about the case.'

'I know, you guys are too close, I get that.'

'It might also interest you to know we've got another bloke buying in, an inspector out of Sydney, Geoff Brown; he'll be taking over the case apparently.'

Josey was familiar with a lot of the Sydney cops, but not this one.

Lester Perkins was one of the city coppers that he knew, and knew quite well; Lester and his family had moved out west to Condobolin years ago after he got the local cop job, a job that initially earned him the level of respect that he deserved.

It felt strange questioning him, not just because he is a friend, but the local head of police. This was something he'd never had to deal with before. The position that he found his friend in now was surreal, a departure from the norm. Back in Sydney they had cooperated with each other on more than a few cases.

Alone in a sparsely furnished room, they sat opposite each other at a two-seater table. Andrew hadn't gotten his wish to be present, because Lester had unequivocally refused to allow it.

Perkins was visibly nervous; not something that was usual for him. Josey wasn't particularly concerned about the nervousness, whereas his annotations were unsettling, arduous - and the confusion he exhibited right from the very start was extremely apparent.

'I hope I can make this clear to you, Cam; not all of it will make perfect sense; not even to me to be honest. How much do you already know?'

'I know it involves your neighbour, Arthur Sheridan, and that he's now missing, presumed dead.'

'And because of that, they think I killed him. I promise you, Cam; I did not kill Arthur, but I do believe he *is* dead.'

Lester's denial of guilt was a real good start for Josey. 'Just tell me exactly what happened.'

His eyes lifted to the ceiling in thought. 'Right, well, it started the morning Arthur woke me out of a deep sleep. He was in a complete panic. Yelling outside my house like a madman. I was still half asleep when I managed to focus on the bedside clock; it was only *six*. He knows I normally surface around *eight*. I tried ignoring him, but the ruckus kept on. I finally threw off the bedclothes and staggered to the front door. When I opened it, at first I didn't even know who it was, his face was smothered in blood; and then, I realised it was my neighbour . . .'

~

'Arthur, what the hell?'

The hapless neighbour explored his forehead with his trembling fingers. 'How bad is it?'

Perkins strode to a land-line that was sitting on a small table nearby. 'It's bad enough,' he answered while hitting speed-dial. 'Did you have an accident in the workshop?'

'This was no accident; that little shit Morgan pinned me to the back wall of the shed with my own bloody car.'

Lester shuddered at the thought of being faced with Arthur's hefty *Ford Raptor*, a massive vehicle capable of doing some serious damage, even without the gigantuous bull-bar that's barnacled to it.

An operator came on the line—

'Robin, it's Lester, we need an ambulance, Arthur's hurt himself - - - yes he's awake and talking - - - yes he is - - - right, I will - - - thanks.'

He left the phone off the hook and went quickly into the kitchen, returning with a tea towel to stem the bleeding. 'Hold this?' he drilled while bunching the makeshift bandage against Sheridan's forehead. 'Why would young Stan do this?' he asked quizzically.

He patted the towel against his forehead and brought it down to gauge the level of blood that had been absorbed. 'Probably because I sacked him.'

There was something else that Lester saw in his friend's

expression. 'Really, why'd you sack him?'

Arthur released an exasperated breath. 'I caught the little *turd* in the bedroom with Arlene.'

If Lester was impacted before, he was blown away by Arthur's crass description. 'What did Arlene have to say about that?'

'She's calling it rape.'

Perkins' expression didn't change as he said, 'You haven't done anything stupid to *him* I hope?'

'If you must know I bloody near killed him - - - he ended up running from the house with his clothes under his arm.'

'Was this before or after he drove the car at you?'

'Before, he came back to get his revenge. I was on my haunches working on the radiator when I sensed someone getting into the car – *I look up and see him, right*, the next thing he's driving forward, straight at me, pinning me against the back wall, if it weren't for an old axle I had leaning there I'd have been crushed . . .'

~

Josey felt the urge to interrupt Lester's story—because so far he couldn't fathom what any of it had to do with the sergeant killing his neighbour—but he held off.

'The following day, Arthur was at my door again, asking me to come take a look at the Raptor. When we got to his driveway, I saw that the nuts from one of the wheels had been removed, apparently while his vehicle was parked there overnight . . .'

~

Sheridan was nervously pacing back and forth at the side of his Raptor. 'I'm telling you, Lester, Morgan did this; he hoped I wouldn't notice. Who knows what else he's done.'

'It'd be a bit hard to miss a bunch of bolts lying on the driveway beside the wheel, if you don't mind me saying.'

'He's playing games; he knows I get in the other side and that I wouldn't see it.'

'I wouldn't call driving the car at you a game, Arthur, but hey, I've seen stupider things in my time.'

'Good - then you'll find the little bugger and put some fear into him.'

Perkins considered the request for a moment. 'Do you want him charged?'

'Too right I do.'

'He lives down by the lake, right?'

'With his mother, yeah.'

'All right, leave it with me, I'll drop by this afternoon and see if he's there or if she's heard from him.' He took a few steps in the direction of his own place, stopped and turned with a reminder for his neighbour. 'Don't forget to put those nuts back on before you drive off.'

'Very funny, thank you Sergeant . . .'

~

'I went to see the kid as promised, but only got to talk with his mother, who wasn't real excited to see me as it turned out. I haven't laid eyes on the Morgan kid from that day to this; no one has.'

'Do you believe he *raped* Arthur's wife?'

Perkins creased his brow and hesitated. 'By any measure, she's an extremely good looking woman; it's not hard to imagine a young bloke might misread the signs.'

'I hear you.'

Lester appeared relieved not to be pushed on the subject. 'Anyway, needless to say Arthur and Arlene weren't getting on too well after what happened between her and young Stan, but they seemed to get past it pretty quickly, it was only a week later that they set off on a road trip. I was out the front when they drove out in the Raptor; they both turned and looked at me all smiles; the perfect couple. What happened after was as far away from perfect as you can get, and more than a bit bazaar – don't say I didn't warn you. I know some of it first hand; the rest, I got from Arthur later . . .'

~

CHAPTER TWO
The Road Trip

For an hour, Arthur and Arlene traversed the freeway without incident.

'Well, so far so good,' she said tartly.

'Give it a rest, Arlene, I've checked everything.'

'Like you did the wheel nuts I suppose.'

'Bloody hell; that was Morgan and you know it.'

She scoffed; the silence that followed dismissed any chance she thought the car was reliable.

He let it go for a peaceful life, and they sat in silence for several kilometres more. While she was stewing about the car though, *he* was mulling over her fling with a boy twenty years her junior—

Out of the blue, unable to let it go, he picked up the thread. 'Why'd you let that creep Morgan get-the-better of you anyway? He's not exactly Mr Universe.'

Neither are you she thought before answering quietly, 'You promised we wouldn't talk about this. If we're going to argue for the next two weeks, let's just turn around and go back home right now.'

They sat in awkward silence again, speeding north a further hundred kilometres—

The verbal peace and mechanical assuredness blazoned away when the steering wheel abruptly wrenched against Arthur's grip. The car swerved off-line, forcing Arthur to take up the entire road in a fight to straighten up; his grappling efforts gradually managing to bring the vehicle under control, slowing it to a shuddering limp.

Arlene wasn't usually a nervous passenger, but under the circumstance she felt there was a very good reason to become one. 'Arthur, stop the car right now!'

Their subsequent unsteady crawl raised the wrath of a passing motorist that had been forced to slow behind them. Arthur gave *the finger* when the irate driver sped past the Raptor leaning on the horn.

'Arthur – pull over!'

'It's no good stopping here,' he insisted. 'We need to make it to Tullamore before dark; I'm not interested in driving down that track at night.'

'Yes, well let's make it in one piece,' she agreed. 'Stop the damn car.'

In a fit of temper, he did the opposite, punching his speed up to a hundred and fifty; yelling and laughing when he ripped past the angry tailgater.

Another ten kilometres slipped by at this breakneck speed. Arlene's nerves putting paid to further protest; her left hand was attributing deep fingernail indentations to the padded armrest.

Fifteen minutes of Arlene's terrified silence persuaded him to edge the speed back a notch or two—

Again - all hell let loose when the car suddenly spun - skidded across the mouth of a siding and came to rest in low brush, out of sight from the road.

'Are you all right?' he automatically asked his reluctant passenger.

With her heart pounding like a steam hammer, she was totally incapable of speech.

She appeared so statuette that he let her be; deciding to get out and check beneath the vehicle; the way that the car had handled convinced him he would find more lose bolts.

Her eyes followed him as he went to investigate.

Stopping at the driver's side fender, he bent out of sight.

Arlene could hear him scratching around on the ground. 'What is it Arthur?'

'Everything seems fine,' he answered tiresomely; 'don't get out; I'm sure we'll be okay if I take it easy.'

She echoed his dismissive words while leaning back into the headrest in disgust.

Heading to the rear of the car he silently suffered her disapproving rant. 'I wish you'd promise me nothing else will go wrong, Arthur. This is supposed to be a holiday.'

He mumbled *bitch* under his breath, half expecting her to say *I heard that*, but she didn't.

Fifteen minutes later they were back on the road. After a further five kilometres at a crawl, Arlene convinced

Arthur to give driving away for the day by pulling into a familiar garage that was coming up. She wanted to have the car checked by another mechanic. Done fighting with her he gave in. The proprietor of the favoured garage, Joe Magrie, was well known to the Sheridans due to their many stopovers at his adjoined motel.

To be honest, if she hadn't suggested stopping, he probably would have anyway. After booking in for the night, Arthur prearranged for Magrie to take a look at the Raptor first thing in the morning.

'Is there a problem?' he asked noticing Arthur's less than calm state.

He told the mechanic about the strange series of events with the car, and asked that he give the big vehicle a good onceover.

CHAPTER THREE
Further Problems

Following breakfast, Arthur had Magrie check under the car as arranged.

'See anything, Joe?'

'Put your foot on the brake for me.'

He did as instructed and noticed the pedal had a slight spongy feel to it.

Joe's voice filtered up through the floor-well. 'If I didn't know better I'd say someone's had a go at this.'

Arthur swivelled from the driver's seat and slid out to take a peek under the raised body. 'What is it?'

Joe's answer was somewhat flippant, 'Just a break-line half sawn through, take a look.'

'You're kidding.'

'Someone's cut into the line.'

Arthur poked his head under the partly raised hoist and saw Magrie was right. 'Do me a favour,' he whispered, 'don't mention this to Arlene, she's already freaking out.'

17

'Well, you'd better tell her something, you can't drive it like this.'

'Can you fix it straight away?'

'I'll have to get the part in; I could have it ready for you around four thirty.'

Sheridan stepped back as Magrie came out from under the car. Like most people he stood taller than Arthur, and perhaps a little younger. He had clean hands for a garage operator, probably because he ran the motel as well, a sort of jack of both trades. His main attire was a dust coat, something you don't see much these days, but he once explained to Arthur that it suited him because he could quickly switch between mechanic and motel operator. His most striking feature was his full head of hair; presumably as dark and wavy as when he was eighteen. 'You said the car swerved a couple of times; any clue what caused that?'

'It's *kind'a* strange I know.'

'It happens. You might've hit some rubber, oil patch maybe. Anyway, I've checked the steering real good; the last thing you need is a problem down at the cabin.'

'I don't need a *problem* — period.'

Arthur went back to the motel room and assured his nervous wife that Magrie had thoroughly checked the vehicle, especially for any lose nuts or bolts.

They left Joe's garage around four thirty and reached the narrow winding dirt track that led down to the cabin around eight.

The state of New South Wales was at the beginning of *daylight saving*, so Sheridan was still hoping to arrive before dark, especially now with all the troubles he was having with the car.

But, it wasn't to be.

On top of having to drive in the dark, he soon learnt the car had no lights. 'Shit.'

'Arthur, don't kid around, I'm not in the mood.'

'Join the club,' he grumbled through clenched teeth.

She released a frustrated groan.

'You can blame me all you like, but it won't make the lights come on.'

'Did Joe check them?'

'It was daytime, Arlene; any other bright suggestions?'

'Yes as a matter of fact, walk down and turn on the cabin lights, and grab a torch while you're at it.'

It wasn't a bad idea; except for the fact the cabin wasn't in sight due to the winding road; plus he didn't want her getting the better of the situation; he decided to persevere. He yanked the hand-break on and stepped around to the front of the car and began banging on the headlight covers, to no avail. The engine bay was as *black as the ace of spades* when he lifted the bonnet.

'I can't see a damn thing,' he cursed as he slammed the lid.

Arlene thought, *who in hell doesn't carry a torch in their car?*

Coming back to her window, he concluded, 'You can steer while I walk in front.'

She got out in a huff and stood back, as though the Raptor somehow possessed the qualities of its prehistoric namesake. 'Don't *muck around*, Arthur, I'm tired and I'm hungry, and I'm definitely not driving that *thing*.'

Arthur wasn't blind to her beauty and she looked even more stunning than usual right at that moment. Then, the image of Morgan on top of her flashed through his brain like an express train. 'Just follow me,' he told her soberly, 'that's all you have to do - at walking pace - it's either that, or we hoof it the rest of the way and leave the car here.'

She considered the situation, rounded the car to the driver's side and slid nervously in behind the wheel. 'Let's get this over with.' She saw him move out of sight as he passed her window on his way to the rear; appearing again in the mirror before pacing back past the passenger window.

'Just double checking,' he said in an effort to assure her all was well.

His empty pledge didn't wash.

From the nose of the car he splayed his arms toward the windscreen like a zealous stage performer. 'Are you right to go?'

'Yes!' she yelled while thinking, *he's braver than I thought standing in front of this abomination.*

She released the hand brake, selected first gear and eased off the foot brake. The car gently moved forward on the incline, prompting Arthur to begin walking - backward at first then turning to pick up the pace.

They worked their way down the track with visibility getting worse by the minute. He knew that his wife was nervous about driving the car and he kept turning to check she was all right. Everything seemed to be going fine and he hadn't looked over his shoulder for two or three minutes, he could hear the crunch of the tyres as the car rolled across a light sprinkling of gravel, so he was always aware of how close it was. He checked again when the gravel gave way to a smoother surface. With the choir of crickets rising at the conclusion of dusk, he no longer could hear the passage of the wheels, or the idle of the big motor for that matter. A minute later, after they had negotiated a bend in the track, he again checked behind - the car was nowhere to be seen.

Panic set in.

He ran back around the turn and saw that she'd stopped forty five metres back. 'What the hell are you doing?' he called out.

She didn't get a chance to answer, the car leaped forward, heading straight for her startled husband. His foot slipped as he tried diving out of the way. Had Arlene not steered the car away he would certainly have gone under the wheels. But her fast thinking got her into trouble. The car left the track and speared into the surrounding bush, only coming to rest when saplings took a stranglehold on the undercarriage.

Making it to the window of the car, he found his wife bent over the steering, crying her eyes out ...

~

'Arthur told me all this over the phone,' Lester clarified to his patient friend. 'The poor devil was frantic. He begged me to come up to the cabin and look for clues about sabotage, after what Joe Magrie told him about the brake line, he was more convinced than ever that the car was being deliberately interfered with.

'He was so desperate, he asked me to come and stay the night; I guess he thought having a copper at the place would make Arlene feel a bit safer. Arthur sounded so terrorised; I agreed to drive up straight away.

'I arrived around eleven and was met outside by my two very worried looking neighbours . . .'

~

'I see you got the car down,' Sergeant Perkins said noticing it parked beneath a nearby tree.

'The thing is . . . *I didn't*. I don't have the foggiest how the car got where it is right now . . . I haven't said anything to Arlene by the way.'

Lester frowned, aware of why he wouldn't want to scare his wife any more than she already was. He secretly hoped his neighbour wasn't losing his grip.

'You've got to believe me - either somebody's brought it down overnight - or the thing has brought itself down.'

'Let's stick with *somebody*, anything else is—'

'Crazy, I know.'

'Does Arlene know you asked me to come and look at the car?'

'No, she only thinks you're here to get us home in the morning'

Lester considered the parked Raptor. 'You know what; if someone nicks that thing while we're gone, they'll be doing you and Arlene a favour . . . '

~

Josey sensed the sergeant wasn't finished, and patiently waited in spite of an inordinately long pause. Perhaps the next part of his story would divulge why the police were considering him a murder suspect, because according to his men at the station, Sheridan was only considered to be *missing*.

'Getting them back home in my car should have been straight forward, but this wasn't the end of it.

'The following morning, before I even had a chance to take a look around in the daylight, a new development pissed me off more than I can tell you . . .'

~

CHAPTER FOUR
The Cabin

The log cabin was positioned on a flat plot of land that was excavated out of a steep slope, with a rough and tumble cul-de-sac immediately in front of it. It was also the end of the bridle track that led down from the highway five kilometres back. Last night there had been a neat timber rail marking the edge of the cul-de-sac and the beginning of a cliff face, which dropped down to a flowing creek, that rail was now mangled and Lester's car was at the bottom of the cliff half submerged . . .

~

'There wasn't a hope in hell of getting my car out of that creek without a crane,' Lester explained, 'so whether or not I'll ever see my drowned Peugeot again is anyone's guess. Needless to say, I now had a personal interest in finding out who was doing this. . .'

~

From where they stood at the cliff edge lamenting the

unexpected fate of the Peugeot, the half-submerged wreck's disruption of the river's passage sounded louder than usual, so much so that they missed hearing the man move up behind them until he spoke.

'What's happened, Art?'

It was odd to feel suspicious, but Arthur wouldn't have felt less so even if it had been his mother standing there. 'Jimmy,' he responded warily, 'is there something you need?'

Sheridan's cool response took the visitor aback. 'You look rattled, something wrong?'

'You might say that.'

'It's just that I noticed your lights were on at all hours last night, and then at about one-thirty I heard an almighty crash. I haven't been able to get you on the phone, so I thought I'd better come see you're all right.'

Curbing his mood, Arthur waved him over to see for himself. 'Take a look.'

Jimmy abided cautiously and cringed at what he saw. 'Your car?' he asked the stranger.

'I'm afraid so.'

'How'd it end up down there?'

'We're not exactly sure.'

There was good reason to ponder the plight of the car, because the cul-de-sac was reasonably level.

Arthur could see Lester was wondering who the visitor was. 'Sorry, Lester this is Jimmy, from just across the creek.'

Arthur's neighbour was a tall man of around fifty five

with a slim build. His appearance presently was that of a man living the easy life, clad as he was in clean overalls and an equally spotless broad brimmed straw hat. His mud laden gumboots had presumably brought him across the creek at some shallow point. Taking a few steps back from the edge he said, 'Well, look, I'll let you boys get on. Call me if I can do anything.'

'One thing,' Lester said holding him up, 'It's odd that you heard the crash - *we* didn't hear a thing.'

Jimmy gave Lester the once over, trying to figure him out. 'Not really, the cliff would have blocked off the sound to the cabin I'd say.'

'Lester's a cop,' Arthur explained to his neighbour.

Jimmy took a second inspection of the wreck. 'Hmm, looks like you might need one.'

Arthur had a question. 'What happened when you tried calling us?'

'Your phone was dead.'

'There's why,' Lester told them pointing to the cabin, having just noticed that the phone line had been removed from the cabin wall.

'That's happened since I made the call to you last night,' Arthur suggested to the sergeant.

The copper in Lester wanted to point out to the concerned neighbour that he was the only person around for miles, which made him a prime suspect. But there was one clear fact that didn't point to him being the culprit; he couldn't have caused all the things that had gone wrong with *Arthur's* car prior.

'Art, I suggest getting you and Arlene back home ASAP and calling this in.'

Arthur peered at the Raptor waiting quietly under the tree, reminding himself that he wasn't the one who put it there. 'I really don't want to have to go in that.'

'We don't have a choice now.'

The Raptor looked okay to Jimmy. 'What's the worry with the Ford?'

'It's a long story,' Lester answered for Arthur.

'I'd take you up to the highway in mine, but my son's got the car this time of year, he does business in the city. All I've got is a motor bike.' His self-approving laugh got nil response.

'I Guess it's the Ford or nothing,' Sergeant Perkins suggested as he walked across to the vehicle.

'You can come back to my place and use the phone if you'd like,' Jimmy suggested persisting with his offer to help.

The sergeant appeared too busy studying the Raptor to answer.

'Lester,' Sheridan called to attract his attention, 'what do you think?'

'Forget the phone, we'll go out in this – I'll drive.'

Jimmy Sullivan didn't quite understand what all the worry with the Raptor was, but sensed Arthur's friend didn't want him involved.

'It's all right, Jimmy,' Arthur told him, 'thanks for the offer. And thanks for coming by.'

'Not a problem. Well, I'll just head off. Good luck you

guys.'

'Thanks, Mate, I'll catch up with you later.'

'Say hello to Arlene for me,' the neighbour offered as he disappeared onto a concealed trail that had seen little use.

Lester was still preoccupied behind the wheel of the Raptor, pushing and pulling at everything he could get his hands on, presumably testing for faults.

Its hapless owner reached the window, still mulling over the conversation with Sullivan. 'Are you worried about Jimmy?'

'I suggest you get Arlene packing,' he told him ignoring the question. 'I'll have a play around here while I'm waiting.'

'Are you sure you want to do this?'

'Not in the least, but it's clearly not safe here, especially for your wife . . .'

~

Josey was beginning to get the picture; he had to agree something strange had been going on. 'Did anything else go wrong with the car, with you driving it?'

'Let's just call that an understatement. I was soon to pick up on what Arthur had been going through. At first, everything was fine. It had taken a great amount of coaxing to even get Arlene aboard, but she finally sat in the front with me; she said she felt safer there. I'm not sure if she just wanted to keep away from Arthur, I started to sense all was not well between them. But, as I said, the car ran without a hitch for quite a while. Arlene

28

was on edge though, even with me driving . . .'

~

'Lester, please drive slowly, okay.'

'I'll be real careful, Arlene, don't you worry. I'm well aware the car is unpredictable.'

'It's the bloody devil if you ask me,' she protested . . .

~

'The car was anything but devilish for the first three kilometres,' Lester told Josey, 'but that was about to come to an abrupt end. As we rounded a bend that had a bit of a lean to it, Arlene's door swung open and she was left hanging outside the car clinging to her seat belt. I hit the brake and the next thing I hear is the sound of Arlene's belt click open. I only caught a glimpse of her falling out.

'I wasn't convinced Arthur's stories about the car were real up until this; I was beginning to change my thinking on that score - the car did seem to have a mind of its own. I know how crazy that sounds.

'I had my foot hard on the brake, there was pressure, but it seemed to have no effect. I'm not sure, but I think I saw Arthur pull on the hand-brake from the back seat . . .'

~

'Throw it into gear!' Arthur demanded.

'I'm trying!'

Leaning heavily into a wide left-hand curve, Lester heard another sickening click and felt his own door catapult open, pushing out into the rock-face. Sustained gouging ripped it clear from its hinges in a spectacular shower of sparks . . .

~

'I was half expecting the seat belt would release – that didn't happen. Coming out of the turn into an open stretch, I was tempted to take my chances and jump, but I couldn't bring myself to leave Arthur to deal with the car alone from the back seat . . .'

~

Hauling himself back into the car, Lester grabbed the floor shift and attempted to change down by force. The gearbox groaned violently in protest, pulling and pushing against his efforts until he was unable to hold onto the lever's gyrations any longer . . .

~

'I'm no Greece jockey,' Lester admitted, 'mechanically what was happening seemed impossible. The gear-shift was wrenching about in my hand, almost as if the transmission was trying to change by itself. I could feel it fighting me.

'The car was doing eighty with no help from me—'

Lester stopped talking abruptly, taking a moment to try and assess Josey's reaction. He didn't like what he saw. 'You're not buying any of this are you?'

'Please, go ahead, I'm listening - I'll let you know if I have a question.' He had many, but they could wait.

The sergeant shifted his gaze onto the otherwise empty room, restoring the incident to mind as best he could . . .

~

'Are you okay?' he shouted as he straightened in his seat,

again trying to achieve some semblance of control. Arthur didn't answer, and he wasn't in the mirror. A quick glance around told Lester his backseat passenger was no longer in the car; the detached seat belt told him why—

CRASH!

The driver's side made contact with the cliff face, raising a hail of sparks trailing behind like fireworks . . .

~

'It crossed my mind Arthur might have jumped and left me for dead, but I was too busy avoiding being ground to a pulp to dwell on it . . .'

~

A hairpin bend was fast approaching, all Lester had going for him was his command of the steering, or so he thought—

The wheel snapped from his grip and took over the task of negotiating the sharp curve on its own.

He hung on for his life, expecting the worst—

Then, to his astonishment, the ridiculous vehicle began to slow, and eventually, not only had it negotiated the corner successfully, but had come to a complete stop . . .

~

'That was enough for me. I threw off the belt and got out as fast as I could, well clear of the thing . . .'

~

He watched its weird antics in disbelief; the gearbox was crunching angrily, presumably trying to locate reverse. With a massive *Clunk* it succeeded. Its wheels spun wildly, dragging the Raptor back into a small clearing . . .

~

'I recall it was having trouble with first gear again. I'd already suspected that this car was somehow capable of doing its own-thing, but now, with no one inside it, I was certain. I thought; it'll never make it into first, the clutch must surely have given out by now and the gears must be completely wrecked; it sounded like the teeth were being shaved into iron filings.

'I looked back down the track in the hope I might see Arthur lying on the roadway. No such luck. The noise of the resistant gearbox had ceased, the car was only about twenty feet away now, and sure enough it was waiting quietly with the motor idling - it was as if it was taking a rest. I felt the drama might be over. Against my better judgment I decided to approach side on, figuring it would need goddamned castors to get to me . . . .'

~

On reaching the car and peering in via the missing door, to his astonishment he saw the clutch was plunging in and out, apparently working on its own—

The engine stopped for a moment, allowing the gear lever to shift into first, then fired up again, its abilities seemingly improving with each manoeuvre.

He quickly distanced himself when the demented Raptor recommenced spinning its wheels to find traction; clawing and spewing fans of gravel in its wake as it headed back toward the cabin . . .

~

'It seemed bent on finishing what it started. I mean, I was pleased that it no longer was interested in *me*, but somewhere back on the track was Arthur and his wife, most likely injured . . .'

~

As difficult as it was to believe this crazy nightmare was actually happening, and in spite of the confusion, Lester managed to hold onto the idea that perhaps he could stop the car before it caused anymore grief . . .

~

'The track has multiple hairpin bends,' he explained to Josey, 'which meant I could cut through the bush and get in front, and hopefully find the others before the car reached them . . .'

~

He sprinted like a marathon man, stumbling across rocks and skidding over moss covered embankments. To his left he could hear first gear roaring insanely with revs flailing.

Scratched and torn after crossing to the next section of track, his ankle gave way on the sudden incline, sending him skin deep into gravel . . .

~

'There was no time to lick wounds,' he breathed nervously, 'the car was close, roaring like a damn wild animal, sending up clouds of dust that I could see through the scrub. When it came into view, at first it appeared to be deliberately accelerating toward me . . .'

~

Heading for cover while the car approached with wild intent, the Raptor inexplicably swerved away as if to avoid running him down. The tactic brought the skidding vehicle in line with a colossal boulder that extended part way onto the track. There was no evading the collision. Brakes went on, but it powerlessly encountered the immovable monolith, the rear end lifting in its challenge to retain momentum - hovering in failure, it fell, bounced and rebound before settling, stalling the engine.

This gave Lester regained courage to scramble toward the car, to try and embolden his belief that he'd find a driver inside, someone that had been hiding from view somehow.

Nothing else made sense.

Before he could process these thoughts, the engine reignited, spearing the Raptor into reverse in a massive show of dust and gravel.

He ran clear, stumbled and hit the ground; kept rolling until he reached the edge of the scrub, once again a spectator left watching the inexplicable vehicle speeding away, toward the cabin; demonstrating once again that he was not its target . . .

~

'I again tried cutting through the bush, but the damn thing had gotten well ahead of me. I decided to keep to the road. As luck would have it, I found Arlene after I heard her, moaning. She was injured, in the bush just off the track, only about ten feet down. She'd have fallen further if it wasn't for the scrub. When I got down to her I found she was unconscious.' Lester shuffled restlessly in his chair. 'I need to take a break, do you mind?'

'Sure, I'll get some coffees.' Josey caught the eye of the constable through the glass panel in the door, prompting him to open up and poke his head in.

After receiving the order the cop obliged, getting straight onto his pager, which meant he wasn't leaving his post, but he did close the door, giving his boss a quick glance that was laced with a kind of empathy.

'Are you able to carry on while we wait?' Josey asked his friend as he moved to take his seat.

'I'm fine, let's get this done.'

Settling into his chair, Josey waited –

'So, um – I could see she was bleeding badly from a laceration to her right knee . . .'

~

Lester removed his belt and used it as a tourniquet, just above the wound.

She reacted to the pain yet remained unconscious.

'What the hell are we going to do about this car?' he asked of himself.

Tightening the belt as far as he dare, it didn't completely arrest the bleeding; and certainly didn't lessen the pain, causing her to yet again moan in protest. She came round for a moment this time, but her gaze was glazed and empty . . .

~

'Not knowing if she had internal injuries, I was loath to move her. I had to do something. Even knowing that the car had probably gone to the cabin, I decided taking her there was my only option. I also thought I might be able to find my way to Jimmy Sullivan's place, which I was fairly sure the car couldn't reach because the road didn't cross the creek. I built a crude stretcher out of branches to help drag her the distance . . .'

~

Shelter would soon be needed, storm clouds were building overhead, unnoticed until the sun became blanketed, and spits of rain elevated the aroma of repellent dust. The spits became missiles and within minutes a torrential downpour descended. Walking became that much harder, and crossing the creek to reach Jimmy's property impossible.

On arrival at the cabin he paused on the cul-de-sac, waiting and watching, exhausted, checking for any sign of tyre tracks. There were none, and in fact he hadn't seen any on the roadway either. He reasoned that the heavy rain may well have washed them away.

It occurred to him that Arthur might have made it into the cabin ahead of them. Calling out and getting no response, he dragged Arlene across to the awning that covered the timber porch, placed the stretcher down and walked to the door - it was locked . . .

~

'I figured Arlene wouldn't be carrying a key, there was no sign of pockets in her skirt, and the small bag she'd been carrying was more than likely at the bottom of the cliff in the creek. I forced a window, got inside and opened up the door to drag her in. It was then that I noticed she was shivering badly, I placed her in front of the fire place and found some dry wood that Arthur had thankfully stored . . .'

~

Lester got a flame licking, eventually amounting to small timbers crackling and glowing into life. It wouldn't be enough, they both needed to get out of their wet clothes.

His plan was to take advantage of Arlene's insentient state to get her free of her wet clothing, but hesitated at the thought, the last thing he wanted was for her to wake up and have her imagination run wild over what he was doing. Her underwear needed to stay on.

He loosened the tourniquet, relieved to see the bleeding had stopped. But it started again almost immediately it was allowed, forcing him to reapply tension. With a blanket from one of the beds, he covered her from neck to toe. Her constant groaning thankfully confirmed she was still in the land of the living.

Considering he was ostensibly on his own in the room, he stripped down to his birthday suit. Using the back of a chair he hung all his gear next to the fire, and hers he placed on a second chair.

Not wanting her to wake up to find him naked and minus her husband, he gathered another blanket and wrapped it around himself like a poncho. The only clothes he was able to find in the cabin were a pair of Arthur's trousers and a shirt, neither of which fitted his lengthy body. After a moment he sat Arlene up to get her into Arthur's shirt.

She stirred.

'You're all right, Arlene, we're safe in the cabin. You've been out to it for a bit.'

She passed out again, but later would have no memory of coming around for those few seconds.

The action of lifting her buttocks in order to pull the tail of the shirt down caused her to once again stir and reopen her eyes. Her stony gaze locked on him, raising the sense he'd been caught in the middle of some illicit act.

Making him feel even more uncomfortable, she checked under the blanket, clearly taken aback when noticing she was only wearing her underwear. She didn't move a muscle as she tried to understand. She wasn't frightened, just completely blank.

The faint murmur of a car engine outside the cabin snapped Lester's attention away, taking him to a window to investigate. It was impossible to see anything other than his reflection, the storm had turned day to night. But there was no mistaking the idle of a car somewhere close. He cupped his hands against the glass to eliminate the reflected glow of the room, but could see no sign of the car - the rain not helping visibility.

Pulling back from the window, he caught a glimpse of Arlene in the restored reflection, attempting to stand. He went straight to the chair where his clothes sat drying. Without removing the blanket from his shoulders he slipped into his damp trousers before letting the poncho-like blanket slide to the floor, aware of Arlene's eyes

38

flicking involuntarily onto his upper torso.

'Where am I?' she mumbled with very apparent confusion . . .

~

'The way she spoke sounded like she didn't know me. When I turned round to face her, she had the strangest look on her face. I asked if she was all right, but she seemed too frightened of me to answer. She was cowering under the blanket, evidently suffering from amnesia. I had no time to deal with it; I needed to find out if it was the Raptor that had returned . . .'

~

He headed for the closed door fastening his zipper; opened up and stepped out onto the porch. The cool moist air ran chilling fingers over his bare skin, producing a deep shiver. After standing in the open doorway for a moment, he ventured out into the torrent. The cul-de-sac was now a river of mud. With the rushing sounds of waterfalls cascading from the hillside, and draining over the cliff toward the swollen creek below, the motor rumbling in the dark could barely be heard.

As he drew nearer to the weak sound, he saw what he feared, Sheridan's car, motionless in the storm, waiting; rain bouncing off its mangled body. He hesitated; remembering the recent events of the last hour or so. But he'd come this far, there was no turning back.

Not knowing what to expect within this dim veil of night, he flinched when dark clouds exploded within submerged worlds of blinding light, turning night to day.

In this overbearing illumination, Lester could scarcely believe his eyes; Sheridan was back inside the Raptor, now sitting behind the wheel – which made no sense, given he wasn't there the last time he'd grasped the courage to check . . .

~

'I'd started to really believe he was the one manipulating the car externally – and now here he was, back in *control* of the vehicle for some mysterious reason.' Lester eyed Josey in pursuit of a reaction, but received no change in the detective's expression.

Cam's a damn good listener, he thought.

'Anyway, Arthur wasn't done with terrorising us . . .'

~

CHAPTER FIVE
Arthur

B linding headlights stabbed through the rain even as the Raptor's engine roared into life, lunging with intent.

As he turned to run he slipped and fell. Massive wheels burrowed into the mud either side of where he lay, with little to no control before skidding to a halt.

Heat from the underside of the Raptor hovered overhead. Gears crunched destructively inches from his face, culminating in a loud clunk that sounded like reverse may have successfully engaged.

He rolled out from under and ran like a man on ice, yet managed to keep his footing and make it to the open door to slam it hard behind him.

Arlene was trembling from a cocktail of cold and fear.

'Have you got any weapons here?' he shouted at her.

Her voice shook. 'Oh my-god, what's happening?'

'Arlene,' he barked impatiently as he started searching,

'we need to protect ourselves.'

They heard a loud CLUNK; followed by an approaching roar.

Recognising the Raptor was charging, Lester scooped Arlene clear of the doorway as would a footballer; in time to avoid an almighty crash that splintered the door from its hinges. The remnants landed on the floor where the duo had stood a moment ago.

Spreadeagled and still in line with the gaping doorway, their attacker's steaming bull bar was clearly visible, vibrating to the rhythm of the V8 engine, recovering from the effects of the impact.

The steam withered in the cold air, revealing to Arlene the sight of a man draped across the bonnet; his head and shoulders protruding through the shattered windscreen - blood pouring from him like a tap. She had no idea it was her husband, but the frightening image was enough to raise a pronounced scream.

More urgent crunching of the gears; quicker this time, gaining reverse successfully before drawing the Raptor away. The awning, left dithering against the roof of the vehicle, collapsed in a heap on the porch, partially blocking the doorway.

CRUNCH, CRUNCH, CLUNK—

First gear! Roaring and sliding like a demolition car, it came again.

Again, Arthur's body flung about on the bonnet like a rag doll. Lester's conviction that Arthur was the driver no longer rang true – the Raptor was driving itself somehow, it tried several more times to break through the front wall of the cabin. Each time it backed off, Lester's only thought was *it's never giving up.*

After reversing from the cabin some distance away, for what he hoped would be the last time, it became quiet. The headlights doused and the engine stopped.

With the ordeal momentarily over, he became acutely aware of Arlene sobbing. He got her to her feet and onto a chair, out of sight of the Raptor. She was confused, but he wasn't to know by how much.

'Who's driving that car?' she pleaded. She knew it couldn't be the bloodied person on the bonnet ...

~

'Arlene still hadn't recognised Arthur; she was very obviously still suffering from amnesia. She again asked me who I am. This was the last thing I needed; I felt I was dealing with the situation on my own.

'I'm not sure how long I stayed at her side, trying to think what to do. I knew that if I was to have any chance of getting help, I'd have to leave the cabin and make it to the highway, but that wasn't an option because it wasn't safe to leave Arlene by herself; and with her bad leg, she had no chance of walking out of there ...'

~

Arlene's expression was both blank and fearful.

'I know this is hard for you to understand,' he told her, 'I can't explain it myself.'

'Wait, where are you going?' she suddenly responded with alarm when he got to his feet and headed to the doorway . . .

~

'I waited there, studying the car, and Arthur; the top half of his body lying across the bonnet - either dead, or dying. There was one thing that had to be done, one thing that I didn't feel right about avoiding, I needed to find out what could be done for him, which of course meant approaching the vehicle yet again. That hadn't gone so well on previous attempts. I thought about Arthur's handiwork, aware he had built the cabin himself. He'd made his uprights from substantial tree trunks; they looked to have had the basic strength of telegraph poles. I felt confident the walls of the cabin would stand up to any onslaught the car had to offer . . .'

~

Lester drew a deep breath and stepped out onto the porch, waiting within reach of the damaged doorway.

The car remained eerily quiet.

He mustered the courage to venture from the safety of the cabin, and then to arc his way cautiously round to the driver's side of the car.

Worried Arlene might be following; he took periodic glances over his shoulder to make sure she was still inside.

Preconditioned to expect no driver, he held onto the hope that this time there might be someone he could confront. This thought also frightened him. What if he had a gun? But then he thought, why bother with all the constant ramming if he could simply enter the unsecured cabin and blast away.

As close as he dare stand next to the missing door, he once again saw that there was no one in the front seat, except for Arthur's legs and buttocks; steadfastly lodged above the broad dashboard by some means. He checked the ignition – no keys.

What to do?

The sight of Arlene framed in the gaping doorway of the cabin, experiencing what appeared to be a complete breakdown, spurred him on. He needed to find out if Arthur was alive, if only for her sake. And if he was, he would attempt to release him from whatever was holding him in place.

There was no avoiding it, he would have to reach across from the bonnet and feel for a pulse - it was that, or climb onto the front seat and reach through the broken windscreen.

That's not happening, he thought.

He had no intension of reaching the bonnet via the bull bar, to do so would position him in its path; he opted to climb the front wheel. His blood ran cold as he did so, imagining it might suddenly rotate and take him with it; that didn't happen either.

This allowed the crazy idea the spree might be done with, or perhaps whatever was empowering it was somehow decommissioned; yet the warmth of the idling engine filtering through to his abdomen gave no reason to believe this was true.

He skulked across the bonnet no further than was

absolutely necessary to reach Arthur's blood-soaked wrist. 'Arthur, can you hear me?' he asked the stony face before him.

Lester knew where to look for a pulse, as a copper he'd had to do this many times, but with the blood, and his fear, it wasn't easy.

His perseverance found nothing!

With the result of his investigation inconclusive, he was forced to give it up, but not before trying to release Arthur from whatever was holding him. Resigning to failure, Lester allowed his body to glide on the grizzly lubrication provided by the thin spread of blood; to reach the edge of the bonnet, from where he dropped to the ground. Without taking his eyes from the Raptor, he walked backward, giving it a wide berth, tracing his footsteps toward the relative safety of the porch, all the while expecting he might have to suddenly run for his life with the real risk of slipping in the mud, as he had done unfailingly.

His fear intensified at the sound of the engine revving, the high-beams suddenly painting through the rain resembling search lights. All preparation couldn't prevent his falling yet again, or the Raptor taking advantage by racing forward. He tried getting up, but it was too late. He lowered his head and waited for the inevitable. He heard the wheels skim past and felt the mud soar into his face, but there was no crushing blow; both mud tracks had traced their lines to his left, ending where the Raptor had stopped – between him and the door; its lights blaring in at Arlene as though delighting in her screams.

Lester lay in the mud pondering his next move, a brief moment of inaction to rationalise what was happening. His attempts at rationality failed, he put his mind to survival.

Think!

With the car parked in his pathway to the door, he needed another way in. As yet he hadn't been to the rear of the cabin and wasn't sure if the back door would be unlocked.

'Arlene!' he yelled over the rain and the revving engine. 'Check the back door is unclipped!' Even as he gave her this instruction it occurred to him the vehicle might actually be able to hear him, it obviously could *see*.

Arlene took a while to respond, she wasn't in any condition to move quickly; she finally did, appearing at one of the two windows, perhaps beginning to accept Lester was friend not foe, her eventual compliance confirming his assumption. 'Yes, it is!'

'All right, I'm coming round!' he waited to see if the car showed any sign of understanding. The fact that it wasn't moving didn't really answer the question; it had a habit of waiting for the right moment. If Lester was to outsmart this thing, he would have to do the same. Whatever the plan, he would have to execute it with exactitude.

'Okay bolts for brains,' he mumbled aloud into the mud, 'let's see how good you are.' He launched to his feet and sprinted as sure-footedly as possible toward the right side of the building. He could hear the wheels spinning without grip, giving him the time he needed to round the corner of the cabin in the lead. Glancing over his shoulder he saw the car spin-out and go wide, losing more valuable time; more time for Lester to increase his lead.

When he rounded the back corner of the building he was alarmed to see Arlene exiting the door. His yelling at her to get inside was to no avail, compelling him to force her to comply. He slammed the door shut; instinctively believing it too would end up off its hinges. His instinct happily proved wrong. From a rear window he saw that the car wasn't getting sufficient run-up to accumulate enough speed to do any real damage, due to the close proximity of the bolder lined forest, but it tried, managing to shake cutlery from cupboards and picture frames away from the walls when it hit. 'Who the hell are you?' she screamed out of the blue, seemingly more concerned with the man she didn't know, than the crazed assailant behind the wheel of the car outside . . .

~

'I didn't have time to deal with Arlene's amnesia. I stepped to the window, sensing the thing was taking another rest. I could barely make out the bizarre-vehicle waiting in the dark; its headlights doused, almost like it was sleeping . . .'

~

When Lester turned from the window to assess her state, he noted she was still deeply afraid – more or less as he'd expected, but not just of the car. He agonised over whether or not to tell her, uncertain about how she might react; would it help her to learn the truth about this crazy nightmare. Either way, there was no avoiding it. 'The man on the bonnet is your husband,' he told her with blunt honesty. 'I'm not sure how he ended up on the bonnet like this.'

His explanation brought about a sudden bout of anger. 'Bullshit! I don't believe you.' She pushed past him.

Headlights that had been dimmed, possibly to save on battery life, immediately lifted when she appeared in the doorway, a reminder that the thing could *see*.

Even as Lester was pacing over to stop her, Arlene was stepping from the porch. The Ford gave what sounded like a joyous rev and fishtailed in the mud, on the attack.

She was already reconsidering the senselessness of her actions when Lester grabbed her around the waist with one of his powerful arms, clambering back across the rubble left lying on the porch; tripping and sliding back through the open doorway as the car collided with the jam.

They were left lying on their backs facing the angry lights and the deep growl of the engine – Arthur, still spread-eagled on the bonnet like a horrific mascot.

For a moment, Lester thought her memory might be returning; even with Arthur's face totally covered in blood, he was still recognisable - and only five feet from where they lay. But, it was not Arthur that had her attention. With the headlights again dimmed, Arlene could see there was no one behind the wheel of the vehicle, no one driving. Even more confused than before, she turned to face her dubious rescuer. 'What game are you playing?' Her voice was a desperate whisper.

Lester ignored her while dragging a tall cupboard from where it stood adjacent to the gaping doorway.

'Please tell me what's happening?' she asked with fear returning.

'Stopping it from looking in,' the comment sounded wrong even to him.

'It can *see*?'

Her confusion was becoming tiresome. 'I can't imagine why you find that so hard to believe, Arlene, after what you've already witnessed.' He had to shake his head to have his own wits return; at least there was a new level of understanding in her expression now. She was finally grasping that there wasn't a person out there, only the car.

Lester dared putting his arm around her in an attempt to regain her trust—

He'd misread her state of mind badly.

'Get your hands off me!' she warned . . .

~

'Arlene was getting more and more difficult to deal with at this point, but at least she'd calmed enough to think things through with some semblance of rationality when it came to the car; that's if rational is the right word in this case, the whole thing was completely surreal - for both of us. She continued to have massive mood swings; one minute trusting me, and then lashing out. Though when all is said and done she was the least of my problems, I think she was simply driven by fear . . .'

~

'How're you doing this?' she pleaded in hope of an answer that made sense.

'I'm not – can't you get that.'

She hardened in the face of his inadequate answer. 'I may have lost my memory,' she ranted angrily, 'but I'm not stupid, and I don't believe a word you're saying.'

When she tried rounding the cupboard, attempting again to reach the doorway, without a word of explanation he took her under the arms and dragged her with brute force across to the iron stove.

She screamed abuse, but he felt ignoring her protests was mandatory. With rope that Arthur had hanging on the wall next to the stove, and against her writhing, he managed to bind her wrists. Now on her back with arms above her head, he fastened her to the leg of the iron stove. This was the only way he could think to prevent her from leaving the protection of the cabin . . .

~

Josey thought, *why would Lester consider tying Arlene up? Surely there had to be another way to convince her to stay away from the car, especially since she had no understanding of what it was.*

Lester's attitude to what he'd done didn't really differ from Josey's. 'Her reaction was perfectly reasonable,' he admitted, 'there was nothing in the least acceptable about the way I was behaving. It goes without saying, I became concerned she might hurt herself; she'd clearly forgotten about her injured knee.'

He fell silent for a moment, mentally exhausted. His glazed eyes had found focus on the floor, yet his mind seemed not to have left the memory of his harrowing experience.

On a despondent sigh he said, 'In hindsight, perhaps we *could have* headed straight into the scrub at the back of the cabin to get away. But I honestly considered walking out of there with her would have been impossible. She wouldn't have made it a hundred yards, with or without the car chasing us, let alone through the bush.

'Anyway, the Raptor once again went into hibernation, silently waiting in the dark. The storm was really going off; the track became more of a river than a road. That's when we heard the police siren. It was hard to believe a patrol car had managed to make it down without spearing off into the creek.

'Through the window, I could see the Raptor slowly backing up. Without turning on its lights, it eased around the cabin. At the back window I saw it enter the forest, a path I thought it might not be capable of taking. Clearly it could.

'No more than fifteen seconds later, the coppers pulled up right outside the front window with their headlights in my face. When they doused the lights, I could see it wasn't Mathews and Beasley from Condobolin. I didn't know what station they were from at that stage, or how they knew to come.

'Apparently, someone had called Condobolin, my boys didn't know who – the line went stone dead before they could find out, but they said the guy sounded frantic. Constable Mathews decided to put the call out for someone closer to the location.

'I thought to untie Arlene before they came in, but there wasn't time. When the coppers saw a half-naked woman tied to the stove, you can imagine what they thought, and how I felt. And frankly, I couldn't believe or prevent what she then did - she was babbling like a mad woman, making it sound like I was some sort of pervert . . .'

CHAPTER SIX
Andrew Perkins

Sitting opposite Lester Perkins, Cameron Josey had listened patiently to his avowal. 'I'm told Arlene's changed her story on that score, she's dropping her accusation against you. How'd *that* happen?'

'You tell me; all I know is she was still highly confused when the police arrived, for the reasons I've explained.'

Josey thought about that, and his next question was, 'You haven't mentioned why the police think Arthur is dead, or why they think *you* killed him.'

He scoffed, 'They wouldn't have even known he was there if I hadn't told them the story.'

'And yet in spite of having nothing more than a missing person on their hands—'

'That's exactly what I've been saying; if you look at it logically, this is all about not knowing what to make of our story. Coppers get nervous when they think one of their own has crossed the line.'

Josey studied his friend for any hint of deceit. Although detecting something hidden in his manner, it was far too early to make mention. Before quizzing Perkins any further, he wanted to determine if Arlene's account completely buttressed that of the sergeant's, like he claimed.

He stood, picked up his brief case and slid in a laptop he'd been using throughout the interview; made it to the door, stopping for a moment to look back at the man he'd known for around twenty years. The story he'd just been told was unexpectedly absurd, and didn't conform to the type of person he knew Lester to be. But it was fair to say, the absurdity was as new to the well-respected policeman as it was to Josey. The vulnerability that he saw in his friend was in deep contrast to what would be expected of him. He said, 'I'll see you tomorrow, buddy, don't expect too much, I'll need some time.'

Perkins eyed the detective with mixed feelings. 'I guess I can be thankful you haven't bolted after hearing this – or is that what you're doing.'

'Rest assured you're story is definitely worthy of closer investigation, I'd still be here even if it wasn't.'

'You'll look into it then?'

'I promised I would.'

Perkins exhaled heavily. 'I can't ask for more than that, thank you.'

'Don't thank me yet.'

He watched Josey go; a guard replacing him in the

mouth of the door.

Josey proceeded down a long corridor, at the end of which he met up with a second uniformed man, who ushered him down yet another long corridor that was adjacent. Their progress was being monitored by a remotely panning security camera that hung from the ceiling.

The two men came out onto a grand white marble staircase, revealing that Lester Perkins temporary place of residence was an old eighteenth century mansion.

Josey bid his chaperone good-day, took a few paces toward the late model Audi that was waiting on the horseshoe gravel driveway and sat in beside the driver.

'How'd it go?' Andrew asked him.

'Your brother tells an interesting story,' was all Josey wanted to say as he clipped into the seat belt.

Andrew Perkins took his grey Audi along the driveway that led to the razor wired fence. 'What have you decided?' he asked while they drove.

'Let's see what Mrs Sheridan's got to say.'

'You'll see she's lying.'

'As your brother's lawyer that's what I'd expect you to say, but if I'm to believe your brother's opinion, it's likely her story will match his.'

'Really, something's changed then, because she put the acid in when police found her tied up at the cabin. She told them he'd molested her. Sound *familiar*?'

It did, Josey knew he was referring to the Stan Morgan rape accusation.

'It's completely unlike anything expected of my brother. You know him as well as I do. Why would he even think of doing something so disgusting when in fact he went there to help them?'

'Off hand, I'd say he wouldn't. But, if her story has changed, it may have something to do with her amnesia.'

This was news. 'What amnesia?'

'They didn't tell you? The police apparently found her in a state of confusion; having suffered what they believe was a bout of temporary memory loss. As for tying her to the stove, we have to consider he may have snapped for some reason. People do.'

'Yeah well, people need a motive to snap.'

Josey took his point, yet he needed Andy to understand their friendship mustn't stand in the way of objectivity. 'Then again as he said, perhaps it *was* the only way to stop her from harming herself.'

Lester didn't have a lot going for him Josey believed, not just his story—or the fact he was a policeman who was perceived to have crossed the line—but also the suspicion that he had something to do with Sheridan's disappearance, *or death*. Not being able to convince his own people he was telling the truth didn't leave him with much of a defence, other than insanity, and Arlene Sheridan too if she in fact corroborates his story. Clearly the local constables didn't believe he was crazy, but the District Police in Orange did, most of who wouldn't even know who Sergeant Lester Perkins was.

The Audi reached the main gate and entered onto the

road back to town, brick pylons displayed the brass plaque which designated the big homes original name, *Condominium*—surely a joke by some *Cockie* who struck it rich enough to build a mansion—now known as the Condominium Psychiatric Facility.

CHAPTER SEVEN
Arlene's Take

Fifty minutes later they pulled into the Condobolin Hospital car park; took the concrete path that drew a line across paddocks of red clay, crossed the cool of a broad patio that surrounded the muddy green structure and entered via its gaping doorway.

Outside room two one six, a nurse cautioned the men to be brief. 'She's not a well lady. Try not to be too long,' she concluded.

'We will be brief,' Josey assured her as he slipped into the room with Andrew at his heels.

Arlene watched them through eyes weak from trauma as they approached her bedside.

The tiredness and the injuries aside, Josey immediately saw how right Lester was in assessing Arlene Sheridan to be an attractive woman. 'Mrs Sheridan, I've brought Lester's brother so that we can hear your story together, will that be all right?'

She looked at young Andrew and tried not to gage his appearance. She knew him of course, but found him a little chubby for her liking, not to mention he had a weird haircut. She didn't much like the expression on his face right now either. She thought Josey was gorgeous, and that's why she favoured keeping her eyes on him. 'I suppose that will be alright,' she said quietly, 'I mean he is the sergeant's little brother.' She looked at him then. 'I don't really think your brother's done anything wrong, Andrew.' She saw that *less-than-happy* look on his face again.

Josey gave Arlene a noncommittal grin. 'We won't be staying long. Please let us know if it gets too much.'

'No, that's fine.' Her eyes fell on Andrew again. 'But not for your brother I'm guessing.'

'Don't count him out yet,' he told her caustically.

Josey glared at him and tossed his head toward the door, indicating it might be better if he left.

'Let him stay,' Arlene insisted. 'I want him to hear.'

'Hear what, that you lied and told the police he acted indecently?'

'That was a misunderstanding; give me a chance to explain.'

Josey was having second thoughts about keeping Andrew in the room, but relented, giving his brash young friend a silent warning to behave.

Arlene took her eyes away from them and stared at the foot of the bed. 'Well, where should I start . . . I gather you've already spoken to Lester, and you're aware of the circumstances of how we came to be out at the cabin?'

Josey knew a whole lot more than that, he'd learnt about the personal problems the Sheridans were having from the constables, but he simply told her, 'Yes.'

'It's difficult to explain how or why, but on our journey we experienced several mishaps with the car. Arthur's a mechanic and even he couldn't understand what was happening.

'Anyhow, later that night . . . the night we arrived at the cabin, I told Arthur to ring Lester and ask him to come to the cabin and investigate . . . '

~

Lester Perkins pulled himself away from the TV to deal with the interruption. 'Who *th'hell*,' he muttered trudging into the hall to snatch the phone off the wall. The caller ID told him who it was. 'Arthur, what's happened?'

'Where do I start, we've just had the most horrendous time with my car. Everything went wrong that could go wrong. Arlene's beside herself; she thinks someone is trying to kill us.'

'Maybe it's time you bought a new car.'

'Believe me it's on the cards, but can you come anyway; I know this's a big ask, buddy.'

'At ten o'clock at night - you're right. Where's the car now?'

'It's here, at the cabin.'

'So you made it there.'

'Yes, but—'

'Arthur, listen, what exactly do you want me to investigate; like I said you're the expert.'

'Yeah, and I'm telling you, things like this just don't happen to a car for no reason; not unless someone is making it happen.'

'Again, you're the mechanic, have you seen any evidence the car's been tampered with?'

Arthur went quiet.

'Art . . . you there?'

'I'm here, and yes I've had a guy look at it, he found the brake line's been deliberately cut.'

Lester had to admit, this on top of the removed wheel nuts didn't look good. 'Wow, if this is Morgan doing this like you say, how's he pulling it off?'

'He isn't that bright a mechanic, so I have no bloody idea.'

'Right, okay, I'll come first thing in the morning. In the meantime, don't drive the car. Lock yourselves in the cabin and get some rest. I'll do the same; I've had a bit of a long day myself . . .'

~

'I wasn't happy with that,' Arlene revealed. 'I insisted Arthur tell him to drive straight up and stay the night. I didn't feel safe there with just Arthur to protect me.

'In any case, Lester did come, and he stayed the night. The next morning, before we even knew that he was up and about; he was banging on our bedroom door shouting in a panic . . .'

~

'Arthur, wake up — my car's in the creek!'

'*What* - what'd he say?' Arlene asked her husband half asleep.

'Get dressed,' he told her as he hastily slipped into a pair of jeans. She quickly put on a light gown and followed on his heels. When they stepped into the main room, they caught a glimpse of the sergeant heading outside.

Stopping at the window, Arlene saw him arrive at the cliff edge and look down; Arthur came to his side near where the white timber rail had been annihilated. She didn't know it was Lester's car that had plummeted into the creek at this stage, but she heard Arthur saying, *'Holy shit, you are kidding me—'*

'*Morning-gents.*'

It was Jimmy Sullivan, who was no stranger to Arlene; he seemed to know all about the car. She couldn't hear every word, but he was saying something about hearing a crash around 1am. He reached the cliff edge and joined in on the inspection of what Arlene now gleaned was Lester's half submerged Peugeot stuck in the running stream . . .

~

'I watched them through the window talking to Sullivan. They were talking about the phone lines being down. Jimmy left after a while, but they stayed out there talking.

'I went back to the bedroom and got dressed. About ten minutes later they came in and told me we were leaving in the Raptor . . .'

~

Arlene was standing back from Arthur's car as though it might bite. 'Are you out of your minds? No way am I getting in that bloody car.'

'What choice do we have, Arlene?'

'Get Lester's car out of the river or call someone,' she suggested quite reasonably.

'Our phones are dead.'

'Are you telling me we don't have one single mobile that's working?'

'Not unless we find your bag, which is probably in the creek.'

'Sorry, Arlene,' the Sergeant apologised, 'my cell's in the creek too.'

She glared at her husband. 'And yours?'

'I tried charging it on the way up, but didn't gain a single bar.'

'You see, Lester,' she said facing her neighbour, 'this is all the more reason not to trust that car . . .'

~

'Arthur somehow managed to convince me that with Lester driving we would be safe, and we started up the track. After three kilometres without incident I began to relax. I was praying the car wouldn't do anything weird, because that track can be perilous, it's been carved into the hills most of the way, with dangerously steep sides.

'Lester seemed to be going too fast as we approached the first hairpin bend and I had to tell him to slow down, but he wasn't listening. I don't know if he was trying to lessen the time spent in the car or what.

'In any event, as we sped around, all my weight was pressed hard up against the door . . .'

~

Arlene heard a sharp click – felt the door swing open - and Arthur's hand touching her shoulder from the back seat, yelling something, but it was too late, she was already falling from the car, becoming airborne . . .

~

'I must have passed out because the next thing I was aware of was Lester calling my name.' She patted the sheets above her injured right knee and told them, 'He had this to deal with so it was decided we should make our way back to the cabin. Neither of us had a clue about what was going on with Arthur's car.

'That's the last thing I remember before waking up in the cabin with Lester. Except I didn't know it was him. I didn't even know who *I* was. All I saw was a complete stranger crouching over me . . .'

~

'You're all right now, Arlene. You've had an accident.'

She rubbed her forehead trying to recollect what had happened, to no avail. Even though there was an open fire burning close by, she couldn't stop shivering, and became cognisant of the prickliness of a blanket against her skin. She looked beneath the cover and noticed she was only wearing her underwear, soaked. She assumed that the pounding rain outside must be the reason. Afraid of the stranger's intentions she tried pushing him away, which she quickly recognised was a mistake; pain blazed through her leg, the leg that he was holding.

'Arlene, lie still or you'll start the bleeding again.'

At least he knows my name, she thought. 'Who are you?'

He didn't answer immediately, and that worried her, and then he said, unconvincingly, 'Someone who's not a threat.'

'Bullshit!' With her left hand, she reached beneath the blanket that she assumed he had placed on her, and urged his hand away. Her fingers brushed across the tourniquet, at the same time noticing he was minus a belt in his trousers.

He tried bringing his hand back onto her knee, but she instinctively fought the gesture, discarding the blanket as she struck him hard across the face.

With Lester still smarting from the shock of the blow, and Arlene confused by his even-tempered response, the faint sound of a car engine drew a new focus for the both of them.

This sent Lester to the window in a panic.

His fear passed to her. 'What's happening? . . .'

~

'I had no idea what was making him so frightened, or who was in the car. While he was at the window I noticed some clothes were sitting over the back of a chair, women's clothes, I decided they must be mine, which could only mean he had undressed me. I could see the skirt had blood on it – and I started to understand it may line up with my wound. He suddenly ran outside to have it out with whoever was in the car . . .'

~

Sitting up on the floor grasping her blanket, Arlene faced the door that Lester had left open. Framed there, the rain sparkled like a sun-shower, floodlit by the car's headlights gouging through the torrent; and Lester carving his way from sight. She snapped her head round to movement at the corner of her eye; on the back wall, a grotesque shadow of a figure running. The Raptor's engine was howling insanely as it approached at speed, its menacing charge sending Lester's silhouette climbing the wall; bending onto the ceiling like a cardboard cut-out.

The Raptor hit the wall a second after Lester slammed the heavy wooden ingress behind him. The oblique angle of the massive bull-bar catapulted the doomed door from its hinges, burying Lester beneath it, along with some splintered timbers that speared through the gaping jam.

It was then that she saw the man on the bonnet. Arthur's bloodied eyes were staring right at her, but she had no idea who he was . . .

~

'Lester didn't think Arthur was dead, but we both thought he looked like he should be. Of course I had no memory of Lester or Arthur – or anything else in my past at that point. I have to tell you, none of this was making any sense to me, and I'm still waiting for someone to tell me what's happened to Arthur—.'

'We were hoping you could tell *us*,' Andrew cut in sharply.

Josey reined the young man's sentiment in with an appropriate answer. 'He's still missing; we can't say much about that right now.'

She weakly arched her arm through the air dismissively with eyes on Lester's young brother. 'I understand,' she whispered.

'Please continue your story,' Josey requested.

'Well anyway, Lester went back outside, which I thought seemed a little crazy. I saw him heading around the car to reach Arthur's door, well, actually there was no car door; it'd been ripped off somehow. The next thing I know Lester is climbing onto the bonnet and reaching out to him. I couldn't be sure if he was trying to help him or harm him at that stage.

'Of course I now know that he was simply trying to find out if Arthur was alive. At first I believed there was someone driving, someone that wanted to kill us, clearly it wasn't whoever the man on the bonnet was, which means, it wasn't my Arthur.

Josey didn't let on that her answer opened his mind to a possibility, he simply said, 'Arlene, can I ask if you think it was young Morgan causing all the problems with the car?'

'How could he, for a mechanic he was as *useless as*.'

Josey liked that she was underhandedly letting the kid off the hook, in spite of what he did to her.

'Why do you think the police are pointing the finger at

Lester?'

She squinted; doubting the detective himself believed his client was innocent. 'I hope you realise I'm not blaming Lester, and I don't believe Arthur would either if we could ask him; otherwise why would we have called him to help us.'

'Do you think it was because of the way in which the police found you that they decided to charge Lester?'

'Initially, but I will say, I didn't help with some of the things I said at the time – I was off with the fairies. I explained all this to the police later.'

'I understand,' Josey promised.

'Those blokes had blinkers on,' she added curtly. 'There I was, tied to a stove with hardly a stitch on, with a man I'm telling them I didn't know. Then there's him telling them he had to tie me up for my own good because there was an out of control driverless car trying to kill us, which I didn't believe any more than they did. Then there's our story of a man on the bonnet covered in blood, dead or alive we didn't know. Lester tells them the man is my husband; I tell them he's talking bullshit. I mean, you could hardly expect me to tell the cops what a sweet guy he was, given my state of mind.' She was shaking her head reflectively.

'Poor Lester, to the cops he probably wouldn't have looked very innocent to them.

'But it was the blood they discovered all over the ground and on the porch that sealed Lester's fate eventually. Once they tested it and realised the blood was my husband's, and that Lester's was our next-door neighbour, it was case closed as far as they were concerned. Like I said; *blinkers*. Look,' she concluded, 'I'm really sorry for the way things have turned out for Lester . . .'

~

Walking the corridor of the hospital Andrew asked, 'Well what's your take on it now?'

'Although Arlene's story about the reason for her being tied up now matches your brother's, it's too soon to make any sort of call on it. We have to accept that her ordeal *could* believably explain her confusion about his intentions; and we have to keep in mind that she has readily apologised. Bottom line – Lester's biggest problem is the blood, and the fact it belongs to his missing neighbour, who just happens to be the husband of the woman the police found tied up and next to naked.

CHAPTER EIGHT
The Investigation

The two men had no trouble understanding why Lester would have found himself in cuffs; Arlene's injuries were more than enough to warrant his being apprehended by police, at least until all parties could be questioned.

'Not completely different stories,' Andrew suggested as he and Josey walked the corridor to the hospital exit, 'but enough to tell me she's trying to make it sound like my brother's been less than a gentleman.'

"Maybe.'

'Sorry, Cam but it seems clear to me.'

'A piece of advice young Andy, you don't build a case on what people tell you, you build it on what you *find-out from what they tell you.*'

They exited the hospital and strode back across the clay stained pathway to the curb.

'So, what now?' he asked Josey as they boarded the car.

'We can take a trip if you're up for it.'

Not only was he *up-for-it* he was dressed for it, having swapped his slacks and sports coat for a T-shirt, blue jeans and a baseball cap.

They headed north in the direction of the log cabin. Josey didn't mind at all that the sergeant's young brother's head was full of questions; some of them were the same as his own.

'Do you expect to find something up there?'

'Who knows, we're just taking a look.'

'The cops have given the place a thorough going over from what I've heard.'

'Maybe we'll get luckier, perhaps have a little chat with his neighbour Jimmy Sullivan.'

'Do you think *he* could be involved?'

'Not especially.'

Andrew noted the detective seemed guarded, which was fine, but it was hard to figure why he wasn't so centred on the Raptor story. 'Do you believe what my brother's saying – about Arthur's car?'

Josey appeared appreciative of the question. 'I believe it either happened exactly the way he says it did, or he has a reason for modifying the detail.'

Andrew studied the passing houses in silence.

'Don't get too hung up on the questions at this stage,' Josey advised, 'it's early days. We need to work out the truth for ourselves. Let's just wait and see what we find at the cabin.'

Lester's predicament was really eating into the young man.

'I think in fairness to your brother, although his account of the events aren't what I'd call coherent, same with Arthur's wife, I believe there's truth in there somewhere, but possibly not exactly the way they're telling it.'

Andrew did a little thinking. 'He's pretty upset about being accused of killing Arthur you know.'

'And why wouldn't he be. Andy, for what it's worth, I don't believe he's killed anyone. As you know, the cops found blood on the ground that was Arthur's, but no real evidence that he didn't just up and walk away, missing doesn't mean dead.' He snuck a quick peek at the young man. 'We've heard two stories that don't make total sense - now it's up to us to develop our own story.'

The Audi turned off the highway and cautiously moved on down toward the cabin, slowly negotiating the steep dirt track that had Arthur and Arlene feeling so nervous.

'I'm beginning to get a picture of their nightmare,' Andrew observed from the driver's seat as he studied the flowing creek at the base of the drop off.

The steep incline had Josey's window hard up against the rock face, creating the urge to lean away; and from time to time try and get a better idea of what was around the many blind corners that the track offered. 'You're right, Andy, the nightmare they experienced on this road isn't real hard to grasp.'

The weather now was very different though, clear blue

skies and warm, which of course may present embossed tyre marks with which to clarify exactly what happened with the Raptor.

It took the hour that Lester warned it would to reach the holiday shack; Andrew pulled the car up immediately in front of the porch, or what was left of it. 'Well at least this part of the story rings true,' he mulled.

He was referring to the fact all the earmarks of a car having rammed the front of the cabin in the manner described, clearly bore fruit. As expected, the awning hung drunkenly across where there used to be a door.

'It'd be interesting to know where Sheridan's car got to after it left here,' Andy said wistfully.

Concentrating on the baked tyre tracks, Josey answered mechanically, 'With a bit of luck these tracks will talk to us.' He walked around for some time with Andy in tow, trying to untangle the many sets of tread marks that had been set in the mud, separating the Peugeot's indentations from the Ford's.

'What're we likely to find that the cops couldn't,' Andy asked sounding doubtful.

'Ye of little faith.'

Josey's confidence gave Andy a noticeable bolster.

They came to where the Peugeot's tracks ceased at the cliff edge and peered down to the semi submerged vehicle.

'You don't think somebody could be in it do you?'

Josey understood he meant a body. He traced all the

74

signs of damage that repeated the story of how the car ended up in the creek. 'That's covered, the police found nothing. Check it out again though if you want.'

Andy took in the tall banks and couldn't see any way down. 'Who do you reckon pushed it?' - With no answer he turned to find the detective missing, and then noticed he'd gone inside the cabin, moving through the frame of a window, barely visible behind the reflected outdoors. He took one more look at his brother's car before heading across to join the detective's scrutiny of the interior.

On entering he saw him bent across the metal stove trying to lift it.

'What are you doing?'

'Seeing if Arlene could have gotten herself free.'

'And?'

'Not a chance.'

Josey straightened and panned on the room to make sure he hadn't missed anything, after which he stepped to the rear door, saying as he went outside, 'This is the back way Lester talked about.'

Andrew hastily caught up with him. 'You're buying that story then, about the car being able to actually see what they were doing?'

He was rounding the western edge of the back wall as he elaborated, 'Given the Raptor's existence is real; that much we know, obviously it was here creating havoc, the question is - can we believe it had no driver.'

'And if it didn't?'

'If not, there had to be some other way it was able to do

what it did so successfully, which includes being able to see.'

He pointed to a fairly well-worn foot-track. 'This adds up,' he said distractedly, 'that's the path he thought to use to avoid being seen.'

He led Andy back inside and crossed the room to the gaping door jamb to study the damage to the contact points surrounding it. 'This all gels.'

Andrew nodded agreement as he followed Josey over the destruction and out onto the baked earth, to once again examine the car tracks, brail left frozen in time, albeit temporarily.

Andrew's mind was preoccupied. 'Cam, with the stove thing, are you thinking Lester's lying about something?'

'Not necessarily,' he finally answered, 'but I do think he's hiding some of the details.'

Andrew wanted to believe the detective was wrong, but was more interested now in what Josey was pointing at. 'What is it?'

'See, these car tracks are coming away from the door for the last time, then they lead off, around to the back with no further disturbance. If we can follow them to their conclusion we might just find the car.'

'How do you suppose the cops missed this?'

'I'm not saying they did, but from the reaction I got in talking to them, although they don't believe your brother is guilty of the charge, I'm fairly sure they also don't believe a word about the Ford Raptor.'

Andrew put ten years on his features by screwing up his

face. 'I'm having trouble myself.'

The tracks took them around to the back of the cabin, just as Josey predicted, and this time they found where the car had entered the bush, vaguely evidenced by brush that had regained its stature after having been laid flat. As they followed the damaged foliage they realised it didn't go far before swinging to the east and joining up with a more substantial, yet barely used track that was partly grassed over, wide enough for a car.

Broken twigs and a skid on the grass indicated a car had recently turned onto the tight track and headed north.

'Are you happy to drive,' Josey asked his *shiny new Audi* owner.

'It's not a Raptor, but let's *give it a shot*.'

Two minutes later they were rounding the cabin in the scratch free Audi, armed with their prior knowledge gained from trudging through the scrub on a short reconnaissance. At the point where they met up with the newfound track, the disturbance from car wheels could clearly be seen from across the bonnet as Andy edged the Audi forward. The tracks ceased over jagged rocks, but started up again not more than a hundred yards ahead.

'Do you think it was Sheridan driving?'

'I'd have to agree *someone* was, if not driving - *controlling*.'

Andy looked out the window and studied the rugged surrounds, 'Who the hell could pull that off in country like this?'

He had a point, even back near the cabin it was hard to

imagine someone could control the Raptor externally, but right here the vehicle would almost certainly need a driver. Given the story about Arthur being badly injured on the bonnet of the Raptor, Josey had to concede the most recent driver of the Ford probably wouldn't be him. But then in the absence of an alternative he decided to assume Arthur quite possibly recovered and was able to drive away. He also assumed that Arthur might not have been as injured as he appeared to be. The whole thing could have been a ploy designed to have people believe he was dead; what a way to disappear. Problem was, if his plan was to kill his wife, then at the point when he was seen lying across the bonnet, one could be forgiven for thinking the success in carrying out the proposal was already a failure.

Josey snapped out of his thoughts when Andy was forced to apply the brakes—

Although the going had been fairly easy for about a kilometre, their wheeled pursuit had gone as far as it dare. In front of them was a steep gradient, which led down to a rocky outcrop, ending in more scrub that proceeded up the opposite bank to an even greater height than where they'd stopped.

Their vantage point enabled them to see where the car's passage had brazenly continued into the recess, and then onto a distant climb.

Josey slid out the door while saying, 'Feel like a walk?' He bent back down to gage Andy's reaction. 'Or you could wait here and mind the Audi if you'd prefer.'

Making his choice he turned off the motor and got out to follow Josey's purposeful stride. 'I'll be coming thanks very much.'

At the base of the rocky outcrop they found evidence of a disturbance.

'It looks like he hit pretty hard just here,' Josey mulled. 'The drop probably wasn't noticed till the last minute, after one hell of a ride down I'd say. But, the vehicle was able to carry on it seems.'

The track that was made by the car as it climbed up the steep incline was relatively easy to follow, the torn earth and scattered rocks indicated great difficulty in climbing the bank. At the top of the rise the density of the brush intensified, so much so that it was hard to believe a vehicle could have made its way through, it wasn't only brushwood, trees were adding to the mix, and rocks—.

An unexpected sound grew, distant but closing fast.

'We're near a road,' Andrew said stating the obvious.

'Yep, sounds like we've met up with the highway.'

The thing was, although the road sounded close, the Raptor had turned to the left to continue pushing through the scrub. They had the choice of following the laid down brush or locating the roadway.

Josey offered, 'My guess is he didn't want to break out onto the road right here.'

'What should we do?'

'He wouldn't have come this far if he wasn't intending to reach the road, let's break through here and search for where he came out.'

79

With more energy now, they pushed and scratched their way through the remaining bush for a few metres. The single car that they had heard was long gone.

The thick scrub had risen above their heads, pushing past one blinder revealed another, presenting no warning of how close they were getting to the now eerily silent highway—

They punched out onto the wide clearing just as a freewheeling cyclist appeared.

The startled fellow swerved at the sudden sight of two men stumbling heavily into the deep easement that lined the road. He had managed to reach such a phenomenal speed with the aid of the steep gradient; he either had no chance of stopping or had preferred not to.

As if their hearts weren't racing enough, a long blast from a horn at their backs warned they were spreadeagled dangerously close to the white line. They scrambled back as a B-Double rocketed toward them and sped by, the lethal vehicle's sight-and-sound diminishing as quickly as an express train. Soberly turning to each other they considered their close call.

'Terrific, we could have bloody-well driven here,' Andy moaned.

Josey smiled at the young bloke's annoyance and got to his feet. He began walking along the easement as though he'd seen something. 'Up here,' he prompted.

They reached a grate that lineated the end of the ditch, the point where Sheridan must have chosen to bash through onto the highway, probably aware of the open drain. Judging by the tyre marks in the soft shoulder the car had gone north, the opposite direction to Condobolin.

Well accustomed to regret, Josey led the way back into the scrub. 'Come on young Andy, there's no more to be done here.'

CHAPTER NINE
The investigation gathers momentum

They drove past the point where they'd emerged from the bush and pulled into a small eating house called *Eat and Run*. It stood to reason Arthur might have stopped for refreshments, or simply to respond to the call of nature.

The place was close to empty when they went in. The shop attendant looked at Arthur's picture as though trying to remember if she'd seen him, but in fact was more concerned with who wanted to know.

'I'm sorry, we're not police,' Josey told her as he gestured to Andrew. 'I'm trying to help Andy here to find his uncle, that's the man in the picture, he's gone missing.'

The make-believe *uncle thing* was new to Andy, but the strategy was clear.

'We get a lot of customers,' she said blankly.

He pocketed the photo and showed her another of Sheridan leaning against the bull-bar of the Raptor. 'What about the car? Seen anything like that; it would have been badly damaged?'

The question about the car attained her interest. 'Yeah, I remember that, it was hard to miss; it came in and parked right out front here – about a week ago - just as I was closing up.'

'Did you see who was driving?'

She shook her head. 'It was there one minute and gone the next.'

Josey gave her a warm smile and pocketed the photo. 'All right, thanks.'

'Sorry I couldn't help,' she offered as they turned to go.

'It was a long shot anyway,' Josey quietly told Andrew once they were outside.

They had no way of knowing if the car proceeded north or south when it left the eatery, but it was decided to carry on north, driving until they reached a garage forty kilometres away.

The attendant in the shop was shown Arthur's picture, but he just shrugged. 'No, never seen him before.'

'What about the car?' Josey asked.

'A bit hard to say,' he told them sounding disinterested, 'it was a fair bit knocked about compared to the one in that picture.'

'Forget the damage,' Andrew said unable to disguise his eagerness, 'was it a Ford Raptor?'

'Maybe?'

'Look, it belongs to the man in the picture,' he pointed out impatiently, 'you must have seen him if the car was here.'

'Not necessarily,' the guy said touching on a little of his own impatience with young Andrew's pushy attitude.

Even Josey was getting confused by the attendant's *double-dutch*, but he responded with his usual diplomacy. 'You didn't see the driver, right?'

'Bingo.'

'But you saw the car, and it looked battered.'

'That's what I said.'

'Did you see it leave?'

'Nope, it's still here.'

Andrew kept his mouth shut, unable to trust what he might say.

'I can take you round back for a gander if that's what you want.' It was a helpful enough offer, but still lacked enthusiasm.

Josey showed the guy his pearly whites. 'Hey, that'd be fantastic, thank you'

He led them to the rear of the garage and there it was - Sheridan's wrecked Raptor.

Josey circled the vehicle under the watchful eye of the informant.

'Do you mind if we take a look over it?'

'It's no skin off my nose. Knock yourself out.' He seemed thrilled by his dismissive tone, clearly not done with irritating them.

A car horn sounded for service and he left without

saying another word.

'Mr Personality,' Andrew decided as the guy receded from view, and earshot.

The irksome guy was already out of Josey's mind, he'd recommenced his exploration, starting with a quick look at the open tray. It was empty except for an extra-large metal box, presumably carrying tools - *padlocked*.

The locked toolbox gave Andrew a grizzly thought. 'Maybe there'll be something in there we won't like.'

Josey thought, *the kid's obsessed with finding dead bodies.*

But he decided checking inside it was advisable. He didn't have to look far; via the smashed window of the pillion door, a ring of keys practically jumped out at him from the open glove box. He reached in and grabbed them without touching any part of the body; he knew the car would end up having the police crawling all over it.

There was no guarantee the padlock key would be amongst the others. He could already see there wasn't an ignition key.

Leaning over the wall of the tray he found a key that at least slid into the lock – turned the key and the lock sprung open. Exposing the dim interior of the aluminium chest, suddenly summoned the foreboding Andrew had felt a moment ago. Josey wasn't expecting to find a body though, and he didn't; the big box was completely empty, not even a single tool.

'Good'a gents, what can I do for you?' The voice was that of a grey haired man, who it appeared might be the actual owner of the garage, not another flunky like the last guy.

'Morning,' Josey said comfortably reflecting the man's demeanour. 'We happen to know the owner of this car, or used to. We're trying to figure out how it got here.'

'My son brought it in early on; we've rung the police about it.'

While wondering if the *son* was *Mr Personality*, Josey handed the presumed owner a card and flashed his ID.

'Private detectives,' the man observed while handing the card back.

'That's all right, you keep it.'

'I thought you might be,' he admitted slipping the card into his overalls and returning a friendly hand. 'Roger, Roger Barton.'

Josey put the ID away and asked, 'How did your son come by the car?'

'Bobby found it about a kilometre down the road in the bush, looked like it'd been hidden. There was no one around so he decided to bring it into the garage. I let him know he should have left it where it was, but you know *kids*,' he said with a bit of a glance at Josey's young offsider. 'The cops should be here any minute, why not stick around and talk to them about it.'

'We might just do that. In the meantime do you mind if we keep poking around while we wait?'

'Sure, take your time. . . Let me know if I can help you with anything,' he concluded as he left them to it.

Josey was keen to check for the blood he expected to

find on the bonnet, but a quick once over suggested there wasn't any. He reasoned it may have all been washed off by the heavy rain. Closer inspection though found traces of dried blood caught in the headlight covers. With a penknife he scraped just enough to slip into one of the tiny plastic bags that he always carried, leaving enough blood for the police to locate and collect for themselves.

'Let's see if this is Arthur's,' he told Andy as he pocketed the bag, moving back round to the side of the car to begin checking the seat-belts. He slid into cotton gloves, and with the driver's door missing, he was able to do the test without the need to climb inside; the belts worked perfectly as far as he could see. Circling the car and checking the mechanisms on the remaining belts and door locks, he found that although badly battered, they were not faulty or tampered with.

He was about to give the exterior inspection away when he noticed something inside. 'Take a look at this.'

Josey had levelled himself beside the rear window just behind the driver's seat, allowing Andy to look over his shoulder.

Leaning in to get the sun off his face, Josey gained better focus. 'This's interesting wouldn't you say?'

'Is that a bullet hole?'

'Yep,' he told him as he rounded behind Andy and looked in through the front window, pointing back at the head rest. 'It's gone right through, which means there might be a bullet imbedded here somewhere.'

Josey checked the dashboard, but there was no sign of a

87

bullet hole, indicating the shot must have gone straight out through the windscreen, perhaps suggesting the glass was blown out by the slug, and not Arthur's body going through it. Equally, it suggested that Arthur may have been hit, ending up on the bonnet as a result.

He took a closer look at the headrest and saw that there was no blood. 'A gunshot doesn't fit in.' he mumbled to himself. 'Not from what we've been told at least.' He straightened and headed toward the front of the garage. 'Come on, Andy; we need to check out where the car was dumped.'

Unbeknown, their passage from the rear of the garage was being covertly observed from a red phone booth at the edge of the highway. The man may well have been listening to someone on the other end of the line, he certainly wasn't talking to anyone though. Either way, he was intently focused on the two men who were currently meeting up with the owner near the front door to the garage; their conversation as silent to him as the dead phone.

'Roger,' Josey was saying, 'any chance someone could show us where your son located the car?'

'I'll take you down myself - in the wagon.'

The dubious caller watched from the booth, hanging up when the garage owner drove away with his visitors aboard.

The wagon was a truck with a small crane mounted on the back, heading south, back toward where the Raptor had exited the forest.

It took only a few minutes to reach the location where the discarded Ford was eventually dumped. The vehicle had only been taken a kilometre from where it came out onto the highway, heading north before re-entering the forest on the left.

Roger sat in his truck and let the detective and his friend have their *root around in the bush*, which is the way he referred to what they were doing when his son called him from the garage with some startling news.

To Andy, the search was a hopeless task. 'I can't imagine what you hope to find here.'

'I'm looking for an ignition key, or maybe a footprint that might tell us who the driver was'

It didn't take Andrew long to realise that picking up footprints on the dry leafy ground was like finding a needle in a haystack.

'What about the bullet?' Andy asked.

'That'll be back at the cabin somewhere – and even harder to find—'

Their attention was drawn to the sound of a vehicle pulling up in a hurry up near where Roger was waiting in his wagon. Out of the dust appeared a small army type Jeep, even at a distance they could see that the young driver wasn't Mr Personality. They watched him talking animatedly to Roger, but couldn't hear what was being said.

Out of earshot to the investigators below, the young bloke was saying, 'Dad, someone's just heisted that car those two blokes are interested in, heading north.'

'Did you get a look at the driver?'

'Not a chance, it was out of the yard like a shot—'

Josey yelled from the gully, 'Everything all right?'

'Someone's taken the Raptor,' Roger yelled back, 'Do you want to go after it?'

They made their way up to the road double-time. 'We're coming.' To Andrew he said, 'I guess we weren't about to find that key.'

'Go in the Jeep,' Roger told them as they reached the top. 'It'll be quicker on the bends and Bobby my son here is a bloody good driver.'

They boarded the Jeep and hung onto whatever they could get their hands on; Bobby was already skidding onto the bitumen before they could reach seat belts.

They'd only travelled five kilometres when they caught sight of Sheridan's car up ahead; snaking in-and-out of view on the bends.

'Can you see if there's anyone behind the wheel?' Young Andy asked Josey without thinking how it might confuse their Jeep driver.

Bobby glanced in the mirror at his back seat passenger, then asked Cam, 'What's he on about?'

For Josey, the innocuous question was a reasonable one, but of course he couldn't subscribe to the idea the Raptor drove itself, which left the *real* question – how was it being controlled, and by who? For the time being he elected to believe that right now it was being driven either by Sheridan or someone else.

They were driving blind at times; entering in and out of

the black smoke Sheridan's car had begun spewing from its exhaust.

'You might like to ease up a bit, Bob,' Josey suggested.

'Relax, Detective, I could drive this road with my eyes closed.'

This was clearly intended as an exaggeration, but the black smoke was making it seem like that's exactly what he was doing. All the skill in the world wasn't about to help him stop when they cleared the smoke to find the Raptor spreadeagled across two lanes, it wasn't clear if this was a deliberate manoeuvre.

Full credit for Barton's reaction, he was instantly on the brake, turning the wheel in the direction of travel, bringing the tail around ninety degrees to take the impact.

On contact the Jeep spun past the obstruction, left the road and ended up in a shallow recess.

At first there was disorientation and the throbbing effects of adrenalin, followed by the gradual gaining of wits, and growing concerns about who might be hurt.

Josey was fine; saved by his seat belt, which he'd managed to slip into before the collision; Bobby's head was leaning on the horn, at the very least, unconscious — and bleeding.

It wasn't until Josey got to his feet outside the Jeep that he noticed Andy was missing from the vehicle.

While desperately darting around to help Bobby, he kept his eyes peeled for any sign of young Andy lying on the ground, thinking he may have been thrown some distance.

On reaching the driver he gently eased him from the horn to assess his condition. He'd suffered a fracture to his head from having impacted with the steering wheel.

The high pitched sound of wheels scrubbing against the roadway drew his attention back to where the Raptor was doing donuts; intimidating - showing them who-was-boss.

Woomph!

Josey swung toward the new sound — the Jeep had ignited — small flames licked from beneath the bonnet, quickly spreading through the firewall. With his jacket held over his head to ward off the heat, Josey attempted to pull Bobby free, but a shoelace had become snagged by the brake pedal—

Flames spread to the kid's oily overalls, aided by the ingrained accelerant.

Intense pain awoke him to the nightmare; vaguely aware of someone reaching in; grappling in the flames - beneath his knees. It was then that he realised his foot was stuck. Flames hungrily ate into his overalls - the penetrating heat demanded he escape – yet his foot remained wedged.

Helping hands that were free to escape were forced to do so—

They obstinately returned - taking hold of his upper torso - tugging violently; again and again.

His foot broke free, free of the brake pedal, and the flames, but not the pain. He was being dragged across the ground away from the burning Jeep; he didn't know by whom. Finally he felt the cool relief of being mercifully immersed in a pool of water. Steam rose as if from a thermal spring - flames doused, and his own screams along with them. He saw the face of his rescuer - the detective now in the water with him, holding his head above the soothing bath.

The ear-splitting squeal of tyres coming from the donut king on the highway drew their attention, taking on a new sound as clouds of rubber gave way to stone and gravel. Sheridan's car had left the bitumen, now charging over the shoulder and down the embankment toward the pond.

Instinctively Josey separated from the kid to draw the driver's attention away. It worked, but that left him with nowhere to run. His only playing card was to sidestep in the hope the Raptor wouldn't be as sure footed. That worked too, but his winning hand vanished in an instant when a patch of marsh swallowed him right up to the knees – stuck fast.

At a hundred and fifty metres he saw the car turning to face his way.

The engine growled and the wheels spun, drawing the Raptor into full attack.

But then with threatening calm, the brute rapidly lent on the brakes, skidding into a crawl, opting to approach with agonising certainty. There was no escaping the intention to bury Josey deep into the mud.

Closer now, it was expected he'd soon see Sheridan, or at the very least somebody, peering through the smashed windscreen. If it was the mechanic, this would be laying eyes on him for the first time; till now he had only ever seen his image in a photograph.

The Raptor *came to a gentle standstill,* its meaty engine angrily grumbling at the edge of the swamp, ready to enter – waiting for the right moment.

He realised the reason for the hesitation, the heavy vehicle ran the risk of becoming bogged itself.

Josey's point of view across the bonnet should have allowed him to see the driver by now, but there was no one.

Perhaps it's the angle?

With the driver's seat presumably empty, only one thing made this possible – the Raptor must be being controlled remotely.

But if so, how was that possible while speeding along the highway? Where was it being controlled from?

Whatever the means, it backed away a measurable distance and came to a stop, changed gear, revved, and charged, accelerating with each approaching moment, perhaps fast enough to traverse the bog without becoming stuck.

That's exactly how it played out.

Josey felt the heat of the undercarriage as it pressed his body into the mud, deep enough to block out light – and air.

He knew enough not to panic, not to try and breathe. That was fine at first, but in each passing moment, the quagmire drew him deeper, sucking away all hope of survival.

His swampy prison felt like quicksand, the more he

struggled, the better it held him within its dark abode – darker – and darker—

Is this how I end? . . .

. . . Out of nowhere, a flash of light heralded a gunshot. Josey was no longer suffocating in the mud; he was on a callout, a decade and a half ago.

He instinctively looked over his shoulder to his partner, to see if *Faraday* was all right. 'You okay, *Freddie?*'

'I'm fine,' came his response from somewhere in the dark.

They were in an alleyway. An armed suspect was in the vicinity. The assailant was known to police and the order was to seek and apprehend. Not so easy when you're being shot at.

Faraday came to Josey's side and whispered, 'What's the plan?'

Josey looked to his right and saw a narrow gap between two buildings that was just wide enough for humans and rats. 'I might be able to flank him through there. You keep watch from here.'

Keeping watch meant staring into the pitch dark for any sign of movement.

From Faraday's point of view his comrade in arms vanished from sight. He strained his eyes into the murky blackness, from where the last gunshot had come from. Illusionary blotches swam in the gloomy limbo; forcing repeated blinks in an attempt to discard the obscuring images.

It was hard to make out given the distance and lack of detail, but he thought he saw light glint off a figure moving in from the right; from behind the edge of the wall that terminated the alleyway.

Was it Josey? Freddie aimed his gun at arm's length, ready to shoot.

Headlights swept past the mouth of the alley behind him, sending a momentary glow to where he'd seen the movement. He was right, the figure was his partner, but the gunman was already aiming point blank at Josey's back.

Faraday squeezed the trigger with little opportunity for accuracy. He saw Josey fall, he'd hit his own man. With the temporary illumination from the street gone, he left his cover and ran at the dark.

From the dark came the glow of the assailant's weapon.

He felt the bullet in the worst possible place – the chest.

He heard Josey cry out his name as though somewhere in the distance.

Josey had no energy left to prevent what was about to happen.

Faraday lay helplessly at the gunman's feet with the weapon aimed at his head . . .

~

Josey jumped convulsively; the shot acting as a wakeup call, alerting him to his present and dire predicament.

Freddie's untimely death had once again signalled the delivery of a conjured colleague, a metaphysical partner on constant call.

With every ounce of his strength, Josey pushed against the wet soggy weight that was holding him. It was difficult to even lift his arm, but he figured that if he could just disrupt the surface he may be able to leaver himself free. Air finally touched the skin of his right hand, bolstering his resolve to lay his arm across the surface of the mud.

He was out of air, and strength.

Pushing down against the mud, he was able to sense his torso moving upward. Progress was unbearably slow, but he daren't stop because he really needed air right at that moment, without it his next breath would have been a choking mud-meal!

He came into the light wearing a surreal mask, still firmly trapped but free to breath; enough to cough out the words, 'We made it, Freddie—'

Talking to his dead partner like this, proved once again that Josey believed in something beyond the grave, but not so as to damage his healthy level of scepticism.

Gouging the sticky muck from his eyes with his fingers and spitting out as much of the muddy soup that he could, he panned his head as far as allowed, fully expecting the Raptor wouldn't be finished with him.

What he saw didn't make a lot of sense;

Bobby Barton's chard body was sitting back behind the wheel of the burnt out Jeep, which is not the way he remembered the events ending.

And Andy was still missing; so too Sheridan's Raptor.

Being buried in mud is the only thing that matched the

facts. Well, not quite the only thing - his last annoying memory—before being buried in mud—was what he'd seen inside Sheridan's car, or to be more precise—

What he hadn't seen!

He blacked out.

CHAPTER TEN
Josey loses grip on the Investigation

Josey awoke to find his wife and daughter at his bedside. For some reason they appeared worried, and their stares didn't add up to an answer.

He moved from their faces to take in the room - - - not recognising where he was; he came back onto their astonished expressions and marshalled an uneven greeting, 'Hello, what are you two doing here?'

Molly appeared decidedly concerned; Rebecca relieved. 'Hello to you too,' his wife said with a slight frown. 'Welcome back.'

Her comment confused him. '*Back,* back from where?' Swinging his eyes to his anxious daughter, he sought her help.

'You've been passed out in that bed for a week, Dad.'

He rotated his head slowly to the left and flinched. Pushing through the pain he came back on them.

Although realising his family were the only people present, distinctive hospital sounds and smells drifted in from the corridor.

'For *a week*?' he said in disbelief.

Rebecca's nodding confirmed the news; a little tear in her eye showing how upset it made her.

'What happened?' he asked blankly.

'You've been in a bad accident,' his wife told him.

He thought carefully about that, and in a flash, most of what happened came back in a vague sort of way.

'You're in the Condobolin hospital,' she added.

'You've come to Condo?'

She told him they'd travelled from Sydney overnight after receiving a call from one of the constables at the local police station. He half listened to their story while recalling his own; *the Raptor, the mud, the fire, the absurdness, and the resurgence of Freddie's untimely death.*

The absurdness made it hard to imagine what their level of disbelief would be, once he told them the full story about the car. He was having trouble dealing with it himself, yet logic told him his forthcoming explanation would satisfy even the largest sceptic.

'It's coming back to me,' he said tiredly. 'How much have you been told?'

'Quite a lot,' Rebecca volunteered with an odd tone.

Attempting to clear his mind, he imagined someone must have already explained it to them, but the truth of it was far more intriguing.

'You came round an hour ago and told us the *whole thing,* sweetie.'

They were nodding at him like dashboard dolls.

This gave him a solid clue that he was in a hospital bed for good reason, and not as lucid as he believed. Aware those pieces of memory were eluding him, he put his mind to work, concentrating on what that might entail. The effort was worth it. His arched brow indicated he was having some sort of success. It took a few minutes, but he eventually remembered telling his family the bizarre story. 'You do know that I don't believe the car drove its self, right?'

'Dad,' Molly scolded, 'this is *us* you're talking to.'

Rebecca spoke on a quivering breath. 'The police aren't quite so on-side unfortunately, they don't believe a word of it.'

The mention of police brought his mind back to the story he told the cops about young Bobby Barton, and the Raptor. Putting himself in their shoes; it wasn't hard to understand why the young constables would be wondering why the detective, who was supposedly here to make sense of the whole stupid affair, was now telling the same rubbish story as their sergeant, who was being held in a psychiatric institution. Josey hadn't yet been given a chance to explain how the control of the car was orchestrated, or how it fitted in with the attack.

Dispersions could easily be placed upon his account of the crash and Bobby's subsequent death, and probably were by now; it wasn't hard to understand why.

How did Bobby end up back in the burnt out Jeep, when it was clear in Josey's mind that he had dragged the young man out of the flames and into the safety of the pond? And what about himself, how had he escaped meeting the same fate as Barton?

These are the obvious questions the police would be asking – a sudden troubling thought came to mind.

'Did I tell you about Andy?'

'You did, and he's still missing I'm sorry to say.'

Andy's plight, along with the mystery of how Bobby Barton somehow ended up back in the Jeep after he'd saved him from the fire, were Josey's biggest worries. Yet Andy's disappearance was far more settling than being found dead near the scene.

His wife and daughter confirmed they knew all about that too, and *their* worries far outweighed his. 'You could have been the one who died in that Jeep,' she said quickly to beat the emotion that was controlling her throat.

Josey didn't want to encourage this line of thought. 'How worried are the police about my involvement?'

'Thankfully they see you as a victim, and so far they haven't laid any charges.'

He glanced off toward the day-lit window. 'But they think I'm as crazy as their sergeant.'

'I don't think they know what to think.'

'I can tell you what they *should* be thinking.'

His wife exhaled knowingly. 'Why doesn't that surprise me?'

Her mother's exasperated comment made Molly smile;

102

she also knew not to dismiss it if her father thought he'd worked something out. 'I bet I know what you're thinking, Dad.'

'That's my girl,' he said with his eyes on his wife.

'It's autonomous,' Molly told her father proudly, 'right?'

A doubtful expression rose on Rebecca's face. 'Really? The way you tell it that hardly seems possible.'

Josey flicked up his eyebrows while adding, 'Well, that's the problem right there, isn't it; how was it being controlled, and by whom?' He went on to assure his girls that as soon as he got out of hospital he would get to the bottom of those two questions.

'Yes well, you can forget that. Apparently you've been forbidden to involve yourself further in the case; you're a party to what's happened their saying.'

Her answer didn't require further explanation, Josey fully realised the view taken by police would have been mandatory; at least he wasn't going to the *psycho* ward. There are plenty of reasons why he might have been a contender – like a boy dead at the scene, or the car and its missing owner, and last but not least, the missing brother of the station's sergeant.

'How is Lester; have you heard.'

'He's still in that place, if that's what you're asking?'

'We wanted to go see him, but they wouldn't let us. You're lucky they didn't put *you* in there.'

Molly let out a laugh ahead of regaining a straight face. 'Sorry Dad.'

Belinda's disapproving expression was reminding her daughter that a young man has been killed. Back on her husband she told him, 'Sheridan's wife is still in hospital too.'

'Yeah, I figured she would be; she was a bit banged up when Andy and I went to see her.'

'And so are you - which means - you've got yet another good reason to turn turtle.'

He knew she was right, he certainly didn't feel on top of the world. Plus there were X-rays and MRIs to contend with yet; his injuries were still unconfirmed. He'd been getting bad headaches from something that was going on inside his neck, possibly a pinched nerve. And then there was an inflamed tendon in his right foot, which had caused him to limp the last time he tried walking.

'I guess you're right, looks like I'll be in here for a while yet. You girls can go home, I'm sure you've got things to do. Once I'm out of here I'll be right behind you.'

'If you believe were leaving before you're well again, you are out of your mind.'

'I thought you'd say that. Actually I was thinking we might treat this as a family holiday, what do you say?'

For Rebecca, this rang giant alarm bells, Josey hated holidays. 'Don't worry about that now. I've made the Motel booking for a week. Let's see how things pan out.'

Josey saluted, 'Yes boss.'

This gained a scoffing groan from his daughter. 'I don't think he's too badly hurt, Mum – he's still being a bit of a

Dad.'

Josey chuckled while saying, 'I've been called worse, now get out of here the both of you and let me get some rest.'

Rebecca picked up her bag from his bed, ready to leave. 'Good thinking – we'll come and see you in the morning.' She lent and favoured him with a light kiss.

Molly followed suit, after which she told him, 'I've got some time off, Dad – so we'll do that holiday, okay?'

He pulled her back in and kissed her gently on the forehead. 'That's okay by me, Pumpkin.'

When they got to the door and turned back, Josey had already closed his eyes.

'Look at him;' Rebecca said on a sigh, 'he's totally exhausted.'

The Motel was only a short distance from the hospital in the same street. They walked arm in arm, exulting in each other's company.

'Are you going to tell me?' Molly asked.

'Tell you what?'

'Why Dad came way out here in the first place.'

'The less you know the better probably; and we're not supposed to be talking about your father's case.'

'What case, he's off the case.'

'He is, and so are we.'

'Mum, I'm not a kid, fill me in.'

Rebecca's quivering breath released the words, 'All right, but you needn't repeat any of what I say.'

She zipped her lips.

'Dad heard about the trouble Lester was in on the grape vine. We talked about his coming here and agreed the least he could do is pay him a visit. He was already on his way when Lester's brother, Andrew, called and asked for your father's help; do you remember Andrew?'

'I vaguely remember meeting him;' she recalled, 'and his family from memory.'

'You would have, Andrew's aunt was one of the teachers from your school?'

'Yeah, right.'

'So Dad's been hired by Andrew?'

'I'm not sure if that's true, especially now.'

Aware Andrew was missing, Molly wondered, 'Do the police know what's happened to Andy?'

'Apparently not; it seems they don't know what's happened to Lester's neighbour either, but I can almost guarantee there's more to it than we're being told, both by police, and your father.'

By the time they reached the Motel and finished a coffee together, Molly knew as much as her mother about the details of the *Non-Case*.

The moment his girls left the hospital room, Josey went-out like a light, but sleep was jam-packed with muddled half-awake dreams about the poor kid that had lost his life trying to help, Bobby Barton. The confusing dreams were most likely being born out of the muddle about why the young man was in the burnt-out Jeep and not in the pond where he'd left him—

A shrill purr snapped him back into the hospital room, to his bedside phone commanding he answer it.

He fumbled for the receiver to stop the noise, scoffed and brought it to his ear. 'Hello?' While listening to the caller with growing interest, he slowly wiped away sleep from his eyes, adjusting the pillow in an attempt to sit up. 'Who is this? - - - No, no – I'm listening - - - I understand - - - 'Where are you? - - - I've got it – trust me - - - Thank you, yes, yes - - - you've helped more than you know - - - can I reach you? - - - no of course not - - - you have my word - - - yes, bye.'

Josey hung up the phone with a grin on his face, one he would have to lose before his wife walked in—

'What are you smiling about?'

Too late, she was standing at the door with Molly.

'Oh, um,' he stuttered, 'that was Carl - - - he rang to see how I am.' This was a cloaked lie that he'd sort out later when the time was right.

Carl, Josey's Man Friday, was presumably at the office in Sydney working away on cases, along with Josey's remarkable partner, Maxine. He could have used either one of them to throw his family off the scent.

Rebecca didn't look convinced as she meandered over to his bed. 'And how *are* you?'

'I had a good night's sleep,' he lied again

'I can see that, you look a lot perkier.'

If she knew the real reason, he'd be in the immediate bad books.

He mustered every ounce of patience to keep his mind on his wife and daughter, as they spoke at length about Andrew Perkins and their connection to the Perkins family.

Josey's mind was on his totally unexpected phone call. They watched him eat his breakfast as eagerly as if he hadn't eaten in days.

Rebecca knew there was something other than a good night's rest that was lifting his spirits, but wasn't about to raise the issue in front of Molly.

When they left, Josey tried getting out of bed, but was forced back – his head was trapped in a vice, brought on by the slightest movement of his neck. He spent the rest of the afternoon impatiently resting, because he knew that if he was to continue with the case, rest was needed, preceded by some seriously effective pain killers. His drowsy mind wasn't going to stop him going over the facts, or so he thought.

CHAPTER ELEVEN
The Facts

Against all determination to continue building the case in his mind, he eventually succumbed to a sort of semi-slumber.

When he pulled himself out of it two hours later, Arlene's story had superimposed over Lester's to become one. The combination was so synchronised that it was either the truth, or it was a complete collaboration between the two of them. He would have given his right arm to hear what Arthur Sheraton might have had to say about their story.

He took his mind back to the beginning of Lester's telling of it;

He thought about the loose bolts in the driveway – who had access? The answer was unhelpful. There was the obvious person, Stan Morgan, the accused rapist. But anyone could have removed those bolts, albeit with less of a motive than the kid. Based on pure logistics, there was Lester, Josey's client Arthur, and even Arlene.

Although Arlene hadn't mentioned the wheel nut incident, she did confirm that some weird things were happening. The most damning of all was the cut brake line; again confirmed by Magrie the motel owner.

The electrical problem with the headlights, confirmed by Arlene, was most likely Arthur's doing – that's if we're to believe Arthur had it in for his wife.

Contenders for pushing Perkin's Peugeot in the creek, if one is to consider all those present, are the neighbour Jimmy Sullivan, Lester himself, or perhaps even Arthur and Arlene. All things considered though, none of them are *likely* suspects.

Whatever the case, whoever decided on putting the Peugeot out of action, was obviously bent on making sure everyone got back into the Raptor.

In the interest of convincing Arlene that the troublesome ford would be safe, Lester elected to drive. Josey had a question here; how was changing drivers expected to alter the atrocious performance of the car?

The drama with the door suddenly unclipping and swinging open was verified by Arlene in no uncertain terms, she had no reason to lie about falling out, and her injuries backed up both their stories.

The struggle Lester was having with the car, was the last thing Arthur's wife witnessed before falling out, making it difficult to argue with their story. Hers wasn't the only door that had somehow been rigged to unexpectedly fly open; both Lester and Arthur had also been placed under threat. Indeed, Arthur had also been thrown from the car; the difference being that Lester never saw it happen. One moment Arthur was there, and then he wasn't.

Arlene saw none of what happened to Lester until she regained consciousness back in the cabin, supporting the injury she had suffered after falling from the car.

If it was even possible that the car was being radio controlled as Josey now expected, the question was - from where? He thought about the path the track took from the highway to the cabin. The lay of the land dictated its course, encompassing many hairpin turns. Imagining it from the air, he envisaged the shape of a snake, creating narrow swathes of bush as it wound back upon itself. A person on foot could conceivably have the time to make their way through the bush in order to keep up with the progress of the big Ford. The proof of this was demonstrated by Lester himself, when he pursued the Raptor as it made its way back to the cabin. It wouldn't have been too hard for the controller to avoid being seen by Lester as he trudged through unfamiliar territory. This raised another question; was the Raptor being controlled by Jimmy Sullivan?

All of these thoughts were void of concrete answers. Furthermore, who was it that modified the Ford Raptor? Was it Sheridan, and was it designed to cover his plan for murder?

The strength of the car's body, with its *Thumper* Bull-bar, a detail Josey had picked up from the sergeant, suggested it was the perfect vehicle to ram its way into a solidly built log cabin. After all, it had endured the blunt force trauma of slamming into an immovable boulder, followed by repeated attacks on a cabin that wouldn't give in. Knowing how well he had built the cabin, would Arthur have settled for the Raptor, or chosen something bigger? Would he have even known the Raptor couldn't force its way through the walls? Or, maybe Arthur wasn't the perpetrator.

It's proved time and time again that the car had no driver, a story that wouldn't have been so easy to believe if not for Josey having seen it with his own eyes. The question isn't whether or not the Raptor *had* a driver; the question is why it *didn't?* Was the perpetrator fixated on trying to make his victims believe Arthur's car had a mind of its own for some reason?

As for Lester's account of Arlene's rescue, it was only from his point of view, no one else bore witness to it – not even Arlene. Following her fall from the car, her next recollection was that of a man she didn't even recognise leaning over her, touching her – was she even *wearing* her underwear, as they had both claimed?

It wasn't hard to understand why she might have gotten the wrong idea about Lester's motives; her state of mind at the time does go a long way to explaining why she could have believed she'd had been interfered with, and then maybe later retracting her accusation once she'd had time to clear her head. It was either that, or Lester *had* done something of a sexual nature to her and in the clear light of day she'd decided to change her story to protect him.

What Josey found odd though, was the detail that Lester had gone into in explaining her wet clothing and her level of undress. Was he perhaps frightened Arlene might say something to police that might incriminate him? And perhaps he made a big issue of his own nakedness for the same reason; even though, the police never saw him in a state of undress.

There's also the fact that Arlene made so little of being tied to the stove, when Lester portrayed it as a major event; designed to keep her safe.

Then there was the standout bruise that the police would have quizzed him about; he clearly needed a story, because he couldn't rely on Arlene remembering the events the way he says they happened – not just between her and Lester, but what happened with the Ford Raptor.

When it came to the part where they both saw Arthur behind the wheel, seemingly incomprehensive, the question has to be asked; how did he get there? Did someone put him there?

Their stories match each other's, almost down to the slightest detail, and if there are any lies among them, they too would have to be a match. That being the case, they would have needed to compare their stories in double time to get them straight before they were forced to talk to police. Oddly, neither one of them seemed to be aware there was a bullet hole in the Raptor's front seat headrest.

Is Arthur Sheridan dead, or alive? Perhaps shot.

If he was dead, it would only explain why he is missing, not the question of what happened to his body.

The other mystery, the most baffling and worrying one yet to be solved, is what's happened to Sergeant Perkin's brother, Andy? All subsequent searches had failed to find him.

It wouldn't have been all that remiss of Josey to walk away from this case, as had been ordained by police and strongly suggested by his own family. He might well have done so, if it weren't for that one very-unexpected phone call, while still laid up in the hospital.

CHAPTER TWELVE
Keeping Secrets

That was a week ago, a week of scan results and medical provisos by concerned doctors. The upshot of his injuries was that he had dodged a bullet when it came to the damage to his neck. He was told that he must take it easy for at least another couple of weeks. And that's what he did outwardly, but inwardly he was working the case.

Twenty four hours after leaving hospital, Josey was once again sitting opposite Lester Perkins in his guarded room at the psychiatric clinic. He'd been driven there by Molly, who had been asked to keep his visit to see the sergeant under wraps. She baulked at keeping things from her mother, but knew enough about her father to appreciate he'd have a good reason for whatever he was doing, which he promised to explain later when more was known.

Perkins looked to have lost a little weight, but still a

very imposing man.

'I wasn't sure I'd see you again,' he admitted to Josey.

'Oh, why's that?'

'That's one of my coppers guarding the door out there, he's not supposed to, but he tells me stuff.'

'Constable Mathews, we've met. So then, I guess you know I've been warned off the case.'

'Maybe you should be listening,' he said sounding like the cop that he was.

'Would you prefer that I did?'

'I'm not in a position to decide one way or the other.' Lester couldn't have appeared glummer if he tried. 'Josey, I have to ask, do you really think you can get me out of this mess?'

'I'm not Hercule Poirot, so I guess I can't say *I'm better than the police*.'

'You might need to be,' he said allowing a grin.

'How much has the constable told you,' Josey asked, 'about what happened?'

'I know how Bobby died; I can't get the image from my head.' Lester's stress forced him to take a deep breath, continuing on an exhale. 'You almost became a victim yourself, perhaps it's time you should back away.'

'That's by the by – I'm here, and I'm focussed on the help Andrew asked for.'

Recognising his mistake in undervaluing the man his brother had spent money hiring, brought an emotional response. Moisture reached his eyes as he flicked onto the constable at the door. 'I was told that you witnessed

Bobby's death.'

'Sort of, it's complicated. Did you know the young man?'

'Only to talk to, but I know his father pretty well. We're on-and-off fishing buddies; do you know how he's taking it?'

'I haven't had a chance to get up there yet, but I will.'

'When you do, tell him how sorry I am.'

Josey was nodding affirmatively, 'Of course.'

Lester hadn't asked about his brother, which led Josey to believe he hadn't been told.

'You look worried, is something wrong?'

Josey expected Lester wouldn't take the news well, especially since young Andy had been in his care so to speak. 'Your brother was out at the cabin with me, and in the Jeep before it crashed.'

'What're you saying?'

'He hasn't been seen since.'

Josey had no idea what he'd heard already, but opted to tell him the whole story. He just listened. He wasn't particularly mummified, not like Josey expected he'd be.

He was as *cool as a cucumber* when he asked, 'Why would you involve my brother in the first place?'

To Josey, he sounded unconvincing, dispassionate, almost like he already knew something. Perhaps the constable's told him, but if so why hide the fact? If Lester was playing games, Josey didn't have time for it. 'No one is to blame for what happened out there,' he told the sergeant, 'other than the person who tried to kill you and

Arlene.'

'And isn't that my bloody neighbour.'

'This is what Andrew has hired me to find out, and I can't do that without your help, you and Arlene.' Recognising his disquiet, Josey added, 'I'm not trying to trick you.'

Lester's face arrested all mobility, deliberate blankness. 'No – then what *are* you trying to do?'

'Get you to level with me.'

'What makes you think I'm not?'

'Because you haven't mentioned spending time talking to Mrs Sheridan on the phone; keeping in touch as they say, corroborating your stories.'

'That's a hell of an assumption, Cam, what's this really about?'

'If you have to ask, then we have a real problem.'

'Cam, I wasn't born yesterday, you're plainly trying to get me to admit our story is made up, but why? You saw what the car is capable of for yourself.'

'I did, and I came to the same conclusion as you, that the Raptor was being radio controlled?'

Lester's eyes became fully rounded, annoyed almost.

Josey was equally annoyed. 'Before you say anymore, I don't want to hear anything that isn't an absolute fact.'

'Why the seesawing, I can't tell if you're working for us or the police. Actually, maybe you should do yourself a favour and walk away; have a careful think about your position. I'm telling you this because I don't want you getting into trouble.'

Josey gave one of his unnerving smiles, because the sergeant couldn't have been more right – he was indeed trying to get him to admit that some of their story, and not just about the car, was a fabrication to cover-up something. His friend's lack of admission added to Josey's growing hunch.

One thing and another Josey had what he came for, and based on his friend's suggestion to walk away, he did, not so much to reconsider his position, but to continue making his *position* crystal clear.

Lester Perkins spent the rest of the day stewing over the odd conversation with the private detective.

How much does he know?

He glanced toward the door to make sure the constable wasn't watching; removed a cell phone from a bag he had resting against the leg of his chair and phoned Arlene. 'It's me; I've just had my detective friend over here; what in-hell did you say to him?'

'Exactly what we agreed on, why?'

'Because he's dropping massive hints that you and I are fabricating our stories.'

'In what way?'

'I'm not sure, because as far as the car goes, he's on our page. He was fishing for something else.'

'And I suppose you got testy with him.'

'Too right I did. I told him to back off.'

'Oh, well done, Lester. You played right into his hands; some copper you are.'

'Give me a break,' he moaned.

'Listen to me, your friend Josey doesn't know a damn thing about anything. He's clutching at straws, trust me.' The line went dead-quiet . . .

Arlene came back with a scoff into the phone. 'So long as we keep our story straight there isn't a damn thing this hot-shot detective can put on us. And you're missing an important point here, Lester; your brother and you hired him to help, why would he turn around and do the opposite?'

'I don't know, he just sounded really suspicious.'

'Bye- Lester,' she told him a second ahead of hanging up.

He held the phone to his ear as though Arlene was still on the line, her belittling words echoing in his head, *some bloody copper you are.*

CHAPTER THIRTEEN
Respite

The coming week was to be the longest of his life.

For a moment he thought Rebecca might be reading his mind. 'You wanted me to relax - this is me relaxing.'

She scoffed, 'That'll be the day. Come on, out with it, what were you thinking about?'

'If you must know; I was thinking, now that I've got more time than I know what to do with, we could take that holiday – maybe a road trip.'

She came and sat next to him on the two seater lounge and placed her hand restfully on his thigh.

She leant back and pivoted her head to see if he was being serious. 'To where?'

'Anywhere.'

In actual fact she was pleased he was thinking of getting out of Condobolin, away from the temptation to wander down to the police station for the occasional update on the case. On that score, the latest was that Sergeant Lester

Perkins was to be held for further questioning. The detective from Sydney that Constable Mathews had told him about was coming out in a couple of days to take over the investigation, seeing as how the local boys were considered a mite too close to the subject.

'And what pray tell are we going to be travelling in?' she asked.

It was a reasonable question, seeing as they had all *flown* into Condobolin, there was the small matter of not having a vehicle. 'I was thinking of a motor home.'

She turned sideways on the chair and looked at him.

'And who's going to drive it, I'm certainly not; and neither is Molly.'

'Drive what?'

They turned to Molly standing outside the bathroom in a towel.

'Your father wants us to take a road trip.'

Her hesitation prompted him to joke, 'If you girls aren't up for it, I'll go by myself.'

'Nice try, Dad,' she quipped before heading for her room. 'Let me get dressed, I need to hear this.'

After she'd gone into her bedroom and closed the door, Rebecca pushed off the lounge and waltzed over toward the kitchenette, saying as she went, 'When did you plan all this?'

'In the hospital, it was Molly's idea remember.'

'And where are you getting this mobile home from?' she asked while filling their cups from the percolator.

'From the old lady I bought it from.'

'You're a dark horse,' she alleged while bringing the coffees over to settle next to him.

Taking up the edge of the lounge she peered at him suspiciously as he took his cup.

'Thanks, cherry Pie,' he smooched. He waited wearing an expectant grin while she digested the idea.

'Do you know what,' she finally said with a tinge of excitement, 'I think I'm looking forward to this.'

He sipped his coffee and told her, 'Good.'

After two days of excited shopping for the supplies the girls thought they needed, Josey had another surprise up his sleeve, one that was about to land at their door. He never let on that it'd been organised, *Mum* was the word. That aside the timing couldn't have been worse. They were in the middle of an afternoon delight at the motel when they were disturbed by a resounding knock.

'Ignore it,' Rebecca breathed passionately.

'No problem,' Josey promised into her parted lips.

Knock, knock, knock — louder this time.

Following their mutual decision to continue, they managed to not miss a beat, determined to finish—

Wrap, wrap, wrap;

'Josey; you in there, Buddy—?' a male voice called from outside.

'Oh shit,' Josey grumbled without stopping.

Belinda pushed on his shoulders, pressing him back to take in his face. 'What should we do?' she laughed.

'Hurry,' was his singular advice, his voice beating

double time to the hastened rhythm; antics so comical that Rebecca's laugh occasioned a sudden expression of passion.

The all too descriptive sound made it through to the front door; where Carl Norris and his wife Nicole were waiting.

'We should leave,' Nicki told Carl with embarrassment.

'Agreed,' he said already pacing away from the door.

They were practically at their insect spattered car when they heard the door of the motel open behind them. They turned to see Cameron clad in his dressing gown, completing the picture. Their collective imaginations envisaged Rebecca hurriedly dressing in the bedroom; into something a little less obvious.

'We're staying here,' Carl called across to Josey, 'we'll come see you later.'

Nicole cheekily appeared in the doorway similarly dressed in her gown, splayed her arms, and announced in a cheery-shrill voice, 'Sur*prise*!'

Josey pointed at them demandingly with the door half closed. 'Stay; we'll be two seconds.'

The door closed with purpose, leaving the visitors hissing with stifled laughter.

Later, the two families were settled at the local Chinese eatery happily discussing the untimely visit. Carl and Nicki showing up in Condobolin was totally unexpected, at least by Rebecca and Molly.

'After talking to Cam at the hospital,' Carl explained,

'We decided we'd hop out and surprise him, see how he's feeling.'

'I'm *feeling* all right,' he joked with the help of the wine.

An amused glance between Carl and his wife set them off again, remembering the assumed coitus.

They'd all known each other for over a decade, their friendships flourishing following Carl's prior eight year stretch as Josey's assistant sleuth. Not only was he an admirable snoop, Norris was a talented disguise artist. He had taken on the appearance of men both older and younger than himself, even a woman on the odd occasion. To see him out of disguise, he was a most forgettable character, whose plain good looks allowed him to disappear equally as well. His expression neither smiled, nor scowled, neither judged nor showed signs of worry, but he could change all that with one single dress up. Along with his altering persona came an array of accents and tone of voice.

His wife Nicole made him even more invisible when she was around, not because of any vicious intent; just because her personality demanded attention. She was pretty, well proportioned, showy yet not boisterous.

One night at a club party, just after Carl had first been introduced to Rebecca and Molly, he came out of the women's bathroom transformed into an extremely sexy woman.

Everyone was wondering how they hadn't previously lain eyes on this luscious female among the other guests.

Rebecca was laughing right up until this sexy siren started making up to Josey. Josey of course knew it was Carl but everyone else had been fooled, especially Rebecca and Molly, who by this time would have recognised Carl straight off. Not this time. That's how good an illusionist he was.

Inebriated laughter accompanied his performance, which ended with a strip-show, in which he ended up clad down to just his male underwear; making amorous advances toward Josey's wife.

Carl's subterfuge brought the house down.

The subterfuge Josey was now conducting was anything but comical, closer in fact to deceit. But it was deemed necessary. Josey needed Carl to help him find Sheridan's car, if not *Sheridan himself*. Meanwhile hiding the fact he was continuing with the case.

A case is what this still was, and most of the detail about it was kept from Carl until he arrived in Condobolin. At the first opportunity that they got to speak alone, they had a meeting.

'What makes you think the car's still in the area?' Carl asked.

'I have it on good authority.'

Carl held, waiting for more information.

'You'll have to trust me on this, its best no one knows where this information comes from at this stage. I made a promise – no exceptions.'

If there was one thing Carl Norris had no problem with,

it was placing trust in his boss, and in whatever that trust entailed.

'Mildura is where we need to be, Carl; but I don't want this causing an upset with Nicole; is she likely to have a problem with you spending a bit of time out here?'

He shook his head. 'She's just happy we're finally doing something together. Mildura's not too far from Wyalong, which is where we're staying; she won't twig.'

Carl's assurance settled Josey a little, but was curious to know, 'What's at Wyalong?'

'She has an aunt there with a few acres just out of town. I sort of instigated an invitation to stay.'

'Nice.'

Across the way in Nicole's room, Rebecca could see Carl and Josey deep in discussion. 'I was really surprised to see you guys here,' she said to Nicole.

Nicole gave her a cheeky stare. 'We're sorry about that.'

Rebecca laughed it off. 'You know what I mean,' she tittered while gaining composure.

'I have to say I'm surprised we're here too, Carl's not real big on holidays.'

'Those two are peas in a pod on that score. When did he come up with the idea?' The expression she got from her friend prompted Rebecca to focus across to their husbands at the other side of the car park.

'Are you worried about something?'

She turned her head back. 'Maybe I'm being paranoid.'

'About what?'

'The timing of your visit.'

Now Nicole was looking at their partners; she took in a deep breath and paused, open mouthed for a moment. 'You don't think . . .'

Rebecca was slowly nodding, 'I do; according to Cam, Carl called him at the hospital. I get the feeling they're up to something.'

She could only suspect that Josey had been untruthful about Carl's supposed call to the hospital, and wonder who else might have been the caller.

They both fixed on the sight of their husbands in discussion.

'He can't let this go – is that it?'

'He says he has, but I'm not convinced.'

Nicki settled into thought. 'Come to mention it, Carl's been unusually excited about this trip. Now you've got *me* wondering.'

Rebecca turned her head sharply. 'Don't say anything just yet, in case we're wrong.'

'Maybe we *should* say something, I mean is Cam well enough to be involving himself in the case?'

'That's never stopped him before.'

'I can see what's got him so interested, it's a damn puzzling story.'

'And he thinks he's got it sorted.'

'And you don't?'

'I don't know, but I do know he's a bloody good detective; maybe he has, and he probably feels he's letting his friend down by pulling the plug.'

Nicole reached across to Rebecca and patted her arm. 'I

wouldn't worry too much, I'm sure that if we're right about this, he's not the sort of guy to place his family in harm's way, or us for that matter.'

Carl glanced across at the women and caught them looking. 'Do you think Bec' might work out what you're up to?'

'Maybe she will – but let's cross that bridge when we come to it.'

Carl was studying his hands, interlaced fingers to seemingly avoid unnecessary gesturing. 'What's the plan if I find the car?' He looked up to receive the answer.

'Don't do anything other than let me know. If you need to contact me, just make up a story that I'll recognise and text me; Maybe say, *you've found a great place to eat*, and where. I'll call you back when I get a chance. If we get sprung, I'll just come clean. Whatever happens don't take any risks, or let anyone know what you're doing, but if Nicky gets suss, let me know and I'll explain it to both of them.'

'And if things get rough?'

'That's when we send them home.'

Carl thought for a moment and said, 'Perhaps we should do that sooner rather than later.'

'Okay,' Josey responded playfully, 'I'll let you be the one to tell them the holiday is off.'

Carl's grin contradicted the frown on his forehead. 'Point taken.'

They turned in unison toward the girls, who sat framed in the open doorway of the motel room.

'Are you certain the caller's information is reliable?'

'Because of who it is; I am.'

That was code for I'll explain later.

'Right, game on.' They clinked stubbies.

The wives saw the gesture and wondered if it might indicate an agreement of some sort, or perhaps it was just two blokes happy to be sharing their time on a rare and unexpected holiday.

When asked later what they were talking about at the motel, Josey told Rebecca and Molly that Carl had a plan to stay with Nicole's aunt, and that they'd worked out a plan to be travelling in the same direction, at least for the first few days.

CHAPTER FOURTEEN
A call from Wyalong

Two days later, Josey and his family were at the house of the mobile home owner, a lady in her late eighties sporting a friendly smile.

They were led through the well-kept house that smelt faintly of age, out into the large back yard where the *home on wheels* sat gleaming in the hot sun.

'An Auto Trail Delaware,' she told them like a salesperson.

The magnificent looking vehicle, maroon and white, had a small hand painted sign hanging from one of the wipers; $110,000.

She saw their eyes on it. 'My grandson paid two hundred and fourteen thousand dollars three years ago; I was happy to give it away but I've been pressured into putting a price on it.'

No one was game to ask who was applying the pressure, the subject seemed finalised.

131

'It's one of those automatic things I'm told. It's got a double bed in there,' then she pointed to the rounded nose above the cabin, 'and up there, there is a single bed for you, Molly.'

'Nice,' Molly approved.

With a titter she said, 'Oh yes, it's nice all right, but I doubt I could swing a leg up there.'

That did it, they all cracked up, it was just too funny not to.

An hour later, following cool drinks, three helpings of homemade cake accompanied by the history of her life, the Josey family were driving away with their beautifully large Delaware with Josey at the wheel.

The unit had three seats if you included the seat-belted chair that doubled for dining when swung round.

Josey could see Molly in the mirror, appearing suitably pleased. The cabin was alive with chatter for the first hour, after which the passing scenery lulled them into a contented silence.

They pulled into West Wyalong near dinner time and booked into a caravan park, the type needed to replenish the needs of the Delaware.

After showers they all met up in the onsite restaurant. With her nose in the menu, Rebecca asked Cam, 'Will Carl be in Hay when we get there?'

'He said he might be, I'm not sure, why?'

'Just curious.'

Molly looked up to gauge if their expressions matched how they sounded.

'Rebecca, I know if you're curious about something you'll come straight out and ask.'

'All right - I find it strange that Carl just happens to be on the same road as us heading in the same direction.'

Molly was frowning. 'What's strange about that, Mum?'

Josey took a short glance at his wife to gauge her reaction.

Which she released on the end of a long exhale, finally saying what she'd been thinking, 'I mean what are the odds?'

Josey scoffed, 'Coincidence?'

Molly agreed. 'Yeah, 'it's a *coincidence* – people run into each other all the time when travelling.'

They left the caravan park early the next morning, next stop, the tiny town of Hay.

Josey's Intel suggested the Raptor might be found in and around Mildura. That could mean it may even be in Wyalong, or maybe even Balranald where Nicole's aunt lives. *That really would be a coincidence*, he thought.

Although his informant hadn't mentioned Condobolin as a possible hiding place for the car, Josey considered it might be worth keeping it on the list.

His cell phone lit up ahead of ringing, fetching his eye to where it sat in its cradle near the windscreen. On noticing it was a text from Carl, he tapped it open.

Let us know when you're in
Hay we've found a great

place to eat.

Josey wasn't expecting to hear from Carl so soon and especially right when Rebecca was showing signs of suspicion. Recognising Carl's message as code for *we need to talk*, he began mentally rehearsing his speal to reveal the big secret to Rebecca and Molly. It wasn't all that important that they not know; it was more about the fact he was disobeying police orders, which his wife would surely interpret as leading their young daughter astray.

Hearing Carl had found somewhere to eat, reminded Molly of how hungry she was; prompting her to ask how far out of town they were—

Her question cut into Josey's mental preparation like an eraser, without the time to develop his approach to the lie, he got right onto what he needed to do. 'Siri, call Carl.'

Calling Carl . . .

Rebecca waited, curious as to why Josey had skipped across Molly's question and why he was showing more concern about the call. 'Cam, what's going on?' Her query was once again interrupted by Carl's voice—

'Josey.'

'You're on speaker, Carl,' he warned, 'I'm on the road with the girls.'

The response was hesitant . . . 'Oh, okay?'

'Go ahead – it's time they knew.'

Molly leant forward gently in her seat belt to reach the attention of her mother. 'Is something wrong?'

Rebecca motioned for her to hold off so that she could listen; she couldn't believe the next words that Carl came out with.

'You need to turn around; they want you back in Condobolin.'

'You're kidding.' Carl's news wasn't even close to what Josey had been expecting to hear.

'The body in the burnt out Jeep, it isn't Bobby Barton.'

The Josey family sensed their holiday was about to take a deep dive into oblivion; over before it even started.

Josey recovered enough to say, 'Who then?'

'They've found traces of *Sheridan's* blood.'

'I didn't see this coming,' he said with utter conviction, well aware of the implications.

'I know, right – this puts you back in the thick of it, not to mention the loss of a suspect.'

An immediate thought popped into Josey's head. 'Not necessarily.'

The news that the garage owner's son wasn't the cadaver went part way to explaining to Josey how Bobby had gotten from the pond alive - to *dead* in the Jeep. But then, that scenario wasn't quite complete, because it would mean Bobby was another missing person – another missing person who had chosen not to contact anyone.

Rebecca and Molly were too mortified to speak.

Josey was already slowing the Delaware as he asked,

'How'd you find this out?'

'That inspector from Sydney called me; he said he'd been trying to reach you. It sounded to me like he didn't trust you'd answer your phone. Be warned, he sounds a bit of a dick; sorry girls,' he hastily apologised.

'Don't tell me, he wants another statement because they think I'm their only available witness.'

'There's that, and then there's the question, why you told the police Sheridan wasn't driving the Ford.'

'He wasn't,' Josey said emphatically. He had no sooner spoken the words, when the problem of whether or not Sheridan was there, actually gave him the answer as to why he may have been driving and why he didn't see him, and how he may have ended up in the burnt out jeep.

He pulled the Delaware onto the shoulder where it was safe from passing traffic and brought it to a halt; he could feel Rebecca staring at him. 'I was waiting for the right moment to tell you.'

He didn't face her until she said, 'You're on the case; I knew it.'

'Not any more it seems,' he admitted regretfully.

'Good, I'm glad.' She was understandably annoyed.

Molly wasn't game to speak.

'Finish your call,' Rebecca said in consideration of Carl waiting on the line.

In his usual style, Josey switched straight back into business mode. 'Carl, I need a big favour.'

'Sure.'

Rebecca imperceptibly descended deeper into her seat;

experience told her that whatever happened now was out of her hands. Her husband was obliged to respond to the police request and would be in strife if he didn't return to Condobolin and face the music.

The upshot was that the favour Josey wanted amounted to his returning to Condobolin alone. There were two benefits the way he saw it, the girls could continue their holiday in the mobile home while keeping them away from whatever his interrogation might amount to. He figured if things got too messy with police that plan could change.

He supposed the girls could stay with Carl and his family at Aunt Judy's property, where there'd probably be plenty of room to stash the mobile home, while he returned to Condo in Carl's Toyota. 'It's a big ask I know,' he confessed to Carl.

'Are you kidding, I don't see you have a lot of choice.'

'No, but you do.'

'Don't be ridiculous, I'll get it setup; Judy will be only too pleased to help. Just get yourselves here as soon as your able, if the inspector rings I'll tell him you're on your way, you can explain why you're late when you get back there. The Toyota's yours.'

Carl was right about Judy; Nicole's aunt was one of the most obliging people they could ever hope to meet. She lived alone on ten acres of grassland and was glad to have the extra company.

The house had five bedrooms, confirming that she

wasn't always alone there. It eventually came out that her husband had died the year after the last of three kids left the nest. Because she had started her family early, she was presently around forty five years of age and with plenty of life left to live. She was a country lady for certain, but with her youthful looks she could be anything she wanted. There was a no nonsense aura about her that demanded respect, yet instantly likable – and not just for her generosity, which she had in spades.

Josey liked that her property was well fenced, and that she had a half dozen German Shepherds on guard. 'They're friendly to people they know,' she claimed, 'but be sure not to do anything that could be perceived as a threat.'

He left the property satisfied that his family would be safe. Pushing Carl's Toyota toward Condobolin, Josey called ahead to get a room back at the motel.

The proprietor was surprised to hear he was coming back so soon, and alone, but quickly gleaned that his customer wasn't in a position to talk about why.

An hour after he left Wyalong, Carl received another call from Inspector Brown asking where Josey was. The city cop's call reached the Toyota only a few minutes later.

'Detective Josey,' Brown's overly officious voice said when his call connected, 'for a while there I thought you'd done a runner.' The self-appreciating scoff that he concluded with sounded contrived.

Carl was spot-on Josey thought, but spoke with a level

voice. 'Sorry about the delay, I had to find accommodation for my family. I'm about an hour away.'

'That'll be a little late for me, come and see me in the morning; be at the station at nine.'

Josey answered him with the same impersonal tone. 'I'll see you then.'

There was no good bye; just the dull clunk of an office land line receiver being returned to its cradle, most likely slammed down for effect.

CHAPTER FIFTEEN
Inspector Brown

At 9am sharp, Josey entered the Condobolin Police Station. He was met by Constable Mathews, the young cop who had been guarding his sergeant at the Psychiatric Centre.

'Sorry about spoiling your holiday, Detective,' he said offering Josey his hand—'

'In here, Detective.'

Josey knew who was making this abrupt command; out the corner of his eye he could see the inspector waiting in the doorway to one of the offices.

After taking his time to complete the handshake with Mathews, he turned and headed toward the man filling the doorway; fully suited, medium build, around fifty; full head of hair that tended to grey at the temples, and momentarily wearing a no-nonsense expression.

With equally blunt countenance Josey presented no eagerness to take his hand unless it was offered.

140

It wasn't, he had already paced away into the room and sat down with his eyes fixed on whatever was taking his attention on the desk. Without so much as a glance from Brown, Josey got a wave toward the seat opposite.

When the City Cop finally did raise his eyes expecting to see his visitor obeying the offer, he noticed the detective had already relaxed comfortably into the chair; this seemed to annoy him.

There was a measure of distaste in his expression; Josey could only assume the guy might have been expecting to see his visitor in a suit, not looking like one of the locals, dressed in blue jeans and an open neck shirt.

This'll be fun.

He was straight to business. 'We'll be travelling out to the location,' he said checking his watch - 'in a half hour.' He folded his palms over the edge of the desk as if his intention was to push it across the floor. 'I've read your earlier statement, which I guess we can throw in the trash can – once you've done the update.' He paused, waiting for Josey to say something, followed by the first sign of recognition he wasn't the only one who could intimidate.

Josey wasn't about to be railroaded, but he also needed to keep this guy on side, especially if he had an inherent dislike for private detectives. He said to the inspector, 'I have to say, the news that Bobby Barton wasn't the victim in the Jeep came as a welcome surprise, how is his father? He must have been pleased to get news like this.'

The blank look on Brown's face told Josey the head cop

hadn't even spoken to Roger Barton, and probably hadn't even enquired about his well-being.

Brown cleared his throat a little awkwardly before saying, 'My directive is to sort out all these somewhat absurd statements. Your account has one standout irregularity, in that you appear to be siding with the story given by the defendant.'

The reference was to having seen the car without a driver. Josey avoided launching into the hunches that he had, because frankly, it was none of Brown's business. All that this guy needed to know was the facts, which if tested on it, would probably see him agreeing, because he didn't seem to possess an abundance of imagination.

'Inspector, I appreciate you must be a very busy man, and I'm here to expedite your investigation as much as I can. May I suggest we continue our discussion at the location; I can walk you through what I saw. Also, with your permission, I wouldn't mind taking a look at the corpse.'

His expression didn't look promising. 'Why?'

'To be honest I can't get the sight of that body out of my head; I promise you I have an indelible recollection of it. If I'm allowed to view the remains, I think it will help me understand why I thought it was Bobby Barton.'

Brown seemed incapable of removing his frown. 'What do you think you'll find?'

'I have no preconceived idea on that,' he lied.

The inspector cleared his throat again. 'Right, well, have yourself back here in fifteen minutes; I'll have a patrol car to take us up to the site. And, if you're even luckier, I'll organise to have you visit the remains upon our return. I can hardly wait to see what that's about.' He was saying all this while heading to the door, whereupon he stopped and glanced back. 'You can wait here, or come back - up to you.' And then he was gone.

Josey wasn't looking forward to sitting in a patrol car listening to Inspector Brown, or worse, sitting in silence with the guy. He put up a bid to drive to the location in the Toyota and got an immediate yes. On the way he put in a call to Carl.

'Hi, it's me.'

'How'd it go?'

'It's still going; I'm on my way to the crime scene now to give his nibs the lowdown.'

'Good luck - is he being the dick I said he'd be?'

'He's no diplomat,' he agreed.

'How long's this likely to take?'

'With any sort of luck I'll be back with you guys for dinner.'

'Well I hope your right because as you've probably guessed I've made some progress.'

'You've found the car?' Josey said with lifted spirits.

'Do your best to get him off your back; what I've found will make your day.'

Josey wasn't sure *getting Brown off his back* was the way it was going to pan out.

When they arrived at the site, he discovered it wouldn't

be easy for another reason, all tyre tracks had been obliterated by further rain, and a subsequent dry spell, even the ashes from the burnt-out car were washed away. As expected, the remains of the jeep had been seized by police. Josey had a good mental picture of exactly where everything occurred though.

Where Josey had been stuck in the bog, although still moist, it was now solid enough to walk on. Brown took a few steps onto it as if to make some sort of point, but in fact his focus remained centred on exactly why the detective had identified Bobby Barton as the one who died in the Jeep. Josey told him it was an honest mistake, and it was. But he wasn't about to mention his hunch until after visiting the Morgue.

'In hindsight, it was a bit of a stretch,' Josey suggested evasively, 'but I figured he may have tried extinguishing the fire, and somehow been overcome and fallen into the flames.'

'So now that we know you were wrong, what's your theory on where the Barton kid is now?'

'I know as much as you do.'

The Inspector wasn't sure whether to buy Josey's story or not, so he moved onto his next bone of contention. The area showed no evidence of where someone could have been deeply buried, especially since the so called *bog* was completely missing, having dried up.

'Just how far into the mud were you?' he asked Josey suspiciously.

'If you mean before the Ford ran me over, I was down

to my knees.'

Brown didn't miss the subtle dig. 'A car coming at you like that should have killed you, yet all you got was a graze and a slight burn to your head; not to mention the burns on your hands by the way, which points to you having put the body in the burning Jeep. You can see why this all looks very suspicious.'

Josey wanted to remind him about the injury to his neck and the head aches, but skipped the effort.

Brown rested his hands on his hips thoughtfully and took a few steps away before turning. 'Explain to me why you wouldn't have seen someone behind the wheel.'

'Any number of reasons, maybe the angle I was at, looking up at a high vehicle.'

'Can you hear yourself, one minute you're telling me the car didn't have a driver, and then you're saying you couldn't *see* the driver, which is it?'

Josey realised he had slipped up in putting himself in a position whereby he'd now have to divulge a portion of his hunch. He also realised that if he was ever going to make it back to Wyalong for dinner and see what Carl has found, he was going to have to give Inspector Brown something that sounded believable. 'Maybe Sheridan was collapsed on the seat, out of my line of sight. Let's not forget that Mrs Sheridan saw her husband splayed on the bonnet of the Raptor at the cabin, which means he was at best unconscious, or he may in fact have been dead.'

Brown laughed at this. 'So now a dead man is driving the car.'

Josey could have lost his composure at this point, but too much was at stake.

'Okay,' Brown relaunched, 'let's say Sheridan is out to it on the seat, and someone else is controlling the vehicle to run you over. I suppose you're about to tell me you know who that is, and how that's done.' Looking for support from his driver he glanced over at young Beasley, and sarcastically said to him. 'This ought to be good, Constable,'

Unfazed, Josey stuck to his guns, 'Clearly it was being remotely controlled. And no, I don't know who was controlling it, and I don't know how Sheridan ended up in the Jeep.' *But I've got some ideas,* he felt like saying.

Brown's laugh sounded closer to a snicker.

Josey had to give him more. 'Autonomous vehicles are a reality,' he said matter of factly, 'it's not such a big stretch to believe they might be controlled from outside the vehicle, like a kid's toy.' Josey knew the Raptor couldn't have been externally controlled while they chased it on the highway, but he didn't want to confuse Brown any more than he already was.

The inspector strode back to where Josey stood and eyeballed him. 'Since you didn't see anyone nearby with a gaming console, let me recap what I think happened here.' He turned his back; took a few steps away and paused for effect; facing Josey he gave his performance. 'Sheridan shows up in the *Raptor* - and tries to run you down while you're dousing Bobby Barton in the pond.' He swivelled around as if in search of the illusive pool,

146

then feigned a confused shrug. And then held his arms out as if to say, *where is it*? 'Look, I don't pretend to know how you turned the tables, or why, but somehow you got Sheridan out of the offending vehicle; dead or alive, who knows, then you put him in the seat of the burning Jeep and—'

'Wow, that's quite a picture, Inspector, why the hell would you think I'd do that? And if I had, I was pretty damn lucky not to have burnt more than just my hands while lifting Arthur back into a burning car.'

Brown's scenario was as solid as Swiss-cheese.

'It's better than *your* bullshit story,' the disgruntle cop breathed out sounding like he was losing steam.

Josey wanted to expand on what *he* thought happened on the day, but decided he'd revealed enough, and moreover it was still just a hunch.

Brown didn't say another word to Detective Josey until after they'd paid their visit to the morgue. The morgue was open, but only in order to receive new check-ins and to dispatch checkouts. The mortician herself was forced away on some sort of family emergency. The coroner only visited from Orange when required.

'I'm still trying to find out what happened to the Perkins kid,' Brown told Josey as they went on their way from the morgue, 'until I do, don't even think about leaving town.'

Josey took it for what it was, a less than official request.

Before a light meal at the motel, he wrote out a new

report, which wasn't all that different to the first, just adding a summary of his day out with the Inspector.

After a good night call to Rebecca he was off to bed for a night of sleep. He left at five in the morning, not for Wyalong to learn what Carl's exciting news was, but for the cabin; he wanted to have a chat with Arthur's neighbour, Jimmy Sullivan. It was too early to be waking people up, so he decided Carl's news could wait. He didn't expect his excursion would take all that long.

He also didn't really expect Inspector Brown would be keeping a watch on him, except for putting out a search if he found out his order had been disobeyed; he took the back roads anyway.

CHAPTER SIXTEEN
Jimmy Sullivan

The dirt track maintained a bad feel about it.

Stories of a mad Ford Raptor suddenly appearing out of nowhere to attack was impossible to remove from your mind. It was also impossible not to regurgitate his worry over bringing young Andrew to the cabin, thereby resulting in his demise.

He made it to the cabin without incident, he and Carl's Toyota still intact. Nothing had changed since his last visit with Andrew, except the ground was as dry as baked bread given it hadn't rained for over a week.

After a quick inspection inside, he made his way to the broken fence to take a look at Lester's doomed Peugeot. It looked even sadder now that more of its body protruded above the surface of the water, which had been reduced to a gentle trickle.

He rounded the cliff edge and made his way down the banks of the creek, hoping that he might be able to cross now that the waters had receded. He noticed a large fallen tree, resting atop each bank where the waterline must have reached at the height of the storm. Although it would have taken deft skill to walk across it while the current was flowing practically knee high, Josey assumed that must have been how Sullivan made the crossing to reach Arthur's place.

With the flow reduced to a modest current, he was able to wade in, and by the time he reached half way across, he was still only calf deep. Where the water level rose to just his ankles at the opposite bank, he took a step up and removed his shoes to upend them. He rung out his waterlogged socks and placed one in each pocket before re-donning the shoes for his walk through the bush.

He soon came across the narrow walking trail that Sullivan must have used to reach Sheridan's cabin. The track had a gradual climb to it, unlike the drop-off near Arthur's place. It wasn't a short distance however and took a good ten minutes to reach Jimmy Sullivan's house. It was more like a cottage. There was a car parked in the yard; somebody was home. He called out, but got no response.

Venturing up a single step to a patio, he was then able to see a section of the roof on Arthur's place, half the distance he'd walked as the crow flies.

He knocked on the door; no answer.

Moving back down into the yard he rounded the house, walked past a woodpile that was stacked up against a wall. Beyond that there was an old clothes line that sagged halfway to the ground between two wooden poles. He bobbed beneath it and continued to the front of the dwelling, or was it the back, it was hard to tell. There was another door that looked just like the one on the other wall, with yet another patio, which he was about to make his way up to—

'Hey, anything I can help you with, mate?'

He turned expecting to see Sullivan, but it was a much younger man than had been explained to him. 'Sorry, I'm looking for Jimmy, is he about?'

'And you are?'

'Cameron Josey.' He showed him his credentials.

After a quick inspection he said, 'Oh you're the bloke who's looking into what happened next door.'

'I am, sorry about the intrusion.' As usual Josey exuded approachability, which the young man appeared to take on board with slight relief. 'Is everything all right?'

'I wish I knew, I haven't seen my father since I got back, that's been three days and I'm worried – have you found out what happened at Arthur's place?'

This was a heavily loaded question, and one too complicated to get into. 'Not in any great depth at this point. That's why I'm here; I was hoping to have a talk with your father to see what else he might know. Have you spoken to him on the phone? – sorry, you didn't say your name?'

'*Jerry* – Dad told me about the car in the creek, and that the police were combing the area. That's all I know.'

'Sadly, the car in the creek belonged to the sergeant in Condobolin, do you know him?'

'No, I heard someone pushed it in. That would have pissed him off.'

'Can I ask; is it unusual for your father to go off without warning?'

'I promise you this is very unusual for Dad, he never actually goes anywhere.'

Josey looked about, blindly thinking.

'Does that mean something to you?' Jerry asked apprehensively.

'No, no not at all.' He didn't want to concern the kid unduly. 'Well look, take my card if you would,' he said handing it across. 'Call me when your father returns, it'd be a great help.'

Jerry seemed quite pleased to have this new contact that might end up leading to his father's whereabouts. 'Likewise, if you hear anything, please let me know.'

Josey reached for his hand. 'Thanks for your time.'

'Right, well thank *you* for dropping by.'

Josey smiled, nodded and left.

He retraced his footsteps back to the river; doing the kid's worrying for him. When someone vanishes out of character, it's usually for a very bad reason.

His thoughts slipped onto the backburner as he waded back across the creek, the whole time keeping his eye on the half drowned vehicle. He decided to take a closer look.

He lifted out of the creek and walked the bank until he came level with the car's rear end. The wheels sat on solid ground now, still showing evidence of the flotsam that the flooded stream had generously provided. The subsided surface of the water was rippling against the front door handles now, but the engine and the rest of the frontend remained submerged. What he could see of the body looked fairly undamaged.

The doors were closed but unlocked, which was odd. All the windows were up. Cupping his hands against the glass, he was able to inspect the interior. The dashboard offered nothing in the way of a clue. The floor pan was underwater and all he could see was a reflection of the ceiling and sky from the opposite window. His scrutiny came to rest on the gear lever, protruding from the water like a dead stump.

This's interesting . . .

The stick was sitting in neutral, and low-and-behold the hand brake was lowered to the off position. This solid piece of evidence lifted a light grin to his face as he repeated aloud, 'This is *very* interesting.'

There was no point in conducting an underwater inspection; that could wait until the car was fished out, which he believed was in the pipeline. He waded out onto the bank and concentrated on the car's rear end—

What he saw right then froze him to the spot . . .

Protruding from the narrow gap at the base of the closed

boot was a shred of material. He felt its texture; it was as thick as an overcoat. Unless Perkins was in the habit of keeping a perfectly good coat in the boot of his car, there was something else in there other than an inclusion from his wardrobe. He thought about Andrew's obsession at that moment.

The latch was the type that was always locked unless opened with a key. Looking around for something to use as a lever, he found a fence paling lodged between the spokes of one of the wheels. It had a six inch nail protruding out of one end. He thought to hook it under the lid and prize it open. The paling was just long enough to allow his butt to rest on it once he had the lever in position. Two or three bounces cracked the lock setting the lid free, ending in a rebound that he managed to stave off with his hand.

The sudden stench from the open trunk forced him to step away, gagging and slipping as he fell on the muddy bank. With the back of his hand acting as a mask, even before he built enough fortitude to overcome the unpleasantness, he knew what was to be found, not just what, but *who*. He could see the top edge of something that was a whole lot more than just a coat.

He smothered his face in the welcome dampness of his handkerchief that he'd dunked in the creek, and slithered closer to the exposed contents. As expected he was looking at a body, a body that had been there more than a few days, but dead longer – and certainly not dampened by flood waters.

To appreciate who it was, he had to lean in until his head was completely within the boot space; hovering above the poor fellow like some sort of hungry buzzard.

He once again gagged and pulled back, but not before making a positive identification – the dead man was Jerry's father, *Jimmy Sullivan*. He was able to confirm this after finding a wallet in the coat pocket, and his name on a credit card, all of which he replaced.

He closed the lid as best he could against the broken lock and stepped well away, beyond the mud soaked bank onto dry grass, where he sat looking back at the bizarre discovery.

Now he had a problem. This gruesome find was going to lead to a whole bunch of questions . . .

Firstly, why hadn't the police found the body? The answer to that had to be because when they searched, the body wasn't there, which meant it'd been placed there sometime in the last couple of weeks; after the car had been pushed into the creek following the police search. This was a setback he didn't need, even though it was just as central to the case as anything else he'd found so far.

Josey needed to get to Wyalong to follow up on the lead he'd received from his informant, not to mention see what Carl had unearthed as a result of it. Right now being held up from doing so was a complete inconvenience.

Dare he withhold this latest discovery?

The broken lock was a problem, that hadn't been like that the last time the police inspected the car.

The question was; was anyone currently thinking of

checking the car again?

Josey assumed that would only occur when the tow truck arrived to retrieve the wreck, and Josey knew that wasn't scheduled for another couple of weeks.

Fast forward, and the hope was that he'd have gotten to the bottom of what was going on with the case, and truth be known, Sullivan's body in the boot was helping that outcome in no uncertain terms, not to mention the circumstance the car was left in.

He was thinking of leaving when his eyes fell on two thin leather straps poking out of the mud.

Arlene's bag?

Its shallow grave gave little resistance and he was able to resurrect it without much trouble. A zip held it closed, so there was minimal gunk inside. The golden discovery was a mobile phone.

Josey knew the procedure, waterlogged electronics needed up to forty eight hours immersed in silica Gel to stand a chance of ever working again. Of course the bag and the phone were also evidence, yet they were too good to leave behind, and too hot a potato to mention to police he'd found them. One thing was for sure, he had no intention of leaving it to be lost forever. The contents of the phone might just be the break he needed.

Decision made, Josey hotfooted it back to his car and drove up the dirt track to the highway without raising an alarm. It was impossible not to feel a deep sadness for what Jimmy's son would soon have to endure.

In spite of his anxiousness to get to Aunt Jude's place, he had a couple of unfinished things to take care of on his way to Condobolin. First there was the promise made to Sergeant Perkins to check in on Bobby Barton's father, to see how he was getting along following the death of his son, which of course was apparently no longer true. Roger Barton had been informed of the mistake, and was now having to face the fact his son was a missing person.

The garage was only a short detour to the north of where the track exited onto the highway, so it was easy enough to make the effort, and it would be remiss of him not to.

Roger recognised Josey as soon as he pulled in beside the pumps. Leaving the confines of the shop he walked out to see him. The Toyota was taking on fuel as the garage owner approached.

'Detective; are you just here for gas or to explain how the cops stuffed this up?'

Josey immediately picked up on his anger. 'I hear you, but no. In fairness, they didn't have much to go on. You must have been relieved to learn your son wasn't the one found in his Jeep at least.'

'You didn't need to come all the way out here to ask me that.'

Josey needed to be careful with this man; he was still hurting, and still none the wiser about where his son was. 'Before we knew it wasn't Bobby, Sergeant Perkins asked me to pass on his condolences.'

'Is it true what they're saying about Perkins?'

'I wouldn't believe everything you hear.'

'That's your advice is it?'

Josey recognised why Roger's mood was anything but amiable, boosting his need to climb into the Toyota and drive out of there; appeasing a disgruntled parent was never easy; this was worse, the guy was probably deflecting blame toward Andrew and the detective in the first place. His point of view wasn't without substance, but it *was* hypothetical.

The pump splashed back and Josey returned the nozzle to its holder. 'I wish there was something I could tell you.'

The words sounded hollow, even to Josey.

The gauge showed *$15,* he was trying to hand over a twenty as the distressed man turned his back and walked away. 'Do me a favour and let me know if you or the damn cops find my son.'

One thing was certain; Roger Barton had a lot on his mind, and glib comments weren't about to appease. Josey drove out of his garage on a huge low.

Joe Magrie, the Sheridan's favourite motel owner, had a similar persona, seemingly carrying everybody's troubles on his own shoulders.

'Are the cops getting any closer to finding who's doing this to the Sheridans?' The question sounded the way frustrated people talk to police when they're exasperated with unsolved crimes.

'They are,' Josey lied on Inspector Brown's behalf.

Magrie scoffed. 'I've heard the cops are looking at Condobolin's own sergeant, is that right?'

'As usual the police suspect everyone.'

'Aren't that the truth. What about you, who do you suspect?'

'I'm still working on it.'

'I can tell you one thing; we get a lot of riffraff coming through this part of the world, I'm betting it's one of those backpackers.'

Josey had no idea how much Magrie had been told by Arthur, the guy certainly knew about the troubles with the Raptor, having been asked to check it for mechanical problems, which led to his finding the sabotaged break line. Josey was half expecting him to place the blame on young Stan Morgan, but then thought he probably wouldn't even know about the rape allegation.

'Too early to tell,' Josey mused in relation to the backpacker idea. 'Is there anything else you can tell me, about the afternoon Arthur and Arlene pulled in on their way to the cabin?'

'Arthur's car had been tampered with;' he said sounding like he'd solved the case, 'do you know that?'

'I do.'

'I'd be taking a close look at that little punk that was working for him; Stan Morgan, he had the opportunity I reckon.'

Having made no mention of the rape, may or may not have clarified whether or not Arthur talked about it with the garage owner, but he's shown he knows something about young Morgan.

'I'll shove off,' Josey told the motel owner, 'thanks for talking to me.'

'You take care, and pass on my best wishes to Arlene when you see her; tell her I'm sorry to hear Arthur's missing, and that I'll come and see her sometime.'

Josey had made his way into the car and got the motor running. 'Hopefully we'll find him soon.' He paused to give the motel owner a card. 'Call if you hear anything.'

Joe Magrie saluted with the card sandwiched between his fingers. 'Good luck to you, Detective.'

Back at the Condobolin motel, he paid his bill and kept driving, heading for Wyalong – again taking the back roads to avoid any other unwanted holdups. He would apologise to young Jerry Sullivan for his unavoidable impropriety later.

CHAPTER SEVENTEEN
Wyalong

Josey had plenty of time to ponder the case while driving the deserted routes to be back with his family. Mindlessly keeping his eyes on the road ahead, his brain remained buried in the details of the case, and his hunches; some of which were beginning to raise the possibility of sinister outcomes. He'd be careful not to let these dark spirits show in the presence of his loved ones.

He arrived at Nicole's aunt's place around 9pm and found Carl had gone off somewhere. The two families were gathered around in the living room, actually talking to each other with the TV turned off.

'This looks good,' Josey observed as he strolled into the room.

They'd been talking so much they hadn't heard the car pull up right outside the front door.

Molly was first to greet him; springing to her feet to give him a welcome home cuddle. Rebecca was hot on her heels with something a little more befitting her status. 'Have you eaten?' she asked after the kiss.

'Not since breakfast actually.'

'Sit, I'll make you something—'

The ringing phone shed doubt on her kind offer.

Aunt Jude got to the phone and heeded the caller with the receiver to her ear, - - - 'I'll get him – It's Carl,' she told Josey holding out the handset.

He feigned disapproval while stepping to take it. 'I thought you were giving me a few minutes to say hello to my girls,' he told Carl as he put the phone on speaker for all to hear.

With eyes on Rebecca, he warned his caller, 'This better be as good as you're making it sound.'

'If this was any better I'd be asking for a pay rise.'

Carl considered the chorus of condemnations and knowingly responded with, 'Sorry *Bec*, I'll feed him as soon as he gets here to the hotel, there's something he needs to see right away.'

Josey's eyes were still on his wife, she clearly hadn't been given heads up from Carl, and Carl hadn't allowed time for explanations.

She exhaled on, 'You better do as you're told. Go on, off you go.'

The West Wyalong hotel was the site and smells of promised food. Before they'd even made it to the smorgasbord, Josey became insistent that Carl tell him what he'd found.

'I need to keep my promise to Bec,' he said leading the way to the food.

Josey was so hungry he hadn't the energy to protest, opting to show a little patience.

As they ate, he soothed his curiosity by filling Carl in on what transpired with the inspector, and about his subsequent visit to Sullivan's place. He held off telling him that he'd found Sullivan's body in the boot of Sergeant Perkins car, because he felt it might place him in an incriminating position if later questioned by police.

At the conclusion of the meal, Carl was still holding out on the news that *couldn't wait*. 'If you don't tell me in the next few seconds—'

'It's been staring you in the face since you came in.'

Josey swivelled his head, taking the hint. He suddenly stopped on the assortment of oddments adorning the wall behind the bar, recognising it easily.

The enigmatic letters adorning the Raptor's number plate reflected Arlene Sheridan's name;

R LEAN

'Please tell me the Raptor is parked out back of this hotel.'

'No such luck, but it was the publican here who found the plate.'

Josey dropped his eyes from the registration plate to a rotund man who had just appeared behind the bar. 'Is that him?'

Carl gave a nod. 'Name's Peter Cook.'

'You've spoken to him about it?'

Another affable nod. 'I have; and he's familiar with Sheridan's Raptor apparently, and happy to talk to you.'

Josey pushed back his chair and stood. 'Let's do it.'

Although noticing a measure of disquiet in Josey, Carl opted to let it slide, following his boss across to the bar.

Cook looked up from what he was doing and caught Carl's eye before shifting onto Josey. He spoke with a deep voice, a calm man who might once have been an important figure in some grandiose company in the city, now discharged to quieter times. He looked old enough to be retired, but clearly wasn't. 'I'm gathering you're the detective that wants to have a chat?'

Josey presented him with his introductory smile, his dark thoughts buried from sight. 'That I am, and I thank you for offering your time.'

'Don't thank me yet, like I told Carl here, I don't know much more than I've already told him . . . be that as it may,' he added waving them toward one side of the bar as he headed in that direction.

They met up with him where the bar ran out, and proceeded to follow as he opened a door that led to a back room. 'We can talk in here, it's a little quieter.'

Cook sat his sizable frame in a single seater lounge, facing two padded seats that he offered with a gesture. Carl was closing the door behind him as Cook began the conversation with, 'Fire away, Detective'

Before he could comply, a barmaid appeared at the partly closed door carrying a tray of freshly poured beers, which she spread around to the beneficiaries while they were taking their seats.

'Bottoms up,' Cook offered as the girl left the room and closed the door.

'A steak and a beer,' Josey said after draining a third from his glass, 'What could be better - cheers.'

Cook volunteered to speak. 'I knew Arthur pretty well you know – and his wife; she's a doll, right - too good for him you might have noticed . . . anyway, what else can I help you with?'

Just how-well does this guy know Sheridan, Josey wondered. The connection raised an alarm, but then this was the country, there probably wasn't too many people who didn't know him.

'As Carl has told you, we're looking for his car and hoped you might know where it is.'

'In a word, I don't, but I can take you to the exact spot where I found the plate; it was right there on City Road. As you saw, I collect items of interest for my wall out there. I knew whose it was as soon as I picked it up, that Raptor of his is a magnet for a start, but the plate is a real standout, friends know it's a dedication to his beautiful wife. That was in better times between them.' The light chortle that followed held a secret.

Josey saw Arlene as a woman who was possibly in an unhappy marriage, and now having to deal with not knowing if her husband is alive or dead. On top of that she was under suspicion of collaborating with his client to murder Arthur. Sheridan was still a prime suspect in the reverse scenario; as was Stan Morgan. Now, all that was left of the known associates to the incidents were Bobby Barton, the Jeep driver, and Sergeant Perkin's brother Andrew, both of whom had simply disappeared from the face of the Earth. For Josey, these weren't serious suspects, purely people of interest due to their absence. The present status of the case was only serving to make him feel even more depressed.

Cook noticed his morose expression and promptly offered his help. 'I can run you out there tomorrow if you'd like; maybe you'll see something I didn't.'

It was what Josey was thinking anyway. 'Very kind, Peter, thank you.'

The detective's appreciative grin wiped away his gloom and made the publican feel as though he was doing a good thing.

Earlier, Carl had casually asked Josey who it was that informed him about the location of the Raptor. He wasn't particularly in a hurry to find out, just curious, and now, all in good time, his boss was ready to bring him up to speed.

'You won't believe this, but it was Stan Morgan. He rang me out of the blue while I was still in hospital. I called you straight after.'

'The kid accused of raping Arlene?'

'Not to mention trying to kill her husband. It surprised me too. He denies both by the way. He says he's not responsible for the loose nuts either.'

'What about slamming Sheridan up against the wall?'

'He wouldn't comment, so I'm guessing he might have.'

'Why would he call you with all this, knowing you're working with the police?'

'He says he trusts me more than them. I'm not worried about why that is, my only concern is that the position he's been put in is absolutely integral to the whole case.'

'Fair enough.'

Carl understood the detective often had good reason for withholding certain types of evidence; and not knowing Sheridan's whereabouts could hardly be making him excited, but with a bit of luck, finding the Raptor might go a long way to brightening his boss's mood.

CHAPTER EIGHTEEN
The Raptor

Peter Cook drove Josey and Carl out along City Road aboard his five seater utility truck until they reached the location where the plate was found. The stretch of road was flat-as-a-tack and treeless, swaying grasslands met a clear blue sky as far away as the eye could see.

As they stepped from the vehicle they could only wonder what point of reference allowed him to pinpoint the exact position.

The helpful publican led them away from the front of his vehicle no more than twenty metres, stopped and scanned the surface at his feet like a chook seeking seed. 'Here you go,' he exclaimed cheerily as he gave the ground a little kick, breaking off a bun shaped clod of dry mud.

They immediately saw that the breakaway soil had formed part of a ridge along the edge of a recess that matched the shape of the number plate. This clear clue as to where the plate had become stuck in the mud didn't even come close to explaining how Cook had known exactly where to pull up. Josey and Carl saw nothing suspicious or sinister in this; it just intrigued them.

Josey walked further along the edge of the bitumen with his eyes cast down to the shoulder. From what he had seen, the way the plate had nosedived into mud it must have come off the Raptor while it was raining, or at least had been. He thought that it might have been heard hitting the road before spearing off onto the shoulder, which could mean the driver pulled over up ahead and walked back looking for it. That didn't gel because there were no footprints, but then there were none of Peter Cooks either. There was little point in asking if the ground was dry when the plate was found.

Josey was ten metres from where they stood when Cook asked Carl, 'What's he looking for?'

'Footprints – tyre marks, we have a pretty good idea of the Raptor's tread pattern.'

Josey had gone even further away before stopping and calling back to Carl. 'He's hit the edge here.'

Carl broke into a light trot to reach where Josey was inspecting the hardened mud.

'He didn't stop according to this,' Josey said stating the obvious to Carl.

'Which means he didn't know he'd lost the plate.'

Further evidence that the Raptor had continued on in the same direction was provided by its distinctive tracks, which progressed inside the shoulder for about another hundred metres before swinging back onto the solid roadway.

'Let's talk with our driver,' Josey suggested as he began marching back toward their waiting transport.

Now leaning against the bumper, Cook watched them approaching, their appearance indicating they might have found some sort of clue. He couldn't imagine what it might be. 'Find something?' he asked once they were within clear earshot.

'Need to pick your brain, Peter, if that's okay?'

'Good luck with that,' he laughed.

Josey acknowledged his joke with a cordial grin. 'If you had to guess, where do you imagine the Raptor might be headed?'

He pursed his lips in concentration. 'If she was going all the way to the next stop, I'd say Broken Hill. If she was after fuel, that'd be about twenty Ks ahead. That's about it, unless you were planning to ditch it.'

'And if you did plan to ditch it?'

He thought for a moment . . . 'Hmm, there is a place, a sort of unofficial dumping yard about half that distance. The bloke who owns it, apparently went overseas a good few years ago, and never came back. Even when he lived here, he used to allow people to throw their wrecks on his property. Since then, people just took the liberty of using it to rid themselves of old vehicles and such.'

'Can you spare the time to take us there? We can come back tomorrow on our own and take a look if you need to get away.'

'That's fine; there's *no hope in Hades* you'll ever find the location. Climb aboard, gents.'

He bounced off the bumper and rounded the vehicle toward the driver's door.

Twenty minutes later he slowed the Ute and turned into a grass smothered track that had been formed by time and the occasional vehicle retracing the duel ruts. This snaked around what appeared to be an aimless path at first, but in fact the rout was being dictated by the random placement of old stumps and even older clumps of volcanic rock. It might have seemed like many kilometres to Cook's passengers, but in fact was probably a third of the distance travelled as the crow flies.

They eventually came to a crater-like ditch that held water as efficiently as a dam. It was a curious sight to see the roofs of vehicles protruding from the extensive pond like islands of multiple colours and rust. Some higher than others, and clearly not floating; most probably stuck fast to the bottom. For Josey, and indeed Carl, it was discouraging; there had to be a hundred vehicles, resting in their watery graves.

Peter had taken the utility as far as he dare. 'It shouldn't be too big a job, boys, I don't see too many Raptors out there.'

He was right about that, a Raptor would stand out by fact of its lofty height. The three men stepped out of their car and positioned themselves on the rim of the crater in order to collectively scan what they could see of the sunken wrecks; anything rusty could immediately be ignored.

'There it is,' Josey told the other two pointing to the far side of the pond; 'the red roof, right on the edge.' If anyone was going to recognise the Raptor at a distance it was Josey, having encountered it firsthand. With its nose in the water and its butt in the air it finally appeared harmless. 'Can you get us around to the other side, Peter?'

'Maybe, we might have to ruff it a bit. Hop in, let's give it a go.'

Peter competently took his vehicle around the rim of the crater in an *uphill*-and-*down-dale* obstacle course, occasionally forced to avoid a wreck that hadn't quite made it off the rim.

Near to their destination at the far side of the pond, the sight of the decommissioned Raptor half submerged reminded Josey of Sergeant Perkin's drowned Peugeot - with Sullivan's body in the boot.

The three men stood outside their car with their hands on their hips, a stance that seemed to suggest no one was able to see a way of extracting the massive vehicle from its resting place.

'I can get a tow truck up here if you're serious; where were you thinking of taking it?'

Josey gave Carl an expression that required deciphering.

'I'll ask Jude,' he told his boss.

Peter knew who Judy Green was and wasn't privy to

any complications with planting the Raptor on her property. 'That's doable,' he told his companions, '*Jacks Towing* goes out as far as Condobolin.'

'Will they be able to get their truck in here?' Carl enquired.

'Not a problem, their biggest rig will make its own road, no doubt it's brought some of these babies here anyway.'

Cook wasn't exaggerating, the next day Jack himself drove his biggest bright green monster through the scrub in a straight line, over the rocks and tree stumps and parked back up against the comparatively small Raptor.

It took little more than twenty minutes to lift the offender out of the water and onto the tray. Hanging on the chain with water draining back to the pond in multiple streams, it had again looked harmless – beaten.

By lunchtime it sat on Aunt Judy's property, drying out in the hot sun.

'It'll take a bit more than a sunbake if you want to get her started,' Jack volunteered.

Getting it started is the last thing I want, Josey thought, and then said, 'Basically we just want to pull a few things apart.'

He could see they needed help. 'I can send someone around.'

'That'd be appreciated.'

'I'll get Chris to call; you got a card?'

'Don't spread this around,' Josey told him as he handed the card across to the oily outstretched hand, 'what we're

173

doing here is a wee bit sensitive.'

He grinned and swung up the ladder of the green monster to the driver's seat. His head jutted out the open window to make eye contact with the property owner, 'Good to see you again, Judith.'

He shocked the daylights out of everybody with a blast from the bugle-horn and drove away.

At Carl's side a few paces back, Aunt Jude told him, 'Tell your boss not to worry about Jack talking, his word is his bond.'

Although Jack's truck had dwarfed the Raptor, the Ford again dominated the scene with a decidedly frightening presence, especially knowing its vicious history.

Rebecca and Molly had been watching the action from the front of the homestead, and now stepped into the yard and wandered over to join the others. Rebecca was keen to ask her husband if he thought it was safe having the thing parked at Nicole's aunt's place, but didn't want to alarm anyone unnecessarily.

She didn't need to ask, Josey could see it on her face.

During lunch, Chris the auto electrician rang to say he could be out to see the Raptor in about half an hour.

He was true to his word, arriving right on time in a blue van supporting the name of his company, *Bright Spark Auto*.

Niceties were exchanged and with the aid of a ladder that he removed from his roof rack he climbed up to the engine bay and began looking for what Josey had asked him to find.

Josey trusted he wouldn't need to start the engine for any reason, so he had removed all of the spark plugs in the interest of playing it safe.

'There's not a car on the road these days that doesn't have a computer,' the electrician muttered to Josey as he peered into the bowels of the workings. 'And this one's no exception,' he added as he poked around at the little black box.

Josey was atop a ladder that he had gained from Judith, positioned on the opposite side to Chris. 'Have you had any experience with autonomous vehicles?' he asked out of interest.

'Not much as yet, but I know how they work. This one isn't one of them if that's what you're asking.'

'Could it have been modified?'

'It could have, but it would need a whole lot more than this baby's got.'

'What if the extra bits had been removed, would you be able to tell?'

'Not without dismantling a few things; it's not just a different type of computer I'd be looking for, there's a whole lot of sensors that are required to make the thing work.'

'And if the sensors were removed; would you be able to see that?'

He leaned in as if trying to melt down into the engine bay. 'Some sensors are usually attached to the bodywork; I might be better off taking a look underneath.' He'd no sooner said it when he started down the ladder. Josey followed suit and they both went onto their knees beneath the metre high floor of the Raptor.

With one of his hands disappearing from view, up into where Josey assumed the steering mechanism would reside, he mulled, 'Hmm, we might be on the money here.'

'What've you found?'

'Holes where their used to be bolts.'

Josey handed him his cell phone. 'Can you get a picture of it?'

He looked over his shoulder, reached back and grabbed the phone that Josey had quickly set up, firing off a flash lit photo.

Inspection of the shot told Josey that something had obviously been removed.

The electrician spent an hour finding and photographing similar locations where parts had been taken, and fairly recently due to the empty spaces being quite clean, far cleaner than they would be if removed before their dunking in the crater.

As he was leaving Judith's property, Josey asked him not to talk about the callout; especially what he'd heard and what he'd seen.

For the remainder of the day and well into the evening, Josey opened up about the case. He felt it was only fair to bring everyone up to speed, particularly Aunt Judith, who had been very gracious in providing accommodation and provisional use of her land.

'So you've known about the remote control car from the

start,' Judith concluded after hearing about his own experience with the Raptor.

'There was no other explanation, although before I saw it for myself I believed Lester and Arlene were inventing the story to cover up something else.'

Josey thought, *secrets were still abound, but not able to be mentioned.*

Those surrounding the table listened intently, yet with largely differing attitudes to the story. Belinda was the least comfortable, but kept her silence for the time being. Molly couldn't have been happier, she idolised what her step father did for a living. Carl was as close as anyone could get to being Josey's employee, so he had all the information already, or as much as Josey had divulged or knew so far.

Nicole's aunt had a frown on her face, which prompted Josey to respond with, 'Question, Judith?'

'Apart from not having a clear motive for modifying the car, do you think it's all over with?'

A chill ran through Rebecca's bones and she spoke up. 'That's exactly what I've been thinking, especially with that bloody thing sitting out there in the yard.'

Josey pulled a few of the spark plugs from his pocket and shuffled them like dice in his hand. 'I don't think the Raptor's a problem without these.'

'This is not funny, Sweetie,' she cautioned.

He took her point on the chin. 'I've asked Judith's caretaker to leave the dogs loose overnight, and tomorrow I'll get the vehicle taken away.'

'Where are you planning on putting it, don't you need to show the police what you've found?'

'I've got pictures, but you're right – the police will probably want to hold the vehicle.'

'Call that inspector from the city; he's the one in charge of the case.' She saw the quick glance her husband gave Carl. 'There's something you're not telling us isn't there,' she conjectured suspiciously.

He exhaled on the words, 'There is.'

She knew it. 'Well, come on – out with it.'

'I'm afraid I'm in a bit of strife with our friend Inspector Brown.'

Molly was frowning now. 'What's happened, Dad?'

His eyes drifted onto his wife. 'I'm supposed to be still in Condobolin.'

'He thought you were off the case,' she realised.

'Maybe not now.'

'Oh my God, Cam – this is turning into some holiday.'

'I know, I'm sorry.'

His wife had sunk so deep into her chair; she almost appeared to be sliding under the table.

'I'll get this sorted tomorrow, starting with getting the Raptor back to Condobolin for Brown and the boys.'

Having taken it all in, Molly suggested knowingly, 'You've figured something out haven't you.'

'It's too early to say, Cupcake.'

Mother and daughter knew not to push the point in present company.

Now that he had confirmation the Raptor had been

modified, which wasn't really in any doubt, he needed to move on. He knew that there was a lot to be done back in Condobolin, and not just in relation to the inspector. He needed to talk with Perkins and Arlene and clear up a few things. And he needed to pick up on the abandoned visit to the morgue. As far as present company was concerned, his hunches and his plans would be kept under wraps.

Alone in their bedroom, this was going to be the last hoorah for a while, and he had no interest in wasting time on anything else.

'What are your intentions, Detective?' Rebecca asked interrupting his obvious goals playfully.

He rolled over on top of her, making her laugh a little too loudly. She shushed herself while trying to imagine how thin the walls of Judith's house might be.

Her hand slid beneath the sheet. 'Hmm, I think you've just answered my question.'

CHAPTER NINETEEN
Back to Condobolin

While the others were having breakfast, Josey placed a courtesy call to Inspector Brown to put his mind at rest about his return to Condobolin, and to ask for his help in ridding Jude Green's property of the Raptor.

'Leave that to me, I'll organise to have it impounded. You shouldn't have moved it in the first place. Anyway, it's no longer your problem . . . I guess I should thank you for finding it.'

Josey could have said, *I'm a helpful kind'a guy,* but came out with, 'That's fine, happy to help.'

'A car will be coming for you too, make yourself ready, I need you here.'

'Of course,' Josey agreed, knowing full well that returning to Condobolin was his intention.

Around midmorning, Josey and Carl were looking over the monster when the caretaker's dogs went into a mad announcement that a vehicle was entering onto the property. They heard caretaker John loudly pacifying the animals, doing his best to convince them there was no threat. Josey and Carl considered the arrival of police and weren't so certain that was true. They watched the patrol car making its way from the gate toward the homestead.

'That didn't take long,' Carl scoffed.

Josey slid down from the driver's seat and onto the ground. 'I'd better go and take care of this.'

He was walking away when Carl hailed him. 'Hey, is this a bullet hole?'

Josey turned and saw him studying the driver's head rest. 'It is.'

'And?'

'And it's something else to look into, I'll explain later.'

Carl looked at the singed hole, and back at Josey, recognising he wasn't about to get a further explanation.

With the patrol car coming to a gentle stop near the steps to the house, those inside came out and met up with Josey and the visiting police officer.

After tying up the stressed dogs Johnny came across to see what was happening, immediately noticing Constable Mario Brooks was the centre of attention. 'What mischief are you up to Mario?' he enquired with a grin.

'I'm in the middle of something here, John, give us a minute.'

The caretaker raised his hands submissively without another word.

'I wasn't going to worry you folks till this afternoon,' the officer told his audience, 'but since I was passing—'

'What can we do for you, Mario?' Judith asked with the clear authority of the property owner.

'I've been told I'd find a Detective Cameron Josey staying here with you.'

'You have the right place, Constable; I'm the man you're looking for.'

The officer faced Josey wearing his *official-business* face. 'I've been asked to escort you to the police station in Condobolin; I'm told you'd know why.'

'This can wait a couple of hours,' Judith told the young man affirmatively. 'We're about to have lunch and you'll be joining us, so turn off your motor and get yourself inside for a cold drink – all of you,' she said waving them toward the door.

'It's not a problem, Jude,' Josey assured Nicole's aunt – 'I was about to return to Condobolin anyway.'

'I'm not having my baked dinner thrown to the dogs; we're all having lunch and that's that.'

The local copper became instantly distracted, more focused on the parked Raptor. 'I didn't know you'd brought a new set of wheels, Jude.'

She faced him from the open screen door. 'Do I look like I'd be interested in climbing up into that thing?'

Brooks gave her a short glance then on to all the other faces. 'Look, I'll leave you folks in peace and come back around three this afternoon, how's that?'

'That'll be fine, Mario,' Josey told the rookie like the choice was mandatory. 'I'll be waiting.'

'Good,' he said backing away diplomatically.

They all stood outside in silence watching the patrol car leave the property; all except Jude, who'd gone in to take care of a roast.

The upshot was that Constable Brooks had received instructions from his Sergeant at Wyalong station to carry out an apprehension order on Detective Josey as soon as possible. Common sense prevailed when the keen young constable overstepped Jude's mark by suggesting the order be carried out immediately; sort of a kill two birds with one stone thing. As expected, the order had come from Inspector Brown. As soon as he learnt that Josey hadn't remained in Condobolin as told to, he'd flown into a rage.

Johnny took his leave and returned to his bungalow at the back of the main house, and the others went inside to see if there was anything they could do to help their host prepare the lunch.

With just two hours until Brooks' return, Rebecca used the time talking with Josey about the sudden so called apprehension, and what was behind his plan to return to Condobolin even before being forced to.

He told her about the body in the boot, and that he'd been wrong about including Sullivan in his list of suspects. He held off mentioning who he thought was behind the modified Raptor when she asked about it, because his theory was yet to be tested. He also told her that he had another hunch that needed to be explored. That would take place once he got past dealing with the irate inspector from Sydney

Upon Constable Brooks' return, the officer advised everyone choosing to remain at Judy Green's property, that police would be taking a very high profile presence; the advice to the respective families was to stay put; as it was impossible to guarantee their safety if they didn't. He also promised them the Raptor would be taken off the property sometime tomorrow.

On top of the police advice, their own sensibility dictated that all except Josey would lay low until further notice.

Laying low was what they thought they were doing, but in fact they were in great danger. The police presence was the only thing protecting them from the surveillance that was taking place within the cover of the forest.

CHAPTER TWENTY
Identity at the Morgue

B rown gave no consideration to offering Josey time to have a meal and relax after the lengthy journey; it was once again straight down to business in the office that he had commandeered.

'You don't listen real good do you,' he chipped.

'I had a lead that took me to Wyalong — I wasn't exactly under arrest.'

'That'll be fixed if you try that again.'

'It won't, the case has moved back to Condobolin.'

Brown stared at him the way people consider a smart arse. 'Oh, this is *your* case now is it?'

Josey looked at him blankly, although he was forced to concede the inspector was right to put him in his place, which brought to the fore, the only important thing now was keeping Brown and himself on the same page. 'There are a few things I've learnt that you should be made aware of,' he offered.

Brown's face took on a tinge of pink. 'I'm listening.'

It was too early to tell him about the body in the boot, clearly it hadn't been found, which he'd thought at the time might have been the reason for his ride back to Condobolin in the patrol car, but then realised it was all about the inspector's ego, and that if it was anything more serious than that, he would have been in handcuffs. 'First I need to pay another visit to the morgue.'

'*The Morgue again*,' Brown moaned tiresomely, 'Is there anything else I can help you with, Detective?'

Josey accepted the tinge of humour appreciatively.

His opponent was staring at him again; perhaps it wasn't humour that Josey detected. Regardless, he needed to reign the situation in. 'With respect, Inspector, I have a lead that may break this case wide open, I ask only for your patience a little longer.'

He was still staring. Finally he stood from the desk and said, 'You've got until I see what this cockamamie morgue thing is about.'

Josey pushed back his chair as he got to his feet. 'I appreciate it; can we do it soon?'

Brown gave no answer as he reached the door and spoke to Beasley. 'Make an appointment for Detective Josey and me to see the Sheridan remains, tonight if possible; after I've had some dinner.'

Josey wasn't expecting an invitation to join him for a meal, and was pleased there wasn't one. Or maybe dinner for him was about to be served in the cell.

Brown swept his arm through the open door with clear

instructions. 'You're booked into room 26 at your favourite motel; you'll find an officer outside waiting. Once you go in you don't come out until I call. It might be less than a half hour, so get yourself some grub if you're hungry and be ready; I don't want this to take all night.'

Pearl, the mortician, was a stout woman with a thin face. A slight smile made her appear less severe than she might without it. 'What exactly are you looking for?' she asked Josey as they stood around the burnt remains, which were lying on the side due to the sitting-stance that it had been found in, which was difficult to keep upright any other way, and made the figure appear to be in the foetal position.

'It's just a niggling feeling at this stage, but can I ask how you got Sheridan's DNA?'

'Not easily, and only recently, the fire must have been like hell itself.'

'I didn't get to witness the whole thing,' Josey agreed, 'but the body must have been stuck in the Jeep for some time. When I came round, the seats were already reduced to the metal supports; and things weren't exactly as I remembered them before I blacked out.'

Pearl knew the story; the confusion about how a body had somehow ended up back in the Jeep, not to mention the confusion about who it was; and how the detective had come close to being a victim himself.

Brown was standing back a couple of paces with a look

of contempt; to him Josey's inspection of the charred body was an absolute waste of time.

On the other hand, Pearl was as curious as mortician's get. 'I can tell you have something on your mind that might be important, Detective; I've seen that look before.' She stepped across to a high back chair that looked like it had been moulded to her nicely rounded body shape over time. From the comfort of the chair she said, 'Sometimes we experts get a little too close to the trees to see the forest. Ask what you want and let's see if we can help you.' She'd used the word *we* loosely, aware the inspector wasn't exactly a confederate. 'Tell me why you have doubts about my findings, that's what this is about isn't it – *doubts*?'

'It is.'

This admission brought the inspector back to life. 'Since when?'

Since finding Sullivan's body in the boot of Sergeant Lester Perkin's Peugeot, Josey wanted to say, but that point was next, along with *why.* 'First things first, just let me get past this.'

'Pearl, I'd like to take a close look,' he requested with is eyes on the corpse and his bare hands held up as if ready to sift through the ashes.

'If you want to keep your hands clean put on some gloves, they're on the bench behind you.'

He understood why Pearl wasn't worried about any further contamination of the corpse; the remains were already as contaminated as they'd ever get.

Back at the silver table with the gloves on, he gingerly sank his hands into the ashes, disturbing the incongruous shape that had been sustained by clinging to the structure of the chard skeleton. He checked Pearl to see if the destruction was concerning her.

'Go ahead,' she responded, 'no harm done.'

They watched him sift through the ashes like a kid searching for coins on the beach. When his probing fingers stopped, it was clear he had found something – it wasn't a coin, but it *was* metal. While pinched between his thumb and forefinger he wiped it to make it clearer to see.

Brown moved a couple of steps closer.

Coming to the edge of her seat, Pearl asked, 'What is it?'

'A *press-stud*,' Josey told her rotating the fastened halves in his fingers.

'And that's what you were looking for?' she asked curiously.

'It is. This is off Bobby Barton's overalls; there's probably another half dozen of them hidden in there somewhere.'

She was grinning hospitably. She knew what Josey was driving at but wondered if the inspector was getting it. 'I know what your leading up to, Detective, and you're right; you can't get blood from a cremated body,' Pearl admitted, 'let alone DNA.'

Brown started losing his cool. 'So who the hell are we looking at – Barton or Sheridan?'

189

'Which means,' Josey continued saying to Pearl while unapologetically skipping over Brown's confusion, 'you found Sheridan's blood somewhere other than on or around the bonnet - that right?'

She nodded comfortably, 'Yes, it was found up against the firewall, underneath the dashboard; certain parts of the firewall were covered in asbestos, which I assume protected the blood from being destroyed. The police only came across it after the Jeep was brought back to Condo.'

'I guess you would have matched Sheridan's blood type from hospital records; the DNA too.'

'Yes.'

Josey wasn't really guessing; he'd already had blood tested that he'd collected from the *Raptor's headlight trims*, put there when Arthur lay injured across the bonnet, and confirmed to be Arthur's – which of course did nothing to explain why that same blood was found on the jeep.

Pearl confirmed his notion. 'Your account of what happened at the scene led us to believe the charred remains couldn't have been anyone other than Bobby Barton, the owner of the Jeep. I couldn't prove that without DNA and he had no dental records. Plus, I had no blood at that stage.'

The inspector wasn't feeling comfortable with not staying abreast. 'Let me get this straight, first you *assume* from what the detective tells you, the corpse is Bobby Barton's, then you say you don't know if that's true due to the lack of proof - and now, because the detective again says it *is* Barton, you're agreeing with him—'

She continued as if the copper hadn't spoken, cutting him off mid-sentence. 'Initially, I was intending to test the bones,' she told Josey, 'but the fact is, burnt bones degrade quickly; genetic markers are difficult, if not impossible to find. So, given we had your testimony I put the bones on the backburner.' Still on Josey she added, 'But you'd already figured all this out, right; and now you've done something we couldn't do; proven that the cadaver is indeed young Barton.'

Focusing in on the mortician the inspector wanted to know, 'How come we now seem to have two people in this Jeep, when logically we know there should only be one? You know what; I think I've heard enough of this.'

Pearl cleared her throat to gain the upper hand. 'If I were you Inspector I'd at least wait to let the detective tell us the rest of what he's figured out, I'm damn sure I'd like to hear it.'

Brown gave her one of his intimidating squints. 'Are you really buying into this?'

She shrugged and brought her eyes onto Josey and then the charred remains. 'Tell us what you think may have happened, Detective.'

'The person who died in that Jeep is as we originally thought - *Bobby Barton*. And, as we now know, the blood belongs to Arthur Sheridan.'

'Is what he's saying even possible?' Brown asked Pearl.

'Detective?' she said endeavouring to pass the question

on to him.

The Inspector wanted to hear it from the mortician, not the private detective, but was forced to eat another helping of humble pie.

'The blood was *planted*.' Josey suggested as though it was fact.

'By Sheridan?' Brown asked sounding interested at last.

'Yes.'

'Detective,' Pearl interrupted ahead of flicking her eyes up at him, 'am I right in saying there's something else that raised your suspicion Sheridan wasn't the victim in the Jeep?'

'Spot on, Pearl, it was what I found a couple of days ago, when I went out to interview Jimmy Sullivan.'

She produced a frown. '*Sullivan*, that's not a name I'm familiar with.'

'It wouldn't be; he hasn't really been involved in the case.'

Brown knew who Sullivan was; he'd met his son when the police did their survey of the area. 'And *now*?' he enquired of the detective in an attempt to keep up.

'He's dead; I found his body in the boot of Sergeant Perkin's car – the one that got pushed into the creek out at the cabin.'

Brown was fully alert now, and pissed; this was starting to sound like something he could sink his teeth into. 'You're telling me, that you found a *body*, and you neglected to report it? No wait, I get it; you had a lead that you just *had* to follow up in Wyalong.' He performed a comical jig. 'Gosh, now that explains everything.'

Josey thought, *it sounds worse hearing someone else say it*. But he needed to move on with his explanation.

The inspector didn't give him a chance. 'Let's deal with the blood in the Jeep first,' Brown continued, 'Sheridan's disappearance means he's still our chief suspect.'

'We can't say that.'

'*You* just did.'

'No, given he had been savagely attacked back at the cabin, I believe the careful placement of his blood, which wasn't in short supply, was to make everyone believe he was dead, but I don't believe the ploy was to escape the police, I think it was driven by his fear of someone else.'

'Who?'

'Whoever was controlling the Raptor after Sheridan was incapacitated.'

'And who might that be?'

'I don't have all the answers, Inspector.'

Brown looked piqued. 'You could have fooled me.'

Pearl's mind was still on what made Josey suspect Sheridan wasn't the one in the fire. 'You were explaining why the body in the boot made you suspect Sheridan's blood was planted.'

'He's saying Sheridan was well enough to have killed his neighbour,' Brown bravely ascertained, 'which means he was well enough to have planted the blood on the jeep.'

Brown was wrong about who killed Jimmy - Josey let that go for the moment and filled Perl in about Sergeant

Perkins car being pushed into the creek and the events that surrounded it, leading up to his revisit to the Sullivan's and the doomed vehicle. 'When I found poor Jimmy, I noted that the waterline on the sergeant's car had been above the roof; in other words it had at one stage been totally submerged, which didn't make sense because the body was bone dry.'

Brown couldn't help asking, 'What's that prove?'

'It proves Jimmy's body was placed in the boot, not only after the car was pushed into the creek, but late enough for the swollen waters to have subsided.'

'Proving?'

'Proving the body went into the boot well after Arthur sustained his injuries aboard the Raptor, meaning someone else killed Jimmy, the same person who tried to kill Arthur. That person was the sole reason Sullivan tried to fake his death.'

'And you don't know who this mystery person is.'

'Correct.' - *Except for my hunch,* he voiced in his head.

'Wait a minute,' Brown sprouted excitedly as though he had hit on a winner. 'We only know Sheridan sustained those injuries from what his wife and Sergeant Perkins claimed. No one else saw that, including you, Detective.'

At last, Brown had his brain working, and he had a point, but Josey didn't want to concede until he had a chance to develop his hunch further. 'You're forgetting one thing, Inspector; why would they tell a story that *excludes* Arthur as the killer by exposing his injuries, knowing it would open them up as suspects?'

He thought heavily about Josey's reasoning. 'Well, maybe they *ought* to be considered suspects.'

It was Brown's attempt to save face. He was catching up, but thankfully not catching on.

Josey had another point to make. 'Unlike you inspector, I'm not protected by the liberties offered to police, and don't have the freedom to make that accusation, I'd be left wide open to litigation.'

'Okay, based on your logic, it doesn't stop *me* from charging these two, just on suspicion alone. You're not off the hook either, Detective; not reporting the finding of a body is a serious offence.'

'A little late perhaps,' was the only concession he was prepared to give.

'Be careful, Detective; because you've told us some other stuff that I don't quite buy. For instance, you're the one who informed us Sheridan built the autonomous controls, which means he has to be the one who drove the Raptor to the burial pond outside of Wyalong; I mean who else could it be? How would this unknown person you're on about know how to work the damn thing?'

He's really thinking.

Pearl had never been so entertained within the confines of her morgue, supressing a grin that couldn't be hidden from her eyes.

In spite of having injected some good thinking into the mix, Brown wasn't enjoying himself; he still felt he was in Detective Josey's hands. 'So, what's the bottom line - um, I mean, what's our next move?'

Aware that diplomacy was his best tool in moving onto what the inspector had called - *our next move,* Josey said, 'With your permission, I'd like to bring Sergeant Perkins and Arlene Sheridan together in the same room.'

'Why?'

'I have a story to tell them.'

'A *story* . . . about what?'

'I'd like you to hear it too, Inspector; it might just add some sense as to why Arthur Sheridan has faked his own death.'

As arranged, Judith Green's property was being well protected by police and her own guard dogs. There was no real reason to feel unsafe, allowing them the luxury of moving about freely.

It was this distant scene that became the focus of a powerful lens, and its owner, hidden from sight within the rim of the state forest. The telephoto images panned within the darkness of the viewfinder, providing the operator with crystal clear pictures.

The Raptor, sitting motionless and alone in the paddock was of some interest, but of particular interest were the people, especially two of the women.

The lens held on them as they walked and talked; their intense discussion only to be imagined, their movement frozen in time every so often as their still-life images were committed to the camera's memory.

Rebecca and Molly had no idea they were the subjects of a new and frightening photo collection, a collection that would soon be added to - in a far more dangerous, and intimate manner.

CHAPTER TWENTY ONE
Grilling at the Hospital

Arlene Sheridan was puzzled by the unexpected plan to transport her from the hospital to the psychiatric centre, after two weeks of nursing her injuries she fully believed she would be heading home. Constable Beasley was given the job of explaining the reason, and for providing her transport there in his patrol car.

The last to arrive, she walked in on crutches to be greeted by the other members invited to the meeting.

She was a little surprised to see Josey and the inspector in each other's company; so far all her dealings with the two men had been singular. Arlene had found Josey's questioning much more creative than the copper, a talent that she could have done without. She also could have done without the inspector's presence, she didn't like him.

Her eyes fell unavoidably on her friend and neighbour,

198

the Condobolin Sergeant. 'Is this going to be some sort of railroad, Lester?' She asked suspiciously.

He was in one of those high back hospital chairs, cuffed to its arm. 'I know as much as you do, Arlene,' he answered blandly.

Brown had his arms folded with his butt resting against a built-in cabinet that ran beneath the only window in the room. Josey had been sitting opposite Perkins, but was now standing as Arlene entered. He placed his hand on the back of a chair and directed her to it, holding the crutches while settling her into the seat.

A designated smirk came to her face. 'What's this about, Detective?' she asked like she couldn't guess.

Josey took his seat, and his time, giving Brown a courteous glance before beginning. 'Inspector Brown and I have some news for you both.'

News wasn't what she was expecting, and she noted Lester's lack of expression suggested he might already have been told what it was. He shook his head and shrugged at her, dispelling that theory.

The respective neighbours had their eyes on Josey anxiously.

'There's been a mistake,' he admitted to them, 'of which I am partly to blame.'

They visibly relaxed, as though some miracle of fate had descended from the heavens to exempt them from an expected gruelling. Although no charges had been laid, they were both still under suspicion, mainly due to the recognized absurdity of their story, although some of the incongruity had been accepted on the basis of recent events.

At this point, like most people, Arlene believed her husband might be dead, even after finding out Bobbie Barton had been incinerated in the Jeep. Her belief that Arthur was probably dead was shared with Lester based on her husband's disappearance following the beating he suffered at the cabin.

Josey recalled she hadn't seemed all that cutup by the possibility; in fact she'd almost seemed relieved, which of course tied in with the scenario that Arthur was trying to kill her, and maybe even Lester.

'So, what's this big mistake?' Arlene asked with a tinge of flippancy.

'Blood found just recently by police has suggested the body in the Jeep is your husband's.'

That relief Josey had seen on her face returned. "He's dead then?'

He wasn't sure how she would react to finding out Arthur is in fact still alive, in spite of what police found. 'We believe Arthur has faked his death.'

'You're shitting me.' She glanced at Lester and scoffed.

Lester's expression was unreadable.

Even Josey wasn't sure if his friend saw this as good news or bad. 'We're not sure how, but following Arthur's ordeal in the Raptor, it seems he showed up at the scene. And, we're fairly certain he faked his death by making it look like he was the one who died in the fire.'

'Who would have guessed,' Lester piped up. 'Who

would have thought he had the strength after what we saw.

Arlene was speechless for a moment, and then with fear in her voice she asked, 'How the hell did you people get this *so wrong*?'

Lester too was now showing he was less than relaxed about it.

'My fault,' Josey admitted. 'I'm afraid my testimony originally led police to conclude that Arthur wasn't at the scene. The fact is Arthur tricked us by leaving traces of his blood behind in the vehicle, a ploy that has only just been discovered.'

The inspector, recognising there was nothing new for him in any of this, began to wonder if Josey had hooked him into the meeting on false pretences.

Arlene's voice shook when she asked, 'So he's alive.'

'As far as we know, he could be.'

'Do you have any idea where he is?'

'We don't,' he told her bluntly before glancing across at the Inspector. With steady eyes back on Arlene, his voice began taking on the ominous tone she was expecting from the moment she had walked in.

'The fact is - this meeting is not just about Arthur, and whether or not he is dead.'

'Then *what*?' she asked impatiently.

'It's about you and Lester.'

She deliberately wiped away all traces of a reaction, almost as if the detective hadn't spoken, and then said flatly, 'What *about* me and Lester?'

Josey wanted to blurt the answer out for the inspector to hear, but wanted Arlene and Lester to realise they too were making a mistake, the mistake of withholding information to save their necks. The foreboding that existed between these two police suspects returned in spades.

'Arlene, let's go back to the beginning. Because Lester wasn't personally involved in the events at the start, and in fairness, only knows what he was told—'

'You can stop right there,' Sergeant Perkins protested. 'At the time, I had no reason to distrust what Arthur told me.'

'Shut up and listen,' Brown snapped overzealously.

More diplomatically, Josey said to Lester, 'Let's just see what comes out of our discussion, all right, mate?'

The sergeant had little choice other than to hold his tongue.

Josey allowed an elusive grin directed toward Arlene. 'I'm intrigued about Arthur's call for help – why call Lester?'

She looked at her neighbour. 'Why not, he's a friend, not to mention a copper.'

'Which would be fine, except that Arthur didn't call Lester, *you* did.'

'Is this another one of your theories?'

'You tell me.'

She had the look of a woman not wanting to tell him

anything.

'Let's move on,' he suggested. He had his own reasons for not dwelling on the issue. Arlene's mobile phone, which he had managed to get working following its dunking in the swollen creek, gave him, in hindsight, every call and text that Arlene had made to Lester. For obvious reasons, to mention that now would raise problems with the inspector and bog the interrogation down.

Brown wasn't letting it go though, 'Sergeant; did Arlene call you from the motel or not?'

'What if she did, what the hell does it matter?'

Josey weighed back in. 'It matters because you need to explain why you've been hiding the fact, why lie about the phone calls?'

Arlene sparked. 'You're good at theories, what do *you* think – what is it you're trying to get us to say?'

It was time to put theories to bed. 'I'm giving you both a chance to tell the truth.'

Their silence spoke volumes.

'All right, let's talk about how your car got into the creek, Sergeant,' Josey offered.

'Someone pushed it; I would have thought that was obvious.'

'It is if the car is unlocked, out of gear and with the handbrake off - - - *was it?*'

The question brought awareness to Lester's face that couldn't be hidden, and although he had the chance to pick up the baton, he elected to say nothing.

'If your Peugeot was locked, it could only have been pushed by the person who had the key.'

The comment unsettled him. 'So now you're suggesting I pushed my own car over the cliff; can I ask why you think I would?'

'I'm not suggesting you're the one who pushed it, and I think you already know that.'

He either didn't understand or didn't want to let on because of what he was holding back.

For most people, shock is hard to fake, which is what Josey decided was needed. With his consideration fully on Lester he told him, 'The day I nosed around your car in the creek, I found Jimmy Sullivan's body in the boot.'

As expected, this news hit like a hammer; neither of them could be accused of faking the sudden distress that immediately beset them, especially Arlene. But was the reason for their anguish clear? Were they afraid they'd be next?

It was Arlene who verbalised it. 'Please tell us you know who's *doing this*.'

Josey wanted to be sympathetic to their trauma, but he needed to let them know that none of their anxiety exempted them from complicity in a way that was yet to be touched on. 'Doing what?' he asked cryptically, – *'Sabotaging the Raptor? Pushing Lester's car into the creek? Destroying the cabin? Or trying to kill you;* which question has got you confused?'

'You're talking in riddles,' Arlene said accusingly.

'That's because a riddle is what it is, or was.'

Brown's face was mummified, but he allowed Josey the reins.

'I don't even need to ask if you believe someone was controlling the Raptor remotely, your stories are based on it. You were right to be confused about whether or not that person was Arthur – at first – but then at some point someone else took over control. I don't think there's anyone in this room that hasn't worked that out. So, Arlene, please don't pretend you know less than we do. The question is; at what juncture did someone else take over the task, and who might that person be?'

The inspector couldn't hold his tongue any longer. 'And the answer *is*?'

Josey glanced across at Brown and then on to Arlene and Lester. 'I was hoping someone might be able to tell *me*.'

Brown wasn't sure if the detective was being straight, or once again elusive.

'I don't understand what the hell you're driving at,' Arlene vowed.

Lester was eyeing her sharply. 'Give it up, Arlene,' he demanded. 'We can't keep our heads in the sand any longer. We both know Arthur was out to kill you, and we know why. Now someone else is; and the way Josey explains it makes perfect sense. It's clear Arthur built the Raptor up to cover his plan to kill you, and now someone else has taken his place.'

Josey was nodding in agreement. 'Right, it's fair to say Arthur pushed the car into the creek to assist in his plan, and then becomes a victim himself when someone turns the tables by getting hold of the console.'

Somewhat muddled by the explanation, Brown asked, 'You two knew about this console that drives Sheridan's car, is that right?'

Lester sheepishly elected to answer. 'Not at first.'

'But you knew Arthur had built it, along with the modifications to the Raptor?'

There came complete silence – other than a nod from the sergeant. The knot in the pit of Arlene's stomach surfaced onto her face.

Josey waited, giving her a chance to come clean. But she chose not to.

For Lester, it was bad enough dealing with Josey's imaginative narrative, but for the first time since their discussion began, he became conscious of the Inspector's power to arrest him on suspicion of retaliation alone.

'Arthur must have found out about us,' Lester confessed to Josey sounding trapped. 'For the life of me I can't see how you worked it out about me and Arlene.'

'You don't have to say any more, Lester,' Arlene warned.

Brown didn't know how Josey had worked it out either, but he sure as hell picked up on their discomfort and evasiveness in not wanting to talk about what was starting to sound like an elicit love affair. He focused on Arlene. 'So you believe this thing the two of you had going was Arthur's reason for wanting *you* dead.'

'Perhaps the both of us?' she expressed glumly.

Feeling obliged to ignore Arlene's plea for sympathy, Lester backpedalled. 'Look, I really couldn't believe Arthur was to blame for what was happening with the car, and I certainly didn't know about the automation he'd built into it. Arlene suspected Arthur way before I did. But, like you say, I became convinced she was right when my car went into the creek. Arthur must have got hold of my keys during the night; it wouldn't have been hard, they were in the trousers I'd draped over the chair.'

Arlene looked livid.

Josey focused on Lester. 'Once you knew Arthur's intentions were sinister—to say the least—you began to believe Arlene's suspicions. This is why you elected to drive the Raptor back out of the valley, which you wouldn't have done if you'd known what else he'd done to the Ford.'

Silence soared.

Arlene suddenly released a rush of air, sounding as though she'd been holding her breath. 'The thought that this could be my husband, only entered *my* head when the trouble with the car began on the way to the motel, otherwise I wouldn't have gotten in with him.' Her eyes fell on the sergeant unavoidably, and had to be torn away before she could continue speaking. 'I was too fixated on Stan Morgan to even consider it was Arthur.'

Josey knew her claim was based on feeling trapped, and didn't want to shift focus to Morgan because he wasn't ready to get into that in front of the inspector; Morgan being his clandestine informant was a need-to-know at this point, especially the young mechanic's claim that sex with Arlene was consensual.

Inspector brown cleared his throat ahead of, 'Right, I want new written statement from you two the moment we leave here; is this understood?'

With no argument from either of them, he took it as a *yes*.

It was anybody's guess as to whether Arlene and Lester would put their dishonest affair behind them and go their own way; doing so would have been almost impossible though, given they lived right next door to each other.

Staying in Condobolin was becoming an issue for them; local newspapers were beginning to speculate far and wide about Sergeant Perkins so called *house arrest,* and what his next door neighbour had to do with it.

By far the biggest issue though was their safety, and Josey voiced it. 'Need I remind everybody that there is still a killer out there?'

In the end Josey made a suggestion that they jumped at. 'With the inspector's permission I'd like to take you both to a safe house in Wyalong. We already have police protection there, not to mention an armed caretaker and guard dogs.'

Josey wasn't the only one who saw this as a good idea; Inspector Brown recognised merit in keeping all those involved in the case at the same location, away from Condobolin, and in what he preferred to call, under police *watch.*

Proof that Brown was warming to Josey's abilities surfaced when he gave his blessing for the detective to travel to Wyalong, to be with his family for a couple of days.

The hospital gruelling came to a close and the Wyalong plan was now set in cement. Josey stood and helped Arlene to the door. With the inspector taking up the rear, Josey turned and advised him he wanted to have a private talk with his client on their way to Judith's property.

Brown baulked before saying, 'I had a feeling you'd ask that, somehow I think there's more to learn. Keep me in the loop, that's all I ask.'

Josey was beginning to gain respect for his on-off adversary. 'Of course, you have my word.'

The inspector left, leaving Josey to recall an expression of slight mistrust.

CHAPTER TWENTY TWO
The Untold Truth

Josey looked in the rear-view mirror and checked the patrol car that was following. He would have given anything to know what Arlene might have been saying to her driver, Constable Mathews.

Alone in the Toyota with Lester, it was the perfect place to give his friend a chance to come clean. Purring along the highway was the perfect place to find out just how far he would go with the remaining untold truth.

'I can tell you this,' he told Lester, 'Brown doesn't believe Arthur's injuries were acquired the way you say they were.'

The sergeant was beginning to glean that Josey and the Inspector had been powwowing more than he imagined. 'Can I ask what he *does* believe?'

'He's suspicious you both planned to kill Arthur before he had a chance to kill you.'

Lester's face loaded with disappointment. 'That's what

I thought. Does Brown even believe *Arlene* was injured the way I said she was?'

'Since you ask, no he doesn't; – and neither do I.'

'What the hell, Cam; what's with the toing and froing. What is it you want me to say?'

'Look at it from our point of view. You've admitted to an affair with Arlene, not to mention the cops showing up to find the woman tied to an iron stove half naked. It doesn't look good, and it's not believable.'

'I thought you knew me better than this.'

'So did I.'

Lester's eyes rounded. 'Is this the reason Brown doesn't believe the rest of it?'

'Brown and I are on slightly different pages; but as far as the law goes, you're left with having to prove your innocence, in which case you need to come clean on every aspect of your story, beginning and ending with nothing other than the facts. He's no dummy, Lester, I don't need to tell you coppers like to gauge how suspects respond to questioning; especially about delicate issues like restraining people for unclear reasons, and in this case, involving nudity.'

'What's unclear? She was drenched and in a state of shock. I was trying to protect her.'

'Please don't play dumb, your explanation for tying Arlene to the stove, near to naked, is viewed by police as completely ludicrous.'

'And by *you* it seems.' He sulked for a moment before saying, 'What else has got you bothered?'

'Primarily, the question of whether or not Morgan

actually *raped* Arlene.'

Visibly thrown off guard by Josey's query, he displayed confusion. 'Why ask me that?'

'Because I suspect you don't believe he *did*.'

'Why would I need to make a call on it; one way or the other?'

'Because it makes sense to you that he might not have.'

'And why's that?'

'All right listen, let's cut to the chase. I know as well as you do that he didn't.'

This stopped Lester short. 'And how could you possibly be certain of that?'

'Morgan told me he didn't – he says it was consensual.'

Lester's creased brow didn't come close to hiding his alarm. 'He contacted you?'

'Some time back,' Josey informed him.

This news was completely unexpected, and the worry finally surfaced. 'And you believe him; I mean, why would he contact *you* anyway?'

'Because he'd heard I was on the case and didn't trust talking to the police; basically he couldn't be sure how much sway you had with them.'

Lester bit his lip ahead of asking, 'What else did he have to say?'

'Quite a bit, things you and Arlene omitted from your involvement with her. He hoped I might explain his situation to police.'

Josey recognised his disclosure was making Lester feel uncomfortable, and for good reason.

Perkins maintained the silence of a man who knows he

has been caught out. Eventually he said, 'Must we keep going over this? I've given you all there is about Arlene and me.'

'No, you haven't - firstly, tell me how long you've been involved with Arlene?'

Lester wondered if his long-time friend was feeling a little disgusted with him . . . 'It's, hard to explain.'

'Try.'

'She comes to me when she feels the need,' he admitted hesitantly.

'Who else does she go to?'

'How would I know? It's not like I'm in love with her.'

This was the answer Josey expected. 'It's just sex then.'

'There's no need to make it sound so dirty.'

'Lester, listen to me; if these questions are putting your nose out of joint, you need to get over it. You above anybody would know that to a copper your irritation screams motive.'

Lester studied his friend curiously. 'Have you ever thought there might be certain things about our relationship that I find embarrassing?'

'Like there's more to Arlene than meets the eye you mean?'

'What's your point?'

'That she has an eye for men.'

Lester looked piqued. 'And you can definitely back that accusation up can you?' He studied the detective and realised he probably knew more than he'd given him credit for. He wasn't done with defending himself though. 'Have you thought what this will do to Arlene?'

'I think Arlene is a woman who makes her own bed.'

Perkins exhaled nervously, sounding like a man who was beginning to recognise arguing with Josey was a waste of time. 'I assure you; before Arlene, I'd never done anything remotely like this.'

Although the sergeant hadn't spelt it out, Josey knew that not too many people would guess the *stove-thing* involved sexual bondage. 'While we're on *that*, I need you to take a picture out of my head by promising you didn't have sex with an injured woman.'

Lester took on a whole new approach; he recognised how disgusting that picture was. There was no further reason to hold back. 'You have my word,' he confessed, 'and you can take that image right out of your head, Arlene wasn't injured until later.'

Josey still had a problem. 'Regardless of when her injury occurred, it boggles the mind why you and Arlene would even consider igniting your relationship given you had no idea what had happened to Arthur.'

Movement in the mirror took Josey's eyes to the patrol car following. A black sedan was overtaking it, slowly; windows too dark to see occupants, perhaps even by Mathews. It hung there as if its driver might be interested in seeing who was aboard the patrol car.

Aware Josey had gone quiet, Lester turned to notice him fixated on the mirror. 'Is everything all right?' He looked over his shoulder and saw the black vehicle suddenly pick up speed and rocket ahead to reach Josey's Toyota and pass at high speed, too fast to see inside. Josey also had swivelled round to try, but the car was gone in a blink, receding in to the distance like a bullet to vanish over a crest a kilometre ahead.

'Should we be worried about this?' Lester enquired nervously.

'I wouldn't dispel the idea,' he answered reaching into his coat pocket to gain his pistol and place it on the console as if making it ready.

Lester was no stranger to guns, but Josey's demeanour amplified his take on seeing the pistol and what it suggested. 'That answers *that*.'

'Don't worry about it—'

Josey had spoken too soon – having gone past the crest where they had lost sight of the black sedan and on reaching the crest that followed, the sedan unexpectedly reappeared, angrily spearing back into sight on their right - set to T-bone the Toyota—

It would have if not for Josey's quick thinking—

Lester tensed to accept the unavoidable collision, but instead felt the dizzying spin of their car Catharine wheeling, creating a blur of sight and sound, and disorientation.

Once at rest the bush before them appeared to continue spinning – intense vertigo. How Josey pulled this stunt off was beyond Lester's comprehension.

Extreme engine revs drew attention to the black sedan powering off the shoulder in a hail of dirt and gravel.

Having failed in its attempt to wipe out the Toyota the assailant was hell-bent on leaving the scene, regaining traction on the highway to execute a spin into the opposite direction.

Again the car was too fast, and dark, to see inside it.

They heard the patrol car's siren and saw it turn and take chase.

'What the hell's he think he's doing,' Josey yelled at the sergeant - '*stop him*!'

Realising Josey meant to use his cell, he gathered his jangled nerves and did as instructed without argument. 'Call off the pursuit, Mathews!' he yelled into his phone. 'This is not a request. If I don't see your tail lights—'

There was no need to say more; near to a crest that would have taken the patrol car from sight, the red lights appeared. They hung there as if waiting for further instructions.

Lester's silence urged Josey to turn and face him. 'Relax; it's over.'

He again gathered his wits and said nervously, 'If you say so.'

'I do say so.'

'Sounds like you know what this was all about.'

'I do.'

'Why am I not surprised.'

Mathews came back to where Josey had brought the Toyota out of the roadside ditch, pulling up beside the driver's window. 'What's happening?' he asked his boss looking past the detective.

'It was too risky,' Josey elected to say, 'my call.' He looked at his watch. 'How long to the property?'

'An hour tops. Is there some sort of hurry?'

Josey thought and then said, 'Are there any other roads that take you there do you know?'

'There is one, but you'd have to turn around to get onto it.'

'How far back?'

'About a mile or so.'

'How long would it take to get to the property going that way?'

'In these cars half the time; if you don't mind eating dust.'

Knowing this, Josey now had just one goal, to get to the destination before the black sedan. He asked Lester to instruct Mathews to take up the lead and to use the siren to get them to Jude's as fast as possible. Lester gave no argument and received none from Mathews, even though his sergeant was officially off duty.

'Be quick about it,' he told Mathews, 'our people may be in danger.'

'Can I ask—'

'No!' he yelled back at him, 'just do it constable! – *Go!*'

Mathews skidded the patrol car away as he'd been commanded, seemingly instigating the slower vehicle's chase.

Rocketing along the highway at a hundred-and-forty, Josey graced Lester with time to adjust his nerves to the idea of travelling at the breakneck speed, before then encouraging him to continue with his account of what really happened at the cabin.

Battling the nerves, the sergeant's shame surfaced like oil on water. He forced himself to speak above the noise and fear, his voice quivering, aided by the road vibration infiltrating the car. 'It wasn't like you might think, Cam, we knew Arthur was alive and well because Arlene and I found him on our way back to the cabin, or to be precise; he found us. As I said I found Arlene perilously hanging from the rock ledge. As soon as I reached her she was desperate to know what the hell was going on with Arthur's car. I knew as much as she did at this point, but we both understood *something* had been done to it . . .'

~

'I told you, he's trying to kill us,' Arlene shrieked.

'Well, let's spoil his day by getting you off this rock.'
They reached the safety of a patch of bush mulch, hands still locked tight, and rested . . .

~

'Just as we were making plans to make it out of there, Arthur showed up, just above us at the edge of the track. He was fairly grazed and bleeding, wounds most likely got from exiting the Raptor . . .'

~

'It looks like you've figured out my little secret,' Arthur told the hapless couple, and then he scoffed. 'A lot of good it'll do you; seeing's how I've got you right where I want you.'

~

The Toyota continued to keep pace with the patrol car, desperate to reach Jude Green's property to warn them of the danger they may be in.

Lester's eyes were transfixed on the road ahead with equal intent as his driver, but the adrenalin of travelling fast wasn't being allowed to prevent him from getting on with his story—

'Arthur couldn't resist boasting over his cleverness,' he told Josey. 'He actually gloated over his workmanship on the black box that he built to control the Raptor, and went as far as to give us a demonstration of how it works.

'Like you guessed, Cam, the box was little more than a games console, but it sure as hell worked. We heard the Raptor fire up nearby; heard it skating on the gravel track before sliding to a stop in front of him. We both knew what he had in store for us . . .'

~

'Arthur, don't do this,' Arlene pleaded with him.

'If you weren't such a tart my love,' he bellowed angrily, 'I wouldn't have to. I guess this is what happens when you fool around behind your husband's back. And as for you, neighbour, you'll get to take a nice little dirt nap with your lover.'

'Arthur, think about what you're doing,' Lester advised. 'The cops will figure this out; they'll know it's you.'

'I doubt that,' he said as he bent and picked up a sturdy twig. 'Anyway, you two won't be around to see it . . .'

~

'That's when he pushed us over the edge. It was dead easy for him. The bastard lightly nudged me with the twig; there was no way that we could prevent ourselves from skating across the moss.

'He wasn't expecting me to roll and grasp hold of the cattle-like prod, but the-luck-of-the-Irish saved him when he let it go.

'He clearly thought we were goners because we heard him drive away, back toward the highway.

He wasn't to know, just beyond the rim of the rock ledge we managed to cling to the high branches of a blue-gum . . .'

~

After dealing with the challenge of climbing from their leafy lifesaver, they set foot on the bolder-spotted banks of the creek that wound its way back to the cabin. Arlene knew that upriver would lead them nowhere near the highway, leaving them with one option, to make it to the cabin. The upside was getting out of the storm, besides, a revisit from Arthur and his modified Raptor was highly unlikely. This belief was bolstered by having heard the Raptor drive away toward the highway while still clinging to the lifesaving branches of the blue gum.

By the time they reached the cabin, Arlene was showing signs of shock and hyperthermia. Lester put her into a hot shower fully dressed, while he got a fire started. The warmth stripped away the chill as she happily allowed her rain soaked clothes to drop to the floor of the cubical. What she couldn't discard was the memory of her husband's actions, and her own.

Having left his drenched clothing strung over chairs next to a growing fire, Lester slid into the warming rain to join her. Their recuperating bodies met in waves of ecstasy, ready for love, yet, it didn't feel right. They let the blessed fluid do its gentle job, and tried to forget they had just escaped the hands of Arlene's murderous husband.

Following their shower they settled on the rug by the fire, sharing a blanket. They stayed like that for an age, happily soaking in the warmth and the chance to push the nightmare from their minds. They fully believed they were now safe.

Relaxed and amorous, Lester looked across at the iron stove; its strength and weight – *perfect* - and then at the innocent coil of rope that hung loosely on the wall - *even more perfect.* He wore a smirk as he stood and removed the fastener from its hook, holding it up to his lover inquisitively while he jerked his head toward the stove.

She knew exactly what his intensions were and smiled.

The passionate bondage that followed was clearly mutual – their favourite thing to do together . . .

~

Albeit minus some of the detail, Lester stopped his story there. 'That's all you need to hear about that,' he told Josey. 'We were lulled into complacency when the impossible happened, or at least that's how we thought of it. We figured Arthur must have decided to come back and check we were dead. We couldn't have guessed he'd become a victim himself.'

Except for the more believable explanation Lester gave on saving Arlene, and the bondage fetish, Josey found there was little difference to their original story.

The speeding patrol car, followed by the diligent Toyota, had left the highway and was now raising dust on the way to Judith's property, no more than ten minutes away.

'Anything else you want to tell me?' Josey asked

encouragingly.

'I'm pretty sure you know the rest. I've given you the gist of it.'

'You've given me more than the gist, but you haven't explained how and when Arlene got her injuries, and why she would throw you under the bus when the coppers arrived.'

'You're a hard man to please, Detective. But you'll be pleased to know her injuries happened *after what we got up to.*' He looked at Josey to see if he wanted more.

He did. 'I'm listening – go ahead . . .'

~

The faint sound of a car engine snapped Lester's attention away from his concubine, taking him to a window to investigate. The glow from the fire made it impossible to see anything other than his naked reflection; outside, the storm had turned day to night. He cupped his hands to the glass, but still could see no sign of a car, no sign of the Raptor; the impenetrable rain not helping.

'Lester, what's happening?'

'I'm not sure,' he admitted as he came to the chair where his clothes were, their game of bondage was over, and after he had dealt with the discomfort of getting back into his wet trousers, he headed for the door.

'Don't even think about going out there and leaving me tied up here,' she warned.

He was already opening the door and stepping onto the porch. Moist air sent chilling fingers across his skin, producing a deep shiver.

'Lester, don't; if it's him he'll kill you this time.'

222

'If I don't kill him first,' he countered.

The cul-de-sac was a river of mud, fed by cascades from the high ground destined to reach the creek. And there was the motor, rumbling in the dark, drawing Lester to it. He baulked when it finally came into view, the shadowy shape of the Raptor; as feared, it had returned. *Was Arthur inside, or somewhere nearby with his little black console?*

Remembering the events of the last hour he hesitated, he didn't know what to expect. He instantly got his answer when the sky arced, lighting the ground like day;

Aided by the intensity of the light, Arthur could be seen splayed across the bonnet, his blood dripping away like freshly poured strawberry icing.

Blinding headlights stabbed through the rain even as the Raptor's engine roared into life, lunging at Lester with intent. Its massive wheels burrowed into the mud on either side as he laid flat.

It stopped short of the cabin and reversed, narrowly avoiding crushing Lester beneath its wheels. Skidding like a skater, the deft sergeant made it back through the open door and slammed it behind him.

'Have you got any weapons here!' he shouted.

She was shaking and he needed to get her untied before doing anything else—

The door at Lester's back exploded from its hinges, scooping her lover off his feet.

As though time was being restrained from moving forward, splinters flew left and right of the catapulting door, pushing Lester ever further into the room until its weight took him down.

Helplessly tied to the stove beside the door jam, she at first didn't feel the shard of timber slice into her leg, or the crush of the heavy cupboard that had pinned her in place. Her leg was pumping blood.

The site of the Raptor through the doorway heralded a bloodcurdling scream.

Arthur, lying bloodied on top of the bonnet, was now partly protruding through the busted windscreen; his head and shoulders in a pathetic pose . . .

~

'My regret is that I ran out of time to get Arlene decent before the officers arrived. I might have fared better if it'd been my own boys that attended. When the three Dubbo coppers lifted the cupboard away and saw she'd been tied to the stove in the state she was in, they immediately thought I was some sort of sexual predator.'

Stopping his story there forced Josey to ask, 'And why did Arlene help them believe that?'

He scoffed, 'I had that out with her later.'

'And?'

'She apologised.'

'You accepted that?'

'Like I said, I'm an idiot.'

Josey had listened with interest to the final part of Lester's story with an open mind, accepting that his friend wasn't thinking with his head. 'Recognising your mistake is a good start,' he simply said to him.

Although his disclosures explained a lot, he couldn't help wishing Lester had mustered enough fortitude to tell it *this way* in the first place.

He looked at Josey quizzically. 'You said you know who's behind all this. Can you tell me?'

'I'm not sure I should.'

Lester looked at the pistol sitting on the console. 'Does the black sedan have anything to do with it?'

'My guess - *yes.*'

'Come on, Cam. I've spilled my guts to you, *how about* you spill yours. You owe me that much. Don't forget I'm the client.

Lester had a point.

'All right, don't say I didn't warn you.'

Now the sergeant began to wonder if he ought to take Josey's advice and leave well enough alone.

'Right, well I can't yet divulge who this guy is, but I can tell you *Arlene* is linked to him almost in the same way that you are.'

This was way outside anything Lester was expecting, and it showed on his face. He couldn't speak.

'I've told you this in good faith, mate. And now I have to insist you do *not* discuss this with her; or anyone else, understood?'

'Bloody hell,' he grumbled. 'This all just gets better and better.'

Josey flicked his eyes onto him and then back to the road. 'Lester – *understood?*' he checked strongly.

His hands were tied, 'Fine.'

Five full minutes of Lester sulking brought about a steady breath before saying, 'How much of my story should I be telling Brown?'

'All of it, and don't hold back.'

The truth stuck in Lester's throat. 'You do realise I didn't want my brother hearing about this.'

Josey knew this was another piece of fantasy from Lester, a fantasy that explained why the sergeant hadn't been as visibly concerned about his missing brother as one would expect. 'I know your brother is alive. But you already knew that as well, it was you who helped him disappear. Straight after the Jeep incident, *you* organised a safe house for him. What you don't know, is that he's now hold up with Stan Morgan. That's *my* doing. I brought the two of them together to wait this out, with strict instructions not to make phone calls; to anyone.'

'Wow, you're full of surprises Detective Josey; problem is, now Morgan's spilling his guts about Arlene and me.'

'If he is, Lester, I'm afraid it's something you'll just have to live with; he would have known about it soon enough anyway.'

Having no real combatant against Josey's decision, or his well-founded warning, *what's done is done*, Lester shook his head. 'So long as my brother is safe, that's all I really care about. He'll get over it in time; he may even learn that Arlene isn't really such a bad person.'

Josey knew this to be a dubious assessment. 'I'll say one thing, Lester, you're a forgiving man.'

'Like I said, I'm an idiot.'

CHAPTER TWENTY THREE
Back to Life

Judith Green's property was beginning to look like a mini music festival. The homestead was easily able to cope with the human influx, offering individual rooms to every one of her expected guests. Judith gave the room with the king size bed to Nicole and her husband Carl, the room with the queen to Rebecca and Josey when he arrived, a nice size one with a double to Molly, and a room each with oversized singles waiting for Arlene and Lester. Even Sergeant Mathews was to be provided for at Josey's request.

Jude already knew of the Condobolin sergeant, and had also heard of Arlene and her husband Arthur. She had only been told a smidgen about the affair between the two neighbours.

Josey had filled her in on their bizarre situation and touched on the danger relating to his hunch, omitting the incident on the highway with the black sedan.

It was only after a half hour of sleep that Rebecca awoke to the sound of barking dogs. She rolled and relaxed her arm across to Josey's pillow instinctively; felt it was cold, raising a moment of panic, but then recalling he was still on his way from Condobolin with the new lodgers.

Too awake to go back to sleep now, and wondering *why the damn dogs were barking,* she made her way into the hall modestly clad in her gown. Seeing Carl hurriedly making his way to the front door, she nervously questioned him. 'What is it?'

With a glance over his shoulder he suggested she stay inside while he checked it out.

'Wise choice,' Judith told her guests as she noticed Molly join her mother.

They were a little alarmed to see her carrying a rifle, but at the same time oddly glad she had it. The confident way she held the weapon suggested the firearm was no stranger to her. She was right on Carl's heels as he exited onto the verandah.

Out in the yard the dogs were going off angrily. The half dozen police that had spent the night there had their guns drawn, confused as anybody about what was happening.

'It's Johnny, folks,' the caretaker called out by way of revealing his position in the dark.

They saw him in the glow of his torch, over by the animals with a rifle of his own held ready for use. If there were prowlers on the property that didn't belong, they were probably having second thoughts by now.

'Have you seen anybody, John,' Judith called in a surprisingly loud voice.

He now had the torch aimed at the Raptor. 'I thought I saw someone over by the vehicle.'

'Put one in the air,' she yelled.

He didn't hesitate in sending off two shots.

Everyone stood still then, waiting for a desperate plea *not to shoot*, but there wasn't one.

The officers could be seen advancing into the yard, rim lit by one of their search lights mounted on a patrol car. The orb of light swung from pillar to post, nervously hoping to cover every corner of the extensive field.

Carl kept his voice down as he spoke to Nicole's Aunt at his side. 'Judith, I think we might all be safer inside the house.'

'Good idea,' she said matter of factly, 'Best you join them; I don't want anyone out here that isn't armed.'

Carl clarified with, 'No I mean all of us – you need to trust me on this.'

She looked at him then and saw the fear, not just for himself. 'You think it's that guy Josey told us about?'

He didn't have to think whether or not that fitted in with Josey's hunch. 'It seems crazy he'd try – *but*.'

'I thought the Raptor couldn't start without the plugs?'

'On the face of it, you're right, but if you hear that thing kick over, it's time to hightail it.'

He had no sooner given the warning when the Raptor's starter-motor was heard groaning sluggishly, attempting to bring the evil machine into life.

Instinctively the police closed in on mass, cantering

toward the sound, so too the light from the patrol car, so weakened by distance that they were unable to see into the vehicle.

Even though they'd all been told of the Raptor's autonomous history, their Intel told them there must be a driver. Especially given the advice that had been given by the private detective, claiming the necessary technology had all been removed, not to mention the spark plugs.

Johnny the caretaker fired off another shot into the air, but whoever was in that vehicle trying to start it, wasn't reacting.

Johnny heard one of the officers raise his concern. 'Leave this to us please sir!'

They didn't hear Johnny grumble, or notice that he was ignoring the warning.

Time after time the sluggish starter complained of diminishing power as the police advanced.

From the dubious safety of the verandah, Carl hoped that this might turn into a perfect night, if only the armed cops could make an arrest and end the perpetrator's spree for good – *game over*.

It wasn't to be, the beast emblazoned into life when the officers were only a couple of metres from it, launching into a threatening charge, providing no time to consider anything other than to run clear of its malicious path.

Their scattered positions became their greatest ally, making it so difficult to become its prey; that a new target was decided upon - *the caretaker and his chained dogs*.

'*John*,' Carl shouted as he ran out into the open, 'get the hell out'a there. Don't even think about taking this guy on!'

A driver behind the wheel was the only thing that added up for Carl.

With the Raptor closing in fast, the highly vulnerable caretaker was already taking his advice, his dogs barking in protest against being pulled by their chains into a retreat from the approaching machine; clearly angered by the danger it presented to them and their keeper. As enticing as its spinning wheels became, the three canines resolve to attack weakened as their adversary drew closer, eventually giving up their refusal to run with the caretaker.

When contact was inevitable, Johnny let the dogs free to run their own path and threw himself into a drinking trough, rifle held high and dry in the hope his manoeuvre would encourage the massive machine to swerve clear of the solid concrete tub to avoid demolishing itself.

Johnny's ploy worked like a charm, his head surfacing to catch the Raptor speeding past, accompanied by the angry German shepherds bravely nipping savagely at its wheels, their bravery bolstered by the realisation the monster was running away.

John emptied his rifle into the dark, careful to aim high enough to avoid hitting his dogs.

Judith had more of an advantage, shooting at the Raptor from the front of the house. She scored a hit somewhere around the missing windscreen, creating sparks. But she hadn't hit the driver it seemed, the menace maintained control.

Near to the front of the house where its human targets

were congregated, the menace broadsided with no apparent objective, until readjusting its position with lights blaring into their eyes.

'This thing has a driver, right,' Judith yelled at Carl while firing head-on into the glare.

It was impossible to tell, but unless its remote-control had been refitted without anybody hearing a sound, nothing else made sense. The fact the dogs hadn't barked until recently wouldn't have given the perpetrator time to carry out the refit, but clearly the spark plugs at least had been silently reinstated.

Carl knew Judith's place wouldn't be a match for Arthur's robust cabin, at least the way Josey had painted the picture. 'Don't go into the house!' he yelled to everyone on top of his voice.

Judith fired a couple more shots which emptied her rifle. She reached into the pocket of her gown to gain more ammunition, but Carl gestured for her to give it up.

'Save your bullets,' he advised, 'we need to get clear of the house.' He gripped his wife's hand as she moved up to his side. 'Are we ready?' he asked unobtrusively to those that could hear him.

'Where's Arlene,' he heard Lester asked sounding panicked.

'Check she's not in the house, quickly. Get yourselves back here. Don't even think about staying inside.'

He went and returned empty handed. 'She's not in there.'

'This thing is about to charge, we need to move!'

Judith just had to ask, 'What the hell is it waiting for?'

'Let's not hang around to find out!'

Caretaker John showed up at that moment with an idea that beat all. Spearing out of the dark on a frontend-loader the size of a truck he squared up with the Raptor side on, scooping it along as though levelling a giant bag of compost.

The sideways motion of the Ford's big wheels gouged at the earth as though it were a bulldozer, building a mound of soil ahead of itself. The engine roared in protest at being overwhelmed – tyres spun in an attempt to escape the adversary – at first failing, then breaking away like a speedway dragster into a fishtail - swinging into a series of under-and-overcorrections to avoid columns of hay bales that threatened to block its new out of control path. Scarcely avoiding the cordon by the narrowest of margins, it again angrily focussed on new targets – the scattering police officers.

Like a confused bull trapped in a Mexican pit, it found itself faced with the deft life preserving skilfulness of the nimble footed police.

Above the roar of the engine and the big wheels ploughing up Judith's property, everyone then heard the blast of a horn harmonised with the shrill approach of a siren; the sweet sounding duet attributed to Constable Mathews police patrol car and its gallant companion the Toyota sedan.

Although no match for the Ford Raptor, their sudden and unified presence presented an annoyance that wasn't conducive to the perpetrator's plan.

The aggressor realigned and did something no one

expected, or considered necessary, it raced around to the back of the house. They heard it stop with the motor still running.

Mathews alighted from his vehicle and met up with Carl and Judith over near the house, while Josey followed the Raptor's path around toward the rear of the house on foot.

Everyone shouted dissuasion to try and stop him, including the officers who by now were returning from the torn up field.

But Josey chose to ignore their warnings.

Before he even reached the corner of the back wall he heard the Raptor accelerate and relaunch, forcing him to dive for his life when it reappeared, reversing along its own tracks in what appeared to be a hasty retreat.

It spun past where Josey had tripped and fallen onto his back – continued past the front of the house where the others stood – did a one eighty to face in the opposite direction – crunched the gears violently and powered away - aligned on a final and defenceless target; a *last hit* before its escape

Out of tainted spite, the crazed Raptor tangentially aimed at the mobile home, succeeding in tearing out one whole side as it scooped past, exposing the dollhouse like interior.

Shock was only surpassed by relief. The arrival of the cavalry and the annihilation of the Delaware had brought the destructive spree to an abrupt yet definite end.

The last they all saw of the Raptor was its taillights heading toward the fence line where Judith's property ended and the heavily wooded national forest began.

None of their vehicles had a hope in hell of following it. But given the strong opposition it had encountered, along with the presence of police, there was very little chance of a return attack – not tonight.

Everyone stood in stunned silence, seemingly more surreal now that it was over. John had brought his tractor to a stop but remained seated with it running as though it were merely a temporary reprieve. Judith hadn't relaxed her tight grip on the rifle either. Josey panned from the receding lights in the forest to the faces of those gathered outside the house, all of whom were about to learn that the Raptor's visit had delivered more grief than was yet known.

Among the police that were returning from their near miss with the mad machine, a constable who appeared to be the head man approached Judith and asked her if anyone was hurt. A quick glance drew Josey's attention to the fact Arlene wasn't present, nor Lester.

There's no way they could have slept through the noise, he thought - *Then it hit him.*

He swiftly paced toward the front door of the house without explaining the urgency.

Nicole and Carl were forced to part in the face of his determined stride as he crossed the verandah.

'Josey, what is it?' Judith probed while catching up to follow him inside.

He began desperately shouting his wife and Daughter's names, but got no response.

'Where are my girls?' several people who had followed

heard him ask in a choked voice. They watched on helplessly while he threw doors open as if already expecting they wouldn't be found. As feared, he was eventually right.

Carl had rushed in and met up with Aunt Jude at the entrance to the hallway. She was looking set to have a relapse. He was about to ask what was going on when Josey reappeared, having exited the last room he'd searched. Ashen faced, his expression answered Carl's unspoken question before Jude could muster an answer. Tears reached the surface when sympathetic eyes met; so equally distressed Carl hadn't the strength to console him right at that moment. Instead he began a search of the entire house in the hope they were hiding in fear somewhere. *It was a hollow hope.*

They were nowhere to be seen. By the time he made it back to the hallway to break the news, Nicole and Johnny had joined Aunt Jude to rally around the stricken detective.

With his heart pounding against the inside of his chest like a hammer, he was incapable of thinking what should be done, just extremely cognizant that something *truly bad* had been orchestrated against his family, which he now took full culpability for.

'Cam, I'll get everyone to conduct a search, they could have found somewhere on the property to hide.'

An urgent voice called from outside. 'Hey, I've found someone!'

Hope lifted Josey heart enough to respond by joining Carl and Johnny as they headed outside, arriving just as one of the coppers came around from behind the house. 'Around the back,' he told the group encouraging them to follow.

Josey hung back, afraid of whom it might be. The fact that whoever the constable had found wasn't with him meant that person was either injured – *or dead.*

Carl and several of the police elected to follow the officer. Close to the back wall they found an unconscious male, lying face down. Constable Mathews joined them and lent to check the victim's vitals. 'It's our Condobolin Sergeant,' he announced to the local coppers. He saw Josey arrive and concluded the message for his benefit. 'He's alive,' he told him knowing it was a comparatively small piece of good news that it was his friend.

Judith was at Josey's side, her arm laced in his.

In spite of his stress, his curious mind focused in on the ground beside where his friend laid unconscious, right where the Raptor had parked. He noticed two sets of footprints in soft soil left moistened by water leaking from somewhere under the floor of the house; two prints were from someone barefooted. There was no sign of a struggle.

This told him volumes.

Knowing what he now had to do he gently released the supportive hold Judith had on him and walked away from the group without saying a word.

This worried her enough to say under her breath, 'Someone should stay with him.'

Carl stepped up to the task. 'I'll keep an eye out.'

The two men reappeared at the front of the house and

looked set to face a barrage of questions about who had been found, but Carl dissuaded their efforts. Seeing the state Josey was in encouraged them to abide.

Josey glanced toward the forest to where the distant lights of the Raptor dancing across the canopy could still be seen. It was *beyond sickening* to realise that his girls were in it; being taken against their will—*because of me.*

CHAPTER TWENTY FOUR
Escape to Hell

Josey's cell phone began vibrating against his chest.

There was no caller ID when he slipped it from his coat pocket and looked.

'Who is this?' he asked with the cell to his ear. It was customary for him not to give his name out if he didn't know who was on the line, this time he didn't need to.

'Listen carefully, Detective - I have your little family with me, do your best not to respond in front of those coppers you're with, I do not want any interference from police, or your buddy Sergeant Perkins, if he's alive that is - otherwise, your precious girls are *dead*. If you understand what I am telling you, just say *thank you.*'

An even deeper frost sped through Josey's veins, but with a glimmer of hope that if his family are still alive, he might get the chance to keep them that way.

Even without the distressing-content of the message, the man's voice was chilling.

He'd hesitated on instinct but only for a moment and then quoted the caller, *'Thank you.'*

'Very good; now here's what I need you to do - leave the line open so that I can hear what's happening.

'In the meantime find a way to get rid of the bloody coppers, be careful, and remember I'm listening. Say *I will,* and then put the phone away.'

'I will,' Josey said ahead of putting his phone back into his jacket.

Carl couldn't have missed noticing how odd his friend sounded. What happened next went part way to clarifying it, for Carl the rest would come soon.

'Is everything all right?' Constable Mathews asked as he approached.

Josey urged him away from the others. I need some time alone, I'm not really feeling well; would it be possible to sit in the patrol car for a spell, I just need to get away from everyone to get my head straight.'

It seemed an odd request, yet the detective did look very close to passing out. 'Not a problem, mate; here take the key,' he offered as he took the self-locker from his pocket.

The huddle of attendees that had migrated to the front of the house in support of each other, watched on in distress and concern over the detective's plight, and that of his abducted family. The wretched man faded away from the glow of lights spilling from the house to inexplicably reach Constable Mathews Patrol car, waiting innocently in the shadows.

No one knew why right at that moment; or that Josey now had ownership of the vehicle.

Aunt Jude, who had settled next to Carl, was extremely worried about Josey's behaviour. 'What's he doing?' she asked like Josey's offsider may know.

Carl wasn't exactly sure what Josey was up to either, yet knowing his boss the way he did, the timing of the phone call had to have been what set his strange demeanour in motion.

On hearing the patrol car fire up as soon as Josey sat in behind the wheel, which Carl noticed Mathews had registered to be more than a bit alarming, Josey's closest confidant immediately knew what his boss was about to do.

As gobsmacked as the sergeant, the other spectators watched the vehicle spin away raising tuffs of grass torn from their roots.

With a bemused grin, Mathews uttered incredulously, 'I didn't see *this* coming,' little knowing the man next to him was now totally privy to the seemingly bazaar action.

With Judith's houselights receding from sight, Josey knew he would not be able to rest on his laurels; several police cars with very capable drivers were probably already beginning their pursuit. Yet a mile down the road, the rear-view mirror remained dark, indicating Carl had picked up what was behind the phone call. His talented field-op knew enough about the case to explain Josey's action to the cops, and the others.

Every single surrounding sound during his unorthodox departure had been heard by the caller via the open phone, establishing the police were not being invited to the party.

'Well done, Detective,' the voice in his jacket said in a low muffled tone.

Josey took the phone out, placed it on loud speaker and threw it into the cradle mounted near the windscreen.

The menacing voice continued. 'And now - the fun starts. From time to time, out of the goodness of my heart, you will be receiving a face-time call, just so that you can see your family is alive, play the game and they will stay that way, try being a hero and they are dead.'

Josey could have played the game as the slime bag had called it, one of two ways, *plead or threaten.* From what he already knew, this guy was all about the thrill and on this basis would enjoy being threatened more than listening to a desperate plea.

'I do know who you are in case you're wondering'

The guy laughed. 'But the question is; do you know where I *am*?'

'If I said yes, would you believe me?'

He laughed again and said nothing.

'I'll agree to play this game if you agree to keep my girls safe until I arrive. Agreed?'

He gave a sick gravely laugh this time, 'I really doubt you'll find me, because I'm not where you think I am.'

Josey's mind locked as tight as a vacuum-packed drum.

Fear for his family forced him to plead just a little. 'My family have done nothing to you; they don't deserve to be harmed.'

'No one is completely *undeserving* of harm, Detective, I'm well aware of how good looks can get one into a whole lot of trouble.'

Josey believed this man was capable of seriously bad things, and understood talk alone would only run over him like water on a ducks back, perhaps to even make things worse.

Silence overtook the airways - - -

Josey's panic broke into the awful void of desperation. 'Are you still there?'

A manic laugh confirmed he was. 'Don't blame *me* for the situation your family finds themselves in, you should have thought of what could happen when you decided not to abandon your happy little holiday. But hey, do your best to find me; let's see how good a detective you are. I'll be waiting – don't be long though, I'm not a very patient man.'

'Can I at least —'

CLICK!

He slammed his hands against the steering wheel in a mix of fear and failure; and a deep dose of desperation. A psychologist once told him everybody has vague criminal thoughts at one time or another, her comment stemming out of Josey's attempt to reach into the mind of a psychopath. The feelings he now had, surpassed the understanding he'd previously gained by a thousand fold

– and it scared him. Strangely, self-loathing soothed the grief and allowed his brain to reengage; determination returning, no arsehole was about to get away with taking his family.

He made a call.

'Where are you?' Carl answered revealing he was able to talk without police listening in.

'Heading toward Wyalong – listen, I'll need your help. It'll be tricky for you to get away, but that's what you'll have to do. I can't keep this car.

'Josey I'm so sorry about the way this has played out, this has got to be the guy you suspected, right?'

'It is. Carl, there's not much time, I'll pull in one K out of town and wait for you to arrive.'

'What then? You won't be safe in the Toyota either. Do you even know where you're going? Maybe we should involve police?'

'No police.'

'Can you tell me why; what did this guy say to you?'

'Carl, you know me, I wouldn't do anything to put my girls in further danger; their dead if we go anywhere near the coppers.'

'I hope you know what you're doing.'

'I'm doing what I have to.'

'So what exactly do you want *me* to do?'

'As soon as you get here I need you to go ahead and hire me a car in Wyalong and drive it back; I'll ditch the patrol car in the scrub out of sight.

'Bloody hell, this sounds risky.'

244

'Risk is our only choice to save the girls. I'll fill you in on everything I know and what else I need you to do while you're driving. Believe me, Carl this is our only option.' Be quick, mate; time will run out if we're not.'

CHAPTER TWENTY FIVE
The case shifts

Denham Bourmac looked out of place as he walked past the rows of tenement houses in Surry Hills. His dress sense reflected a style more commonly found in the outer west of the city, well-worn leather jacket over a check shirt – cap and cargo pants; and a nose that could compete with that of a giant ant eater. His expression was more of a sneer than a smile.

The house he finally stopped at matched the rest of the houses in the street, except that it was painted a standout purple.

His knock was heard from inside and responded to. A heavily tattooed young woman appeared. 'Denham?' she enquired knowingly from the opened doorway.

Denham sensed a slight cringe, as if she was repulsed by his appearance. 'That's my name, don't wear it out,' he joked.

'Why don't you come in, my *ol'man's* hangin' to meet you.'

'Why don't I,' he said cheekily brushing across her tight pullover held breasts.

She seemed to enjoy the contact, but cringed again as he passed. 'You look just like your picture,' *ugly as sin she privately decided.*

The old-man as she had called him could have been Bourmac's twin, just as unattractive, his lack of appeal somewhat enhanced by questionable looking *tats.* He took the visitor's hand as you would an arm-wrestler. 'It's nice to make your acquaintance, *bro.*'

'Ditto.'

'Right, right, come on make yourself comfortable; let's get you started, you can call me *Rooster.*'

The two men sat on an old leather lounge that had seen better days, while the lady of the house went to the kitchen to *mandatorily* fetch a couple of beers, apparently needing no verbal request from the master.

'I appreciate this, Rooster,' Denham told him referring to being allowed into their world; 'I can't wait to see what you've got for me.'

He laughed and sounded like a cowboy pulling the reins when he said, 'Steady on partner, you need to calm your bowels, these assets *ain't* cheap.'

Rooster pointed a remote at the TV and brought an exquisite looking young woman to the screen. 'Like I said, don't be too quick to judge, there's over a hundred of these baby's to consider.'

'Wow, if there all as good as *her* this could be a hard decision.' Except for his gravelly voice, Denham sounded like a shameless schoolboy.

They were only about ten ladies into the parade of pictures when Rooster began to get restless. 'Maybe give me heads up on what gets your rocks off,' he suggested impatiently.

'I prefer blonds actually.'

'Who doesn't?' he chuckled salaciously as his mood bounced back up.

The slide show got quicker, now deliberately skipping past brunets. He'd only seen five blonds among the remainder of the shots, and they weren't what he was hoping for.

'Man, you're hard to please; you might need to hit me with more detail - and money if you're not careful.'

The beers arrived and Rooster dismissed his shag with a disrespectful scolding for taking so long. She took it in her stride and left the room.

'I guess it's not just the girl I'm after, it's more the situation; you know what I mean?'

A bright idea made him laugh while suggesting, 'You can spend the night with Mandy if she turns you on.'

'I heard that,' Mandy protested from another room.

Rooster was having a great time with this, and Bourmac thought it best to emulate the mood.

After allowing his expression to relax into neutral, Denham voiced his preference. 'I'm sort of looking for a threesome.'

'How old?'

Bourmac raised a gleam in his eye. 'I'd specifically like a couple of different ages.'

'Let me tell you something Denham my man, a lot of

blokes come in here saying they want more than one woman, most of the time it turns out they can't handle it.'

'I get that, what I mean is; one watches while the other – you know, is with me.'

'Yeah, that'll work.' He turned off the TV and leant back into the sofa to the point where he was almost lying down. 'I might have something for you; they just come in. But I'll have to clear this with the boss; can it wait till tomorrow?'

'I'm happy to pay in advance if you can fast track it.'

'Cool; where're you staying?'

'I'm right here in Surry Hills.'

'If I can get this organised for tonight; can you get your arse to the north-side?'

'Not a problem.'

'All right, leave it with me, *bro*; I'll text you with their pictures. If they're not blond we'll slip in a quick rinse, not just their hairstyles – you get my drift?'

He did. 'Cool bananas,' he laughed.

Denham Bourmac left the abode of Rick the self-professed Rooster and his piece of fluff Mandy feeling a little closer to his goal.

CHAPTER TWENTY SIX
Bourmac's Purchase

Arlene Sheridan walked from the kitchen into the hall and stopped at one of five closed doors. She knocked and entered without waiting for permission.

'Dinner is served,' she announced referring to the food laden tray in her hands. 'Paster curry and sausages; very exotic,' she insisted wryly grinning at the two shackled women.

'Stick it up your arse,' Molly strongly suggested.

'And what about you, Mum?' Arlene asked without a flinch.

'What *she* said.' Her voice shook, unable to muster the tone of defiance her daughter managed so convincingly. Of course she knew her daughter was just as afraid as herself, and how panic-stricken would her loving husband be right now? Cameron hadn't left her mind since their abduction.

Does he even know what's happening to us?

Has he somehow worked out how evil this woman is?

It was difficult to know how much time had passed since their abduction from Aunt Jude's house; they knew nothing of how it was carried out. By what means they had been transported from Wyalong to Sydney was not divulged, they'd awoken in this very room stripped naked and bound by chains.

Arlene was the first person they saw when they recovered from whatever drug they'd administered. 'I know you must be extremely confused ladies,' she said smugly, 'but all will be revealed in time.'

They watched her leave the room and hadn't seen her since.

So far they hadn't laid eyes on her partner, and could only wonder if that person was known to Josey.

He'll come if he does; finding people is his job - - - but, do I really want him to?

What will he do to them if he does – or worse, they to him?

She was terrified they would instantly murder him if he came to the rescue; but if he didn't - - - she couldn't allow herself to think about that, at least not for herself. But the thought of Molly being in this situation was more than she could stomach.

She finally found herself fantasizing that Josey would break in and kill each and every one of their captors, experience reminded her that he was capable of taking a life if it meant saving another. Knowing *him* also reminded her that it's not something he's ever taken lightly, yet this time he'd be easily forgiven if he did.

Arlene finally returned and placed a tray of food at their

feet, aware there was nil chance of them kicking it over, since their ankles were fastened to large metal rings attached to the floor. They were able to lean forward to reach the food but made no attempt to do so.

'I guess you're not hungry enough yet,' Arlene quipped sarcastically. 'That'll change.'

The room was almost empty, furniture replaced by mattresses, cushions and exotic rugs of many colours; several of which provided dubious comfort for the captives to sit with their backs against the wall; hands free to eat if they so choose.

'How do you expect to get away with this?' Rebecca enquired with nervous anticipation, afraid the answer might remove even further hope of a rescue.

'That's a need to know, sweetie,' was the smug reply, 'but I'll tell you this much, you're going to love what happens next. You'll learn things about yourselves you never knew possible.'

'You don't know us,' Molly said defiantly.

'That's not true, I'll go so far as to bet you're still a sweet little virgin – you needn't answer, we're about to find out for ourselves.'

'At least I'm not a slut like—,'

'Molly!' her mother demanded protectively, 'don't encourage her; just be quiet.'

Arlene found their reactions amusing. 'I promise you'll both be making a lot of noise soon.' She turned and moved to the open door, leaving them with one last thought. 'You should build up your strength; tonight you'll be having the pleasure of a visitor.'

Their fearful expressions spoke volumes.

In Arlene's mind the fear and disgust would turn to lust. She looked up at the mounted camera suggestively. 'You'll probably want to watch this over and over, I know *we* will.'

The door closed behind her, leaving them to visualise where this was obviously leading. The absence of hope encased them; the warmth of the heated room their only plus, given that they were already stripped naked in readiness for their mystery visitor.

CHAPTER TWENTY SEVEN
Josey's Torment

He hated the Kia, it was the physical embodiment of the change in his life, a life without the people he loved at his side, people he took far too much for granted; his beloved Rebecca and their sweet daughter, beautiful Molly. It was the beauty that both his girls possessed that frightened him the most. He wished he could will himself to where they were, and his mind be blocked from seeing it.

His biggest challenge right now was holding to the speed limit, yet he knew road-speed alone would not achieve a thing; except maybe in getting a ticket and the disclosure he is wanted by police. He could only imagine the livid expression on Inspector Brown's face. He was beyond ready to include him, yet this option was untenable, it was too soon, but that was about to change.

He cast his mind forward to the jet awaiting his arrival in Orange, and the subsequent Jetstream flight to Sydney.

Then the taxi ride to Wisemans Ferry, and the house where his girls were experiencing unimaginable horrors at the hands of Arlene and her psychopathic accomplice. How he knew these things would soon come to light, but right now the *how* was unimportant.

Casting his mind forward was one thing, but virtually winding the clock back was fraught with compunction and disappointment.

If only.

If only his family hadn't come to Condobolin.

If only he'd sent them home earlier.

If only he'd left for home with them.

But time was a one way street, what horrors would time take him to when he finally reached that house? What terrible things would he see, and do?

If only he'd involved the police sooner, his girls might be safe now; even at the expense of his prime suspect getting away.

The plane left on time from Orange.

Seven hundred kilometres per hour seemed a snail's pace. He wanted to accept the face time calls he had been promised, if only to hear the voices of his girls; but he sensed it would only fuel the foul mind of the captor, so he opted to not answer the calls. At the back of his mind he thought that if he did answer, it might just be an invitation to witness his family being murdered, or perhaps be seen forced into illicit acts.

The stress was showing, a hostess finally asked if he was feeling okay; the question prompted him to ask if there was a seat closer to the exit with a bit more leg

room; just in case he became more ill than he already was
– *he had another reason.*

She quickly left and returned with a bag and a
gentleman in tow with good news. He had a seat near the
exit and was happy to give it up.

While Josey was worrying himself sick aboard his flight
to Sydney, Arlene was answering the door to *their visitor*
at the far away destination. 'Good evening,' she said as
gracefully as a high class receptionist might, 'we're ready
for you, Mr Bourmac.' She took a moment to check the
car that the visitor had shown up in, not the sort of wheels
a man with money would ordinarily drive; an average
looking second hand Hyundai.

He noticed what was on her mind. 'I've only owned it a
day,' he explained.

She immediately calculated it was probably his way of
hiding any record of his visit. It never ceased to amaze
her how men were so embarrassed by their sexual needs.

Denham followed her into the open lounge where he
was asked to take a seat, but not before a not so quick
frisk, part of which included a good-old-touch-up around
the groin, *part of the service,* he assumed. 'My partner
will be here in a moment, would you like a drink while
we wait?'

He knew this to mean she would be staying for the
show. He hesitated as if to consider her offer of a drink,
but in fact was vying for time, nervous over what was
about to happen. 'That would be great, thank you.'

She left and came back with a bottle of rum and a bottle
of Brandy along with several cans of differing soft drinks.

'Help-yourself won't you,' she said offering him his glass.

The bottles were unopened he discovered when he twisted the top on the Bundy, which was somehow calming, because he needed to keep all his capacities. He poured generously and left it straight.

Arlene picked up a glass that had been left on the small table at his knees, filled it with brandy and joined him on the couch, sitting sideway facing him at the opposite end.

She took a large mouthful of the booze, her cheeks were already flushed, which was either from previous drinking, or anticipation of what she was about to watch; the camera on the wall confirming she and her partner were voyeurs, which needed to be nipped in the bud.

'Can I ask that there be no cameras involved?'

This struck a bad note. 'Are you shy? I mean, asking for two ladies suggests otherwise.'

He needed an affirmative answer. 'I'm not in a position to risk being identified; you understand.'

She did, and hated it.

He couldn't be sure if she believed his reason, but asking was the only move he had. If they chose to say the cameras were off when they weren't than he'd just have to put up with that.

'Well, I think we can get started; would you like to meet your friends for the night?'

'Yes of course, I'm looking forward to it.'

Her partner, who he had been advised is *the boss* when talking to Rooster, hadn't yet shown up, but was fully expected to be present before the show got underway. He swallowed the remainder of the rum, revelling in its nerve settling warmth.

She led the way to where his entertainment for the night awaited. She paused, knocked and as usual entered uninvited.

The looks of embarrassment weren't unusual, Arlene loved the way people became self-conscious when naked. She couldn't possibly have known just how embarrassed this lot were.

Denham chose to keep his eyes on his host until she got the message to leave. With the door closed he scanned the room; the only camera he could see was minus its little green light, unlike the one he'd seen in the lounge-room. He looked into the eyes of the naked women and said on a nervous breath, 'Well, this should be fun.'

In Sydney at last, being first out of the plane gave Josey several minutes head start, and with no baggage to pick up he was free to hotfoot it out of the terminal where he met up with Maxine, his very anxious partner from their Sydney office.

Gothic in appearance, Maxine was a standout, not to mention outstanding when it came to efficiency and exceptional reconnaissance capabilities. She'd had little to do with this case, mainly because it was out of town, but she'd been involved in a string of cases in which she had been pivotal to their outcome. But their relationship was far more than business.

She had Josey's Plymouth ready and waiting. The keys were in her hand, but she couldn't resist wrapping her arms around him before handing them across. She was crying.

'Max, I need to move.'

She stepped back, gave him the keys and watched him get in behind the wheel. 'Bring our girls home safe,' she told him as he threw the car into gear.

'Wish me luck,' he suggested.

His voice trailed away as the squeal of tyres took the Plymouth away on its mission of mercy.

'Good luck, Chief,' she whispered to the receding car.

Maxine stood there for several minutes before making her way to the taxi rank, now and again shedding a worried tear.

Josey was putting the pressure on, taking the shortest route possible to reach Wisemans Ferry. The occasional safe driver brought out some uncommon road rage over the unintentional yet extremely disruptive obstacles. He was breaking every speed limit and all the known road rules, but the plight of his family was all that he saw; not the bus he'd caused to brake, or the coronary he'd inflicted upon a cyclist. Time after terrifying time he drove through spaces that barely accommodated the width of his car, a judgement that accrued an accuracy assuring amazing success.

One stunt melted into another, a rollercoaster that he hoped wouldn't draw the attention of a copper who fancied himself a *Jack Brabham*, all the while praying some unforseen mishap wouldn't suddenly bring the reckless spree undone.

It wasn't clear until much later how long this mad dash had taken, aware only of having finally made it to the location. Would he be in time?

Thankful for the cover of night, he parked the car short of the address and stepped cautiously up to the house; widely alert to the slightest movement that might turn out to be an adversary. Even though the location was less than thirty kilometres from the city, the place looked more like something you'd expect to see in the country; large, with many rooms by all accounts, and wide decks all round. It was eight o'clock. Again he desperately yearned not to be too late. Double-checking the bullets in his pistol he slipped it into the back of his belt beneath his jacket.

After making his way silently onto one of the side decks, he held his breath in the hope there were no guard dogs. He had bought an all-black outfit at the terminal in Orange while he was waiting for his flight to Sydney, and now crept like a housebreaker toward a well-lit window.

Inside, he saw a small TV, its glow facing a lounge setting, presumably with someone sitting there watching. The imageries that he knew would be playing on that screen would prove to be disgusting, depictions he never expected he'd ever have to watch; and thankfully, so far the television was hidden at the other side of the couch. The nightmare he knew his girls might already be facing was beyond disturbing.

What Josey couldn't yet appreciate was the layout of the rest of the house. There was nothing he could see that gave him a clue what these people were watching at this very moment, or what was going on in their minds.

In fact those watching the monitor were confused over Denham's decision to designate Molly as the bystander; they could have sworn he would have chosen the younger woman. Clearly the camera in the love room was capable of operating without the giveaway green light, but disappointingly the angle wasn't allowing for a clear view of what the visitor was doing to the mother.

No one could see that from Molly's point of view it was clear Bourmac actually had his eyes closed.

Was this some sort of sick fetish? She thought.

Outside, it was time for Josey to make a move; he began by speed-dialling a number in his cell— *Right then the recognisable cold chill of a gun barrel pressed hard against the back of his neck.*

'What's say we pop inside for a better look,' a man's gravelly voice demanded from behind.

Caught out, Josey dropped the cell phone into a flurry of plants that were rising from a windowsill garden that was mounted waste high. He could only trust the gunman hadn't seen or heard it drop, and that the glow from it wouldn't be seen beneath the shelter of the opportune shrubbery.

The guy continued patting his captive down and located the belt mounted pistol, housing it in his own jacket. A sharp jab into the neck with the gun barrel encouraged Josey to get moving. 'Don't be shy, you'll find the view inside is a whole lot more interesting.'

Calmly accepting the sleazy offer, Josey moved toward the door, he had to start somewhere.

'Knock on the door *arsehole.*'

Josey gave four raps followed by two more, the kind of knock you give on a friend's door.

'You're a very funny man,' the gunman assured him sarcastically, 'I'll enjoy watching you squirm.'

A woman appeared wearing an ugly-devilish mask.

'Hello, Arlene,' Josey quipped knowingly.

Arlene was doing up her dressing gown, and perhaps deliberately too late to achieve modesty, given it was her singular piece of clothing. Although totally unfazed by being recognised, she *was* taken aback by not expecting to lay eyes on the detective quite so soon. She beamed at the gunman appreciatively, 'Nice work, Teddy.'

Hero-Teddy shoved their unexpected guest forward as Arlene stepped out of the way to let him enter.

'Look who just popped in,' she said to whoever was on the couch, haughtily delighted over the detective's early arrival.

In response to her welcome news, a similarly masked man stood from the couch and turned to face the doorway in the full-Monty. He was still relaxing from whatever the bastard had been getting done to him on the couch while watching the TV.

Josey's blood ran cold at the thought of what that might be.

The brazen stance of this guy indicated he thought he had *all of what it takes to satisfy a woman*.

'Fancy seeing you again, Josey quipped flicking his eyes to where the sun normally doesn't shine, 'Well, you know what I mean.'

Joe Magrie let out an appreciative laugh in response to the detective's little joke; just as pleased as Arlene at seeing the detective on his doorstep—having found the location so soon—it came as a tangible *stimulus* for the entertainment. 'I'm impressed; I thought you'd be still pussy-footing around out west, but I have heard you are very good at what you do . . . Hey, you're here now and just in time to watch the show, which if you don't mind me saying, is pretty damn cool,' he finalised like a high rolling promoter. He gestured toward the sofa. 'Please, a front row seat awaits you.'

Josey hesitated, looking for the slightest chance to make a move that wouldn't endanger his family. There wasn't one.

He took off his mask before saying, 'Perhaps you'd rather watch *live,* from inside our *love room.*' With no response from Josey he turned to a draw in the cabinet below the TV and extracted a gun, aiming it point-blank. 'Or maybe you'd prefer I put a bullet in your head right now.'

Josey did what anyone with half a brain would do, he accepted the offer to sit, which he did with his eyes focused on the wall above the TV.

'You're not watching, Detective,' Magrie grumbled; waving his gun toward the screen. 'Is this not your type of porn?' When he laughed, Teddy joined in like a string puppet; he didn't need a grotesque mask, he was unpleasant enough without it; and huge, and thankfully fully clothed.

Arlene drew sick of the entire banter, saying as she threw her mask off, 'Joe, just shoot him and his boring family and be done with it. But do it outside, I don't want blood on the carpet.'

Josey couldn't help eying Arlene with utter distaste.

On the other hand, Magrie's expression was calm and in control. 'Patience my love, we can't interrupt our session in the love-room, too much editing later, and besides, there are a few things I'm curious to find out from our prying detective here.'

She scoffed without taking her eyes from the porn show. 'Like what?'

He swung the gun onto her, demanding she not question him. 'Watch your mouth, Arlene.'

Cracks in the armoury, Josey thought.

Leaving the guarding of their prisoner to his bodyguard, Magrie returned his pistol to the draw and sat next to Josey elbow-to-elbow. 'This isn't turning you on is it,' he laughed stating the obvious.

Josey finally brought his eyes to the screen; there really wasn't anywhere else to look; Baumac was doing his thing, and not one other viewer noticed anything other than fear and confusion on the faces of the TV stars.

Josey wasn't thinking about what he was watching, his mind was on the connection between Arlene and Magrie. Did that connection explain the abstruseness between what happened at Aunt Jude's and now? Was their relationship a love-hate situation?

'So, Detective Josey, I'm intrigued; how'd you find this place?'

'You said it yourself; I'm good at what I do.'

He let out a deafening laugh, capping with, 'Oh well, it makes no difference, I'm real glad you're here – it'll be much more fun.'

Josey considered Magrie wasn't thinking too clearly about what he was watching on the monitor.

What does he think he's seeing?

How long before he becomes suspicious?

That moment looked like it may have arrived when

Magrie suddenly pulled away from the monitor to assess Josey's reactions. What he saw wasn't what he expected.

How could he be so relaxed about this?

Josey's blasé attitude was definitely perplexing for Arlene now too.

Magrie turned back to the image on the monitor, the image being beamed from the love room.

All he could really see was Bourmac's back.

The fact the guy hadn't taken off a stitch of clothing suggested he had some sort of problem. He decided this wasn't working out. He barked at Teddy while pushing off the couch. 'Keep the gun on him,' he warned referring to the detective.

Bourmac spun when the door to the love-room opened brazenly. He knew he was in trouble as soon as he saw the rage on the captor's face. If there was any doubt the subterfuge was disintegrating, it vaporised when Magrie belligerently dragged him from the mother, clearly aware he hadn't been doing what he came here for.

In the viewing-room, Josey had seen all the TV he was prepared to take. He swung on Teddy and relieved him of his weapon in a grasp-and-grab.

Arlene was heading for the pistol in the draw. She had her hand in there when Josey slammed it shut with his foot.

She cursed him through the pain while withdrawing empty and very sore handed, which was fine; now Josey had two guns.

Armed like a Wild West gunslinger, he appeared in the doorway of the bondage room.

Magrie was *ropable* now.

The girls, and especially Molly, who was preserving her modesty as best she could, showed a mixture of relief and embarrassment at the sight of her step father; she had never once allowed him to see her naked, not even when she was a kid—

'Josey!' Rebecca warned, 'behind you!'

He swung and swept Arlene's rifle aside as it went off. The close range explosion raised a resounding echo in the tiny room and an ear-splitting ring inside his head; assigning a trace line where the bullet had extracted a layer of skin across his cheek—

The malevolent woman stood her ground with the smoking rifle as the henchman arrived at her side with a shotgun. She peered fiercely at Magrie with a hungry request. 'Let me kill him before he causes anymore trouble.'

'Why the hell not - go ahead, *lover*.'

The girls screamed so loudly that a wailing siren blaring in the distance was almost missed.

'Do you hear that, Magrie;' Josey said using the only psychological tool he had. 'Better late than never as they say.'

Like a trapped animal imagining a means of escape, trying to decide whether to eat its prey or run from the hunter, Joe the motel owner froze. His eyes fell on Arlene devilishly with an instruction. 'We leave nothing, everyone comes with us. If he gets heroic, kill him and we'll take the body.' With this chilling ultimatum set in stone, he swept across to the captives and with a key from his pocket began releasing them from the ion rings.

Josey perceived Arlene's trigger finger was tightening,

as if not to wait.

Her dubious beau picked up on it. 'Don't even think about it, lover, if he's dead it'll be you carrying his body.'

'I don't trust him.'

'For fuck sake Arlene,' he shouted, 'do like I tell you.'

The siren was getting closer, even as the henchman went to a front window to check. 'They're close Joe, I can see their lights.'

'Get him clear of the door,' *Mad-Magrie* snarled at Arlene.

'Backup,' she demanded swaying her rifle at the tiresome detective, 'into the hallway, shit-head.'

Molly was crying now.

'Teddy,' his boss snapped, 'Go get the bloody car, *now*.'

'I need to go my own way,' Bourmac pleaded breaking his silence.

'You're not going anywhere shit-for-brains.' Magrie was pushing the women ahead of him, showing no empathy for their fear and their naked discomfort. 'Arlene,' he barked. 'Make sure the queer doesn't make a run for it.'

He was at the front door now; unaware Bourmac was already keeping up compliantly.

Arlene had Josey following in the hallway; rifle trained and ready to shoot if he tried anything.

He was stepping backward, keeping his eyes on her; she was presently the only thing preventing him from an attempt to stop Magrie from once again abducting his wife and daughter.

The familiar roar of the Raptor announced the arrival of

the henchman with their means of escape. Its presence here in Sydney had come as a surprise to Josey; Magrie must have brought it from the Central West as cargo, probably to make sure it would never be found again.

Arlene and Josey were almost to the Raptor now; her gun still held fast on the detective.

The police were closing in on the property; approaching from the south – their siren sounding sweeter by the minute to the captives. The safest thing Josey could do now - *the only thing* - was to play along.

Half way through the door to the back seat of the Ford, where the henchmen had allowed the girls to fold themselves up in a blanket, Josey painfully crushed the urge to reach across and take him down right there; instead, plan-B began with a swift kick back at Arlene.

It sent her to the ground - accompanied by the blast of a stray shot as she hit dirt. The gun switched ownership before she had a chance to gather her wits. Now she was the captive and not a bit happy about it.

Josey was fully aware his hold on Arlene had only created a Mexican standoff; the trained rifle on Arlene being equally matched by the henchman's gun aimed at Molly's head.

With the barrel of her own gun in her face, Arlene wasn't sure what Joe would do.

'He won't shoot!' he yelled from the driver's seat. 'Get the fuck in the car you silly bitch!'

Josey helped her decide. 'Do like he says.'

Although confused she didn't argue, picking herself up and hurriedly climbing into the Raptor. She looked back from her window, lamenting the loss of her chance to do her worst with the annoyingly resilient detective, but at least they still had his precious family.

Bourmac had been holding back, awaiting the outcome of the detective's move on *the bitch*.

'You too,' Josey said giving their nervous deviate a push toward the vehicle.

He didn't argue either, he boarded the Raptor by the skin of his teeth with the monster already powering away in a spray of grass and gravel. Squeezed in the back seat, next to the blanketed girls and the henchman, it didn't yet seem like much of an escape.

The last thing Magrie saw as he drove away was the detective standing alone at the front of the house, a dead set fly in the ointment. It was easy to guess he had been the one who called the coppers, who were still far enough away to allow a clean getaway. One thing was clear; the detective's decision to allow his girls to be driven away equated to some sort of smart-arse plan.

'Keep those dames out of sight,' Magrie growled at Teddy from behind the wheel.

He carried out the order under duress; the Raptor was rocking and bouncing as effectively as an amusement park dipper.

'Don't get too comfortable back there Bourmac, I'll be finished with you as soon as we're clear.'

Denham knew what that meant. 'Please, don't kill me - I'll make it worth your while to take me with you.'

Magrie caught him in the mirror, almost like he was considering his plea, but it wasn't that – the little *dip-shit* confused him. 'What's your deal anyway? You pay for two women and can't get it up; is that how it is, *weirdo*?'

'Don't think I can't pay, I'll give you two million.'

Driving blind for a second he glanced in the mirror at his weird-arse passenger.

'I'll give you the money,' the gift giver promised, 'but only on the condition the women come with me.'

This raised immediate suspicion.

Huddled beneath the blanket, mother and daughter cringed at the thought of ending up with Bourmac, yet compared to murderous Magrie he seemed like Santa Clause.

But their captor wasn't thinking about money, or women. This hadn't been a good day for Magrie, and he needed some real stimulation to make it better. He needed to kill someone; that always worked. Maybe he'd do all three of his passengers if he felt like it.

He romanticised about it as he drove, seeing himself *slamming on the brakes, dragging them all from the vehicle, lining them up on their knees and putting a bullet into each and every one of them.*

That was going to happen anyway he decided right then, and the thought made him feel incredibly impatient.

He wished he'd had more time to interrogate the detective; he was fascinated with the process that allowed the bastard to track him to the Wisemans Ferry address.

If Josey was here with him now, he would be the last one he'd kill; after watching his family die.

Then it hit him – getting away from the detective had been far too easy.

CHAPTER TWENTY EIGHT
Death Row

The raptor headed north via the national park, the perfect place to get rid of useless-bodies. He'd do Bourmac first, money wasn't everything, and - just because he couldn't stand weirdos.

Something caught Magrie's eye in the rear-view mirror; a black sedan he decided, it had lit up momentarily as it passed beneath a street light that illuminated the only intersection for miles – the car was innocent enough, but he wasn't taking any chances—

Everyone except the driver got thrown to the side when without warning he made an unannounced turn into a side road – calling it a road might be an over qualification; perfect, the sedan wouldn't have a chance of following.

But it did.

This was a quandary, if the detective was on his tail, it didn't seem tangible, why stay behind and then follow?

They had travelled five kilometres with no sign now of headlights in the mirror, and they had made turns at several junctions. He convinced himself that the trailing car had been pure coincidence and drove on across the potholed gravel causeway.

But the lights reappeared a kilometre later.

A cross road was a last chance to find out if he was being followed by the sedan. Turning left and picking up speed, he reverted to the rear mirror each time the bush lined bends allowed a line of sight; his anxiousness noticed by his passengers, especially Teddy, who became drawn to the rear window just as the lights receded from sight on one of the curves.

Also sensing her *love bug's* continued unease, Arlene twisted in her seat to look back. The pursuing lights reappeared.

'We're being followed,' he told her and Teddy before they had a chance to ask.

The rifle that had been resting butt down at Arlene's feet she lifted into her nervous hands.

Magrie was too busy keeping the Raptor on the dirt track to form an opinion about her action, or to notice Bourmac reach beneath the blanket that was masking the girls in the back.

Within the pitch darkness of their cover, the sudden arrival of his hand raised dread. Light stabbed from the interface of a cell phone, the screen favouring Rebecca. She squinted into the glare – her retinas taking a moment to adjust and allow recognition; incredibly, the cell was displaying a message; the first two words made her heart leap with hope—

its carl i have joseys phone.

In the subdued glow, Molly saw profound relief cross her mother's face; and then the message when the phone was turned for her to read; Rebecca raised a finger to her lips summoning mandatory silence.

If only they'd known earlier, their ordeal might have been a little less terrifying. Carl's disguise was that good. He would explain that later, the risk of disclosure was far too high. He hadn't believed for a second that the camera in the love room was switched off, and promised himself he would do everything in his power to find and destroy the recording that they would undoubtedly have made. He believed the hasty retreat from the house that was forced on them wouldn't have given them time to grab the offensive material.

The display on the phone's interface ended, plunging the captives back into darkness.

Carl withdrew the concealed mobile from under the blanket and covertly returned it to a side pocket in his jacket.

The big worry for Carl now was that the Raptor had been making such good time over the rough road, and given the glow of lights had apparently vanished, it meant Josey's Plymouth had dropped back so far that he may not be able to catch up—

Unsatisfied with this development, Magrie suddenly altered the scenario. 'Stuff this,' he cursed just ahead of jamming the brakes on hard. The Raptor skidded and broadsided into the shoulder, coming to a halt part way into the scrub. He plunged it into first and ploughed a path that took the Raptor forward a few more metres; out of sight from the road.

Perhaps he's planning to wait in ambush, Carl thought.

What eventuated was close to Carl's guess, yet far more terrifying.

By the time Josey rounded the same bend, he was forced to execute an emergency halt—

Confronting him were Mad Magrie's passengers, they'd been expressly lined up across the width of the track, all on their knees with their hands clasped behind their heads; a sick mind's idea of a private little death-row.

Josey noted, *Arlene's not one of them.* In fact she was nowhere in sight.

Still wrapped in the blanket that they'd been allowed to share, his wife and daughter were painfully driven to deep despair, with little to no respite from fear at Josey's timely arrival.

Behind the line-up, along with Henchman Teddy, stood their would-be executioner; his pistol aimed point blank at the back of Molly's head.

Josey couldn't possibly know if Carl had already managed to reveal his identity to the girls, but even if he had, seeing the illusionist here in the same dangerous predicament as themselves hardly provided hope.

'Come on out, Detective,' Magrie scoffed, 'Join us, we have room for one more, or maybe you'd prefer to just watch.'

Magrie's manic laugh made Josey feel sick to his stomach, but he knew enough to do exactly as demanded. With no immediate strategy to save the situation, he stepped out of the car and waited for the captor's next instruction.

'Close the door and move to the front of the car. And I don't need to remind you, your lovely daughter here is dead if I see any sign of a weapon.'

Again, Josey abided without hesitation, feigning calm, a demeanour that clearly unsettled his opponent, he'd do his best to change that; he didn't want to enrage the guy any more than he already was.

Without any provocation or announcement, Magrie swung the pistol off Molly and onto the henchman, shooting him in the back of the head, stone cold dead in an instant – purely for shock effect. *It worked.*

The girls were sobbing, believing they were next.

'A little demonstration,' the psychopath quantified with eyes on Josey, 'just in case you think I'm playing.' The gun came back onto Molly, then onto her mother; back and forth, back and forth.

'Who's first?' he asked in a reasonable tone.

'For God's sake.' Josey's voice had shuddered at the sight of his girls living in such fear, he had more than a little of his own. Dealing with antisocial personalities was never a textbook situation, but this was off the scale. The terror he saw rippling through his family and friend was more than he had ever been forced to bear – he felt completely helpless.

Making it sound like killing people was a normal day's work for him, he told Josey, 'You know what, I'm really pleased you're here, Detective, because I've made a decision, now you get to see your family die before your very eyes.'

It sounded like he was on the verge of shooting, robbing Josey of time to think. There had to be a way of stopping this. Dare he reach for the gun in the back of his belt?

Where's Arlene? Why isn't she here, she wouldn't want to miss seeing the execution; maybe she's hold up in the Raptor somewhere - or lying dead in the bush already.

He saw the beat-up tyre marks leading into the scrub and figured that's where she'd be.

If not dead, she might have her rifle ready for any trouble makers.

Josey's gun-hand was itching, he could feel the pistol pressing against his spinal cord – beckoning. Was he fast enough to get it – to swing and fire before Magrie put a bullet in his daughter's head?

The detective's anguish was doused by the next command. 'Turn round and let's see that gun under your belt.'

Almost relieved by having the decision circumvented, Josey turned and lifted his jacket to reveal the pistol; he'd already been given about thirty seconds more of life than he thought he had.

'Drop it and kick it away.'

We're in a pickle now, Freddie, he said in his head. *Is this the day I see you again my friend?*

'Please don't hurt my family,' Josey pleaded while carrying out the order. 'They've done nothing wrong.'

'Oh, *boo-hoo*, like I give a shit; just shut up and tell me how I fucked up, that's all I'm interested in; how'd you work out I was involved, and how'd you find me so goddamned quick?'

Pleading for the madman's sympathy hadn't worked so

he let his anger show. 'Give me a reason to bother; if you're planning to kill us anyway, what's the point in telling you anything.'

Carl felt his boss might be clutching at straws; it was time to do something. He got off his knees and faced their perpetrator defiantly, bringing all the attention and the gun onto himself. '*I* can tell you how you *fucked up.*'

Magrie considered the weirdo had suddenly lost his mind, was he asking to be shot? 'What the hell would *you* know?'

'Carl, don't,' Josey warned. He wasn't comfortable with him taking the heat.

The penny dropped. 'Oh I get it; you're working for *his nibs* – tricky.' He launched into a snicker, but cut it off when he saw what the weirdo did next—

Carl peeled off his large prosthetic nose, then his ears.

Magrie was completely gobsmacked. 'What the hell is this?' He watched the chin go, the hair and contact lenses. 'Well I'll be . . . ,' he chimed incredulously. 'I know you; you're the wimp that our hero detective uses to do his dirty work. I saw you snooping around in Wyalong, looking for the Raptor. I saw you before that at my motel. Well, it looks like killing you was the absolute right choice.' He raised the gun to do just that, but hesitated. 'No wait, I think I'd like to hear the rest – you tell it so succinctly, which is just as well, because I think the detective is in danger of shitting himself if he even tries to talk.' The insult directed at Josey was clearly aimed at getting him to make a move, a reason to blow his head off; not that he particularly needed one.

Carl had created the time they needed to think, and

Josey knew not to throw it away. He kept his silence; allowing Magrie to bask in what his deranged mind imagined was an upper hand

'Go ahead,' the killer continued, 'speak while you still can.'

'All right - but first, I have to say, in fairness to you, I'm not half bad at disguises, so, not recognising me was probably more excusable than some other things you should have spotted along the way.'

'Be very careful what you say, *Carl Bourmac*;' he warned laughing at the inventive way he'd played with the fictitious name, 'because I'm getting real close to the end of my patience; get the hell on with how your soon-to-be-dead boss found me out.'

'In a word, *bondage*; once he worked out Arlene and you are into that sort of thing, it led him to twenty possible businesses listed on the Dark Web. The money trail led to you in six of them, three of which are in Sydney. It wasn't all that hard to figure out which one you'd taken his girls to.'

'Fascinating.' The revealing story had Magrie positively entertained. 'Go on,' he prompted.

Although Carl was being dead calm in the face of adversity, Josey knew it to be an extension of his friend's many talents.

Carl said, 'Of course, we are aware you killed Jimmy Sullivan.'

This brought a hand clap and a delighted laugh.

'Apart from finding Jimmy's body in Sergeant Perkins' Peugeot, the car had your DNA all over it.'

Josey recognised Carl was deliberately avoiding saying

exactly who made the discoveries; and knew why.

Magrie chuckled, not appearing to pick up on the diversion. 'And I suppose you know why I killed him.'

'Easy; you caught Jimmy spying. He'd seen you take over control of the Raptor after beating up Arthur and placing him inside it. Killing the only witness seemed like your best move.'

'Well that's guesswork, but keep going; I can't wait to hear how anybody thought I'd know how to operate the Raptor.'

'You got lucky with that one; the night Arthur and Arlene stayed at your motel, you just happened to see the little black box that Arthur was trying to hide from Arlene. It made no sense until you heard Arlene calling Sergeant Perkins on her mobile; she'd left Arthur in the room and gone to the laundry. Their conversation centred on her suspicion that Arthur was trying to kill her, using the Raptor to cover up his plan.'

Magrie was smiling like a circus clown.

'You put two and two together and spent most of the night looking over his car for signs of how he might be doing that. You found Arthur's modification, which you appreciated was connected to the black box you'd seen. Add to that your piecemeal background in Electrical Engineering, and bingo.'

'I'm blown away by all this brilliant detecting,' Magrie expressed sarcastically.

'You were a little brilliant yourself,' Carl countered, 'because that's when you hatched the idea to turn the tables on Arthur, because poor old Arthur had no inkling about the bondage fetish you and Arlene had, which was something you helped cultivate in her. But it really wasn't until you witnessed *Lester* and Arlene in the cabin together that your plan for revenge broadened.'

Magrie gave Carl a slow hand clap in appreciation of a story well told. 'All true, I can't deny it – but, who gives a shit really; it's time to move on.'

With Magrie's pistol again aimed straight at him, Carl's only weapon now was Josey's phone, which he removed from his jacket with the tips of his fingers, *cautiously*. 'Here's something you might not be expecting,' he suggested holding it above his head for inspection.

Magrie had no interest in what he was on about, and looked decidedly ready to shoot.

'This is Josey's phone, the one he dumped in the flower box at your house; the one that he used to call police just before your henchman bailed him up. You've probably done yourself a favour shooting that poor bastard, Teddy was it? He wasn't all that good at his job to be honest.'

Magrie wasn't looking quite as smug as a moment ago.

'While you were concentrating on getting away from the police, and Josey turned the tables on Arlene, he handed it to me after he gave me my marching orders. I didn't need to ask why. The police used the GPS signal to track my every move, do you see where I'm coming from?'

Magrie could.

He could also see that beyond where Josey had parked, there were two patrol cars waiting in the distance, having entered onto the track the Raptor had come in on. A short blast from a siren drew his attention to a third patrol car that was blocking the road in the opposite direction.

Rage sent Mad Magrie's blood pressure skyrocketing. Breaking into a run, sheer spite drove him to give Carl a bullet to think about, hitting him in the chest; and then two wild shots over the shoulder at Josey, both of which missed as the detective was diving for his discarded pistol.

Josey somewhat recklessly fired several shots from the ground but the bullets went annoyingly wide.

Magrie was making good progress along the tyre tracks that led into the scrub, toward Arlene and the Raptor. 'Start the goddamned engine, Arlene,' he was shouting on the run, 'we're out of here.'

She was quick to do so.

The engine was growling into life even as Josey was realigning for a more controlled shot at Magrie. He aimed, only gaining a clear shot for a final split second; not long enough, he saved the bullet. Abandoning any thought of entering the scrub in pursuit, he made his way to Carl and the girls; desperately hoping his friend's gunshot wound wasn't terminal.

Blood was pumping from high on Carl's chest, too close for comfort to the top of his heart.

Pressing down hard on the wound, Josey muttered to his family, 'We need to keep pressure on this.' To his brave illusionist he warned, 'Stay-awake buddy, you know the drill.'

The Raptor broke free of the brush like a charging buffalo.

'Keep the pressure on,' Josey reminded the girls while heading for the Plymouth.

They watched him speed away. The sight of their man

launching into the beginning of a dangerous pursuit was bittersweet, and more than a little frightening.

Josey ate the Raptor's dust for a hundred yards; he knew that up ahead the second patrol car might still be parked on the track and that it wouldn't even be close to a match for the Ford, and he certainly didn't want to run into the barricade himself, although the wellbeing of his 1950 Plymouth Special was the furthest thing from his mind.

The Raptor swerved away to the left, revealing the expected patrol car; along with pointed weapons in the hands of three dangerously hyped officers that Josey hoped had time to work out he wasn't the enemy—

After successfully rounding the hapless coppers without attracting a bullet, he kept the pursuit going for another kilometre before Magrie did what was fully expected, he headed off road.

Plymouth's home company would have paid big money for a video of the endurance test their vehicle was about to undergo; these vehicles weren't noted for their rally accolades. But it wasn't tributes Josey was interested in, it was justice. Justice for the suffering this man had put his family through, and for the cold blooded capability he so blatantly exhibited without the slightest empathy for his victims.

Detective Josey thought of Carl lying in a pool of his own blood, of the massive job he had done in saving three lives, and hopefully himself. And before that, in helping infiltrate the sordid realm of forced *salacious human trafficking*.

His mind cast back to the day Carl and he hatched their

plan, the day Josey was racing to the airport to rescue his
girls . . .

~

'For the moment we need to keep Brown out of this,' he
told his offsider, 'but it's crucial he gets involved very
soon – subject to our timing, I'll explain why when we're
both in Sydney. I suggest you leave Nicole with her aunt,
there's no danger back there now.'

'Where are we meeting?'

'We won't be; I need you in Sydney before me, I've
organised a chopper to pick you up from Judith's place.
You'll be touching down at Mascot. Maxine will have a
cab waiting for you on the tarmac. Go straight to my
office, I'll be calling Maxine to fill her in on what's
needed. She'll have your gear there and she'll help you
get ready. Your tricks of the trade are crucial. And buddy,
you're about to enter a cesspit that'll most likely make
you retch . . .'

~

Having to involve Carl played heavily on Josey's mind,
especially now. Hate was an emotion that didn't often
come-visiting, but Magrie was bringing out the worst.
The thought of killing Joe Magrie, the psychopath, was
developing into an obsession, a positive and a negative
one.

His mind drifted to the anguish his two favourite people
have had to endure, he found himself wishing he could
wind back the clock, back to when young Andrew
Perkins phoned and pleaded for help. Admittedly that
part of the ordeal had proven to be a success, at least as
far as keeping his friend out of gaol for attempted

murder. Of course there was no way to escape the disgrace of involving himself with the wife of his next door neighbour, not to mention allowing her fetish to persuade him to take part in what most people considered the seedy side of sexual depravity. Josey was comfortable not making any judgement on that score, but the same didn't apply to Magrie, his degeneracy expanded beyond morality to the depths of malevolence—

These thoughts swept away in an instant, an instant of sheer panic when he cleared the dust and saw the Raptor at a standstill in front of him. He'd been chasing Magrie's tail at close range, the police patrol cars had given up some time back, he almost wished he'd done the same because there was no guarantee he could bring the Plymouth to a complete stop before running into the back of the Raptor.

The Raptor's predicament was made more perilous by the fact it had stopped for a very good reason, left as it was tethering on the oblique edge of a damnably deep ravine, its passengers left staring at their fate, their final destination insistent on drawing them down; Josey too if momentum had its way.

That's not what happened, gravity's impetus was only enough to provide the slightest tap on the Raptor's rear end – enough to shift it—

The opposite and equal reaction stopped the Plymouth's forward slide; at the same time beginning the Raptor's unavoidable plunge – at that very moment, Josey couldn't help welcoming it.

He watched it go; caught a glimpse of Arlene's forlorn face looking back at him through the rear window, perhaps wishing she could swap cars with him.

While their fate drew them to the base of the ravine, it might be imagined their minds were attempting to rationalise the smidgin of life left to them, perhaps enough time to come to grips with what they are guilty of.

The downside in Josey's mind was that their guilt would vanish far too mercifully.

He saw the crest of the explosion rise before him, now without excitement or malice. He couldn't deny there was relief, yet there was still a chance he'd be next. His front wheels were relying solely on maintaining grip on the dangerously lenient earth; hopefully upholding its viscosity long enough for him to vacate the vehicle.

As carefully as a tightrope walker, he began the process, shifting his weight to the back seat with nervous precision, speed wasn't an issue; living relied on the patience of a turtle.

He made it to the rear door handle, touched it ever so gently, hope of seeing his family again looming as an incentive, a potential reality. He turned the handle—

But he rapidly arrested the endeavour as the front end sank alarmingly into its only remaining support.

It's about to go his mind yelled—

Automatically accepting this subconscious advice, he separated from the vehicle even as it clipped his shoe, even as he landed on solid ground while it sped away from view.

He was crawling back from the edge when the second explosion ripped skyward, escorted by a lava-like high rise; lighting the earth beneath him in a shade of rich ochre.

Bedazzled by adrenalin, and by the realisation he had barely escaped death, he lent back on his hands, counting his blessing with nether a thought to the loss of his beloved Classic Plymouth.

That's where he still sat when Inspector Brown alighted from one of two patrol cars that had arrived a few metres back. The Sydney cop strode past him to get as close as he dare to the edge, to where tyre tracks drew a picture of what just happened.

He finally turned and asked, 'Did you have a hand in this?'

Josey scoffed. 'You still don't know me do you.'

'Oh, I believe I do, somehow I don't think you'd deliberately throw that Plymouth Special of yours off a cliff for love-nor-money. Sorry, I had to ask.'

Josey realised Brown had one thing right, love and money wasn't enough to force him to let that car go. 'Or for hate,' Josey countered referring to Joe Magrie's death. 'But I'll be honest, Inspector; I definitely thought about it.'

'Loud and clear, but do me a favour, don't repeat that sentiment to anyone else. If it helps, I'll say I saw the whole thing.'

He had created an unlikely friend in the inspector on the back of a common enemy; something that often happens when felons inadvertently bring down mutual bridges.

'Let's get Officer Fuller to take you back to your family.'

'How's Carl—'

'Your friend's in good hands,' Brown cut in foreseeing the question, 'he's on his way to hospital; the medics say he'll be fine.' He laughed at a thought. 'I wished I'd been there to see what he did with that disguise of his; it certainly impressed your wife and daughter. Apparently the ambulance guys didn't know what to make of all the body parts spread all over the ground.' He laughed again as he helped Josey to his feet.

Officer Fuller had the doors open for them as they reached the patrol car.

'Just a moment,' Brown said as he peeled off to talk with the driver of the second vehicle.

The driver reacted to the inspector's approach by stepping out to talk with him.

'Edwards, you and Collis go see if you can find a way round to the bottom of the ravine. Let me know if you succeed and I'll join you. In the meantime check out the situation. Two vehicles have gone over, check for signs of life, but I doubt you'll find any. Let me know either way.'

'Yes Sir.'

'Good.' He paced back to the other patrol car, telling the driver as he approached, 'Fuller, Let's go.'

The young copper closed Josey's door and dutifully rounded the vehicle double time to take up the wheel.

He spun the car in the dirt, cuing the second patrol car to follow until they returned to the roadway, at which point Edward's travelled in the opposite direction in search of a way into the ravine.

No one knew it yet, but this wasn't over.

CHAPTER TWENTY NINE
It's not over til it's over

The patrol car with Constable Edwards at the wheel, took fifteen minutes and travelled ten kilometres to find a way to the bottom of the ravine. The open expanse was as level as a baking dish with rocky bush covered hills almost all round.

With nothing but grassland to obstruct the view, the location of the carnage was easy to locate, a smoke trail lifting skyward like an aerial signpost was an additional pointer.

Edwards and his partner Collis brought their patrol car to a stop at the edge of a circle of burnt grass, they saw that a few small flames were still licking at remnants of combustible material. There wasn't much to speak of.

Approaching the entanglement on foot, they saw that what was meant to represent a Peugeot sedan and a Ford Raptor was no more than a pile of tangled metal. And somewhere in this mess lay two bodies.

At a metre from the wrecks, heat still reached out to touch the skin, far too hot in fact to begin any sort of close-up search.

Collis called it in. 'We're at the crash site, Inspector. It's too hot to handle right now; do you want us to wait it out? - - - Right, will do - Over.'

Edwards was peering into what he believed was the Peugeot, which looked like it might have landed atop the Raptor and slid off. 'What'd the chief say?'

'He says wait.'

The area looked more like a bomb site than a crash site, car parts were strewn like shrapnel.

'Can you see anyone?' Collis asked.

'It's too hard to tell; like the boss says we'll have to wait.'

Riding in the back seat of Fuller's patrol car, Josey had his eye fixed on the hostage location up ahead, masked within the frame of the bobbing windscreen. As expected, the ambulance carrying Carl had gone on its way, just one police patrol car remained. The back doors of the stationary vehicle swung open in unison, revealing his girls alighting expectantly. They'd been given some rather loose fitting clothing from somewhere, Molly's borrowed copper's jacket clearly belonging to the driver.

Fuller brought his patrol car to a stop a metre away from where they stood.

They were still shaken, yet the arrival of the vehicle carrying their man, alive and safe, raised clear elation. They paced on feet seemingly made light, to greet Josey before he even had a chance to step away from the door he'd just opened. Their bodies collided as he stood, rumpling him against the vehicle. Heartfelt hugs and kisses abounded in a grand discharge of pent up tensions.

Yet, irrational guilt sunk deep claws into the detective's psyche. An Emotional release brought its baggage; tears flowed from a man not prone to easily display fear. He became apologetic; stressed and harassed over the unbelievable danger he had put his family in.

Rebecca held him away. 'Hey, let's have none of that, sweetie. We're fine thanks to you and Carl.'

They held him close, giving him the time he needed to settle his nerves.

Inspector Brown quietly watched on from outside the patrol car, a new and deeper understanding of the detective emerging, and a realisation of what a fortunate man he was.

With tears threatening to spill, Molly finally asked, 'Dad - is it over?'

'It's over, Pumpkin,' he whispered holding her tighter.

Rebecca's voice shook as she asked, 'And Magrie?'

'He's dead; Arlene too.'

They urged him back onto the car seat and stood around the open door while he gathered his composure.

Written on their faces, he saw the question they wanted to ask but couldn't, but they deserved to know. With a degree of hesitancy, he clarified the circumstances around the demise of Magrie and his dubiously faithful offsider.

'They essentially killed themselves,' he told his girls, feeling a little stronger now. He went on to explain the whole grizzly event, leaving out the fact he had almost shared their fate. The death of the Plymouth he would leave till later, he was glad they hadn't thought to ask. 'Is Carl all right?' he enquired changing the subject.

'Yes, he's fine.' She glanced at the policeman sitting in the driver's seat of the car they had alighted from. 'Constable Bentley kept him alive until Paramedics arrived. They were amazed he had Carl already stabilised.'

'I need to thank him,' he said as he eased clear of the open door. His family walked arm in arm with him to where Bentley sat behind the wheel of his patrol car.

Inspector Brown was on the phone a few paces away, and for some reason he did not look in the least bit happy.

His call was to Edwards down in the ravine.

Edwards was talking into his body mike while moving in closer to the bowels of the wrecked Raptor. 'Yes I'm sure - - - yes - - - they're handcuffs alright, singed black; wrapped around the wrist.'

Brown had his voice held low. 'And you can't tell if it's the man or the woman.'

'Not without knowing who was driving,' Edwards was telling him as he pushed his way deeper into the carnage. 'And don't ask me why, but it's the driver's left arm that's been handcuffed – wait for it, to the bloody steering wheel no less. The remains must have gotten thrown about a fair bit because it ended up out on what's left of the bonnet.'

The Inspector was slowly alighting from the patrol car while saying, 'You're sure you've had a real good look around for the passenger?'

Edwards gave the surrounding grasslands a scan. 'Yep; if the passenger's been thrown as expected, he or she has hit the air like a long range missile.'

'Yes, all right Constable,' Brown scolded in a whisper ahead of disconnecting the call. Pocketing his cell while walking to Bentley's car, he felt a knot developing in the pit of his stomach.

'Can I have a moment, Detective,' Brown requested as he meandered up to Bentley's car.

Josey knew by the tone in his voice that something was wrong, but he wasn't about to make the mistake of excluding his girls from whatever it was. 'Is there a problem?'

Brown hesitated for a moment considering the women, and then understood he needed to continue, carefully. 'The men have only found one corpse.'

Rebecca's hand shot to her mouth.

'Which one?' Josey asked with steely calm.

'They have no idea except that it was the driver.'

The image of Arlene looking back at him as the vehicle tipped out of sight over the cliff evoked Josey's memory.

The pose she was in, on her knees roughly kneeling between the seats indicated it was *only her left arm* that was cuffed, allowing her to twist out of the seat and face backward. 'Was the cuff on the left wrist?' he asked.

'It was,' Brown answered with no attempt to hide his surprise at Josey knowing that.

Josey considered her look of despair wasn't any more than expected. But where was Magrie at the time?

Was he even in the car in those last moments?

'I won't try to figure out how you already know, but Edwards and Collis did find the driver was handcuffed to the steering wheel – like you said, by the left wrist.'

'The corpse is Arlene; she was the driver.'

Brown raised a frown, 'She couldn't have jumped free if she'd wanted to,' he murmured.

But Magrie could have, Josey thought.

It was clear they hadn't swapped drivers after pulling away from the hostage site; she would have been perfectly capable of driving, even handcuffed as she was. The bastard remained the bondage-master to the very end. But Josey suspected, not *his* end.

The movie in Josey's mind continued on playback. He considered he may have jumped before the Raptor reached the cliff edge; perhaps even before reaching the parked patrol car's roadblock, through the cover of dust there was every chance of not being seen, *every chance.*

'He's here,' Josey warned agitatedly. 'We're not done.'

No one could fathom what he meant at first.

'You are shitting me,' the inspector swore.

'Why in god's-name . . .?' Rebecca's question was a good one, but there was no time to spend trying to figure it out.

Being the maniac that he was, he was presumably bent on satisfying his lust for killing, Arlene becoming the most convenient cab off the rank. Who was next?

'Inspector Brown wore a weighty expression when he warned Josey, 'I would advise your family leave in the patrol car with Constable Bentley.'

'I'm not going anywhere,' Rebecca told him.

'Mrs Josey, the man is armed and we have no idea how close he might be.'

Josey was assessing that risk as the inspector spoke. The dirt road where they stood stretched into the distance, providing clear vision in both directions. To the north, the road curved out of sight a good thousand metres away. And a similar distance to the south it got swallowed up by forest.

To the west of the roadway, open grasslands spread toward a boundary of tall trees. To the east, and right at the roadside, tuffs of widely spaced grass struggled to survive amongst scattered rocks; a rough and tumble three metre ramp that met a hard edge that marked the beginning of the forest.

If Magrie was close–and Josey believed he was–that's where he'd be. He reasoned that he would have had time to double back within the cover of the forest, and possibly could be looking at them right at this moment, waiting for the right time to make a move, or perhaps take them all out one at a time with a bullet, although that was unlikely in Josey's mind; he'd have to be a damn good shot to hit anything as far away as the forest with only a pistol. But then, maybe he'd gathered something bigger from the Raptor.

Josey ushered the girls to the opposite side of the patrol cars, placing the open grasslands at their backs, and the vehicles between them and the forest, the only possible location from where a shot could be fired from.

'If he's anywhere,' Josey explained eyeing the forest, 'it's up there.'

Brown followed the advice to stand behind the cars without too much urgency, yet believing the detective may be spot-on about Magrie's location. The question was what to do. He phoned Edwards and Collis in the ravine and instructed them to return in order to provide backup. Of course he knew the fastest they could get back was around ten minutes.

Dawn was winning the battle against the night; but entering the dense woodland was still a foreboding prospect, it would be another hour before the sun touched its dark floor. Finding a gunman in there amounted to a herculean challenge. It was decided they would wait for the backup to arrive before leaving the girls with just two armed police officers; considering they'd be a whole lot safer in the company of *four*.

Josey and Brown took separate paths into the forest the moment Edwards and Collis arrived. Edwards was instructed to follow only if shots were heard coming from there.

After penetrating the tree line only a few metres, Josey glanced back down and noticed the patrol cars were already almost out of sight.

The thought of moving ever further from his family gave him the creeps.

He could hear the inspector unavoidably snapping his way through the bush nearby, which meant Magrie had the upper hand, if in fact he'd found a place to silently hide.

No one was to know how big an upper hand he really had at this point.

Yes, Mad-Magrie had plenty of opposition, but the element of surprise weighed in his favour, so much so that he couldn't help smiling. The dim arrival of daylight was his partner, hidden in plain sight and ready to strike; a place that nobody had thought to look, because he'd put himself there even before Josey and the inspector had returned from the cliff.

As still as death itself, he waited – a spider hiding in its funnel-web. He wanted to laugh, yet if he allowed himself the luxury, his advantage would be instantly lost.

The further the two heroes went into the forest the better his advantage became.

With the resonances of their fruitless endeavours diminishing, he decided now was the perfect time to make his move.

He again silently checked his pistol, checked that each chamber showed him those beautiful shining disks, six bullets that he couldn't wait to send on their deadly errand. Satisfied the weapon was fully loaded, he closed the chamber as silently as a Cheetah about to pounce.

The tight space in which he'd placed himself dictated he remain face up, forcing him to slide on his back, using shoulders to progress sideways in short silent advances. The row of feet to his left, told him he must go to the right.

One last slide brought him out of his hiding place, free of the underside of the patrol car, free to do his worst.

From the driver's seat, Constable Bentley saw the movement out the corner of his eye and turned to face it. His window exploded—

Bullet number-one had hit its target. The tiny missile had caught Bentley somewhere in the neck, possibly a fatal hit.

Edwards and Collis were reaching for their housed pistols at the other side of the patrol car in what seemed like compressed time, ducking for cover with the two women, whose screams had not yet had time to draw air;

and with shards of glass still floating away from the point of impact.

The crack of the gunshot had sent a cold chill shooting through Josey's veins like a speeding virus. Tree trunks the size of dinner tables becoming his obstacle course as he ran, with no eyes on the cars, or his girls.

A second shot rang out – a third – a fourth - their echoes reverberating in the forest like ghostly reinforcements.

Breaking free of the forest onto the rocky ramp, he heard Brown a pace or two behind.

Josey prayed his nemesis wouldn't have already fired on the girls; prayed he'd been too busy defending himself against the armed police. It was this belief - *hope* - that allowed Josey to function, and not falter.

Busy rounding the patrol car, Magrie wasn't yet aware of Josey and the inspector's approach, but he soon would be.

From the forest, the hesitant rescuers saw Molly and Rebecca come into view above the roof of the car, terrified; and with good reason, Magrie was now right next to them. They daren't move given he had the gun at Rebecca's head this time. The only reason he wasn't pulling the trigger right at that moment, was the threat from the one copper that remained on his feet near the car; Fowler, aimed and ready to shoot if Magrie acted on his threat; another dangerous standoff.

Edwards and Collis couldn't be seen, suggesting they may have already been brought down.

The sight of Constable Bentley in the front seat of the patrol car, clearly injured or dead, didn't offer Josey a great deal of hope that the other two men were all right.

The whole scene made him feel sick.

Four shots had rang-out; two would have been return fire. With the shooting stopped, it wasn't safe for Josey to recommence the mayhem by firing on Magrie, the chances of hitting him and not his girls were slim at best.

Magrie's defensive body language suggested his present strategy wasn't exactly going to plan; the real worry was; what would he do next. It had to be hoped Fuller would keep a cool head and a steady hand.

Josey signalled to Brown that he was cutting around to the flank and for him to wait until he was in position before revealing his presence. As he executed this risky manoeuvre, he couldn't dispel the memory of the fateful day his partner, young Freddie Faraday, lost his life while saving his. But he made himself a promise; if anyone was to die today, Magrie would be among them.

When the time was right to draw attention, the inspector rounded the cars with his revolver aimed, positioned so that it kept Magrie's back turned to where Josey was crossing the road from behind. Now Brown was able to see that two of his officers were flailing on the ground, incapacitated with undetectable injuries. And Magrie, hiding behind Josey's loved ones, his only insurance, which was more than enough.

Molly considered making a move on Magrie, and might have if not for the risk of his gun blowing a hole in the side of her mother's head.

For the sake of the women, this was not a time for the inspector to be bargaining; *bluffing*. In submission he held his pistol high above his head in order that Magrie could see it being thrown to the side.

As pleasing as this was for the captor, he immediately became focused on the fact he hadn't yet laid eyes on the detective. He was about to turn and check behind when he heard Josey's voice at close range, felt the gun barrel press into the back of his neck.

A gun aimed point blank didn't always amount to a death sentence, but on this occasion, Magrie had to remind himself that the person holding the weapon had had the lives of his family put at extreme risk.

The sick bastard laughed.

Josey's hand twitched in response – his finger jerking *away* from the trigger purely by chance.

This was seen as a weakness by his foe, and Josey knew the pistol held to Becky's head was a loose-cannon that could go off at any second. With this grim thought at the forefront of his mind, he gave no warning of the sharp and precise action that saw him grasp and twist Magrie's wrist, forcing the gun barrel skyward, and the harmless bullet that spat from it too.

Josey wanted to know how many shots were left in the gun. 'Pull the trigger, arsehole,' he ordered.

Magrie was giggling like a school girl at this.

'Take my advice *shit-head*;' Josey warned with a calm menacing tone delivered through clenched teeth. 'Do-it quick or my nervous disposition might cause me to accidently blow your goddamned head off.'

'Ha, like you would in front of a copper.'

'Do what you have to do detective,' Brown told him, 'I seem to be having trouble with my eyes.'

This gave *shit-head* a noticeable chill, but he hesitated in obeying the order to empty his gun anyway. It was enough to prompt Josey to angle his pistol atop Magrie's proud head-of-hair and fire, creating a bloody bald swathe across the arsehole's useless skull.

The encouragement to empty the chamber was then quickly observed to ward off further assaults to his proud head of hair.

'Again,' Josey demanded. By all reckoning the shot that smartly exited Magrie's gun was six out of six. 'One more for good measure,' he said through clenched teeth.

The trigger squeezed, producing nothing more than a light click, confirming the gun was empty. All Magrie could think about at this point was that his brand new hair style was stinging like hell itself.

'Becky, Molly, move over with the inspector.'

They did so happily, accepting the inspector's invitation to come to his side as he retrieved his pistol from the ground.

Now Magrie faced the inspector's gun and Fuller's gun in the front and Josey's at the back; what could possibly go wrong—?

Famous last words the sick bastard thought as he made a swift movement for Constable Edwards' gun, which was right there at his feet, having dropped from the copper's hand when he got shot.

While reaching down, he was thinking this was his perfect chance to come out on top, finally to get one over on these heroes.

It might have worked for him, if not for the three shots that rang out in quick succession as Magrie was rolling around toward Josey with Edward's weapon ready in his hand.

One power-balancing bullet from Brown ripped the pistol from Magrie's hand as it took out a knuckle; the second bullet came from Fuller taking out a chunk of muscle from the upper left arm. A third coming from Josey, took out teeth before exiting somewhere at the back of his neck, and as was discovered later, ended up planted deeply into soil; a blood soaked seed that had no chance on Earth of ever sprouting.

Josey took a couple of steps forward to inspect the result of his shots, especially his.

Incredibly, Magrie wasn't dead, but he was incapable of moving any part of his body, incapable of retaliation, incapable of breathing without blowing blood bubbles – but, he *could* still see.

Vaguely peering up from his place of passing, Magrie construed that the detective's features were as cold as ice, utterly void of the slightest empathy. His was the face of a man who was very much saying, *bon voyage to hell my friend*.

Josey's absolute lack of empathy, or any indication he was concerned that he had just killed a man, frightened Becky to the point where she felt hesitant in approaching him. She quickly got past this reactionary feeling when Molly ran in and wrapped her arms around her father. The spell of hesitancy evaporated, commanding that she join her daughter.

Within the enclave of their arms he trembled, fathoming that *in reality*, he had saved *two lives* - by taking *one* that didn't deserve the privilege.

Adrenalin and fear devoured his strength. His legs gave way, felling him hard up against the support of the patrol car.

He felt the welcome provision of his girls governing his slide to the ground, their selfless efforts to bring him to rest at the base of a rear wheel, where upon he was able to relax his head, and able to observe the inspector checking the condition of the two wounded police officers, a metre from where he lay against the tyre.

'Please tell me they're okay,' Josey offered in deep hope.

'No sweat, we're fine,' Collis answered.

The mere sight of the injured men stirring and talking was immensely pleasing.

Constable Collis was asking the inspector dolefully, 'Is Bentley gone?'

'Just my ear,' was the answer that filtered thinly from the driver's seat

'No great loss,' Collis groaned through his own pain, 'you don't listen anyway.'

'I heard that, but thanks for asking – bastard.'

Brown shook his head at the warped sense of humour of his Sydney coppers, feigning disbelief.

Molly was already rounding the vehicle to see what could be done for the driver. She found him holding a wad of indiscriminate cloth up to his ear; and without a second thought moved the blood-soaked bandage away so as to check his injury, enough to discover a piece of cartilage the size of a one cent coin had been taken by the bullet.

'How bad is it?' he asked distractedly peering up at her gorgeous face.

'It might whistle in the wind,' she told him, 'but you'll

live.'

'Please – don't make me laugh,' he said while unable to stop. He'd been noticing for the past hour how goddamn attractive she is and like any good-looking nurse, she was the greatest medicine a man could wish for.

The smile she returned promised a full recovery, albeit with a branded ear.

Listening to the banter between his daughter and the young cop gave Josey a buzz. Cops hated losing one of their own, and he knew the humour that was circulating was from a respectful place, a thankful place.

Inspector Brown was taking a moment to double-check Magrie was dead.

He was - which was simply *wonderful news on top of all the alternatives*, the threat was clearly over.

Lifting his eyes to Josey and his family, Brown told them, 'This is a good day, folks, don't even think about looking at it any other way, especially you, Detective.'

'Don't you worry, Inspector,' Rebecca promised, 'he'll have me to deal with if he tries.'

CHAPTER THIRTY
Dinner Date

Two months after the drama in the National park, Josey had a few people over to his place for dinner. In attendance were Carl, fresh out of hospital with his arm in a sling, and his wife Nicole. Inspector Brown came along with *his* wife, something the Joseys thought they'd never see. He wasn't the only ring in; Andrew Perkins just happened to be in Sydney and got the invitation to dinner when he rang Josey's office to talk about the case.

The update on Andy's brother was encouraging, because when Josey rang Lester the day after Magrie sent Arlene to her death, the Sergeant was thinking of leaving the force; Andy informed Josey that his brother had had a change of heart following an upheaval of support from the townspeople, and had decided to stay on.

A warm evening dictated the meal be set up on the deck, and they sat around well after the dishes from the main course had been taken away and replaced with dessert and port.

The most curious person at the table was Andy, he'd been ostensibly out of the picture, hold up with his unlikely housemate Stan Morgan, who had also been invited, but declined; apparently he'd left Condo to head across to Western Australia somewhere.

In spite of his young age, Andy had all the confidence you'd expect in a solicitor, and not shy about asking questions; the answer he got about his brother's affair, and the subsequent bondage, didn't faze him unduly.

Lester couldn't have asked for a more understanding brother, Josey thought.

'So Arthur built the autonomous Raptor,' he said to Josey when the subject turned to that.

'It wasn't hard to figure, he was the only one close to having the knowledge to do it. He got a little help in the weeks leading up to using the controller, Condobolin's auto electrician was only too happy to feed him with information. Of course the *sparky* never knew about Arthur's plan to murder Arlene.'

'Magrie seemed privy to it, how did that come about?'

'Once I found out about his somewhat illicit history in and around the world of bondage, it was too coincidental not to be connected to your brother and Arlene. I needed to find out exactly how far that connection went. I had Carl here stop over at the motel as himself so that he could sniff around; that's how Magrie knew who he was when the prosthetics came off. He'd seen him in Wyalong too. Carl found his room was bugged, which meant Magrie could have been privy to private conversations in every room. That wasn't the only way he had of eavesdropping, Carl caught him listening in from his switchboard in his back office.'

Andy scooped in some apple pie while thinking about what Carl had done. 'So Magrie hears the conversation between Lester and Arlene, and decides to, what, turn the tables?'

'Exactly right,' Josey affirmed ahead of a sip of wine. 'That began the morning of the Sheridan's stay at the motel. The plan was to put-the-wind-up Arthur by sabotaging the brakes on the Raptor; this would have confused Arthur no end, because it wasn't his doing and seemed coincidental. It was easy for Magrie to create the leak while Arthur and Arlene slept.'

'Who did all the mechanical stuff that happened to the car after that?'

'It was Magrie who knocked out the headlights, which he managed while fixing his own sabotage on the brakes, but the rest was what Arthur had already built into it.'

The inspector had been sitting quietly beside his wife enjoying the story, but he had a question too. 'Going back to Magrie's connection to Arlene, you're saying she was willingly having it off with him as well.'

His wife, a tiny brunet with big attractive eyes, elbowed him playfully. 'You don't have to be so crude, Geoffrey,' she laughed with the help of her warming whisky.

'Was Magrie jealous of Arthur do you think?' Geoffrey asked Josey.

'Almost certainly, but primarily he was a psychopath, his actions weren't always well thought out. I think he just saw the Raptor as a way of doing what he does best, and getting away with it.'

'You'd have to agree though, he kind of lost it toward the end, going after your family the way he did.'

'I was a fly in the ointment for sure; again, it wouldn't have mattered – he was on a spree. Bottom line, he just wanted to get his thrills, with sexual deviation and murder.'

Rebecca was holding Molly's hand beneath the table and gave it a thankful squeeze. 'We thought we were his next victims, I've never been so frightened.'

Molly smiled at her father with her raised glass of wine. 'Thank you, Dad.'

Prompted by her appreciative gesture more glasses rose in recognition, accompanied by '*Hear hears.*'

After the clearing of the table, Andrew took Josey aside in the lounge room. 'I just want to say a personal thank you for what you did for Lester, you saved his life; his wellbeing I mean to say. I'm not all that cutup about his getting involved with that woman, why he *would* is the real question.'

'Don't let it get to you, Andy, people do strange things when it comes to grief.'

He knew what Josey was referring to. 'You mean losing Mum.'

Josey confirmed with a light nod.

Lester had lost his wife to galloping cancer the year before. Arlene, being what she was, put her hooks into him almost immediately, taught him about the release he thought he needed. He fell for it, she wasn't helping him, just satisfying an insatiable appetite – an appetite that got her killed in the end.

Brown waltzed in to join them. 'I hear your brother will be back on the force, Andy.'

Young Andrew faced Brown with due politeness; he hardly knew the guy. 'All thanks to the detective here.'

'And Carl,' Josey told them catching the illusionist's eye at the other side of the room with the girls.

Andrew took a half step back. 'I'll leave you guys to talk.'

'Thanks, Andy,' the inspector said respectfully as the young man went to join Carl and the others. Back on Josey he said, 'I don't need to tell you about the paperwork involved in being a copper, so this is purely to get a few facts straight.'

'Sure, what's on your mind?'

Rebecca was watching her husband and Brown as Andy arrived. 'What did the inspector want?'

'Not sure,' he answered as Brown's wife was closing in from the kitchen.

She joined them in observing her husband. 'I see Geoffrey is doing his thing over there.'

They sort of picked up on what Geoffrey's thing was; *picking the detective's brain.*

Josey was telling Brown, 'At the cabin, Arthur waited until Arlene was asleep before going out to Lester's car. It was easy enough to keep the noise down; quietly placing it out of gear; releasing the handbrake, and giving it a light push. The crash would hardly have raised a sound inside the cabin due to the sharp drop-off, a point made by Jimmy Sullivan.'

'The object being to make sure they had to drive out of

there in the Raptor.'

'Correct.'

'When does Magrie come into the picture?'

'He made his way to the cabin overnight; via the track Andy and I discovered at the back of the cabin. He would have driven to the spot where the track meets the highway. I dare say he may have even seen Arthur push the Peugeot into the creek. But he began to understand what Arthur's plan was way back at his motel, having heard Arlene and Lester talking on the phone. He didn't know exactly how Arthur planned to kill Arlene as it turned out, until he found the additional computer gear that had been installed.'

'How'd he know how to control the vehicle?'

'Arthur had hidden the gizmo he'd built, the console, in his tool box in the boot of the Raptor. Magrie found it while he was working on the car in his workshop and figured it out. He may have even practiced using it after he'd fixed the sabotaged brakes.'

Brown digested all this and then asked, 'Where'd Arthur end up after he fell from the car?'

'He didn't fall – he'd jumped. From the cover of bush, Arthur was able to control the Raptor without being seen, except by Magrie.'

'And Magrie got the console from Arthur?'

'Yes, that's when everything turned sour. The first he knew he was being watched was when Magrie shot at him.'

'Hence the bullet hole in the headrest.'

Josey was nodding, 'He'd have been dead right there if Magrie hadn't been a lousy shot – it was a short reprieve though, what followed was one hell of a beating before Arthur was sent on his spree in the Raptor.'

'And Arthur told you all this?'

'He did.'

Ordinarily, Josey wouldn't have been first cab off the rank in interviewing Arthur Sheridan at the prison, where he'd ended up, but influence from Perkins and very careful consideration from Inspector Brown had allowed it. Josey had already spoken to Arthur prior to the interview; after finding him in hiding at the cabin.

'How'd you work out he might be there?'

'If he was watching the news, he'd know Magrie and Arlene were out of the picture. I figured the cabin was the safest place for him to lie low – at least in the short term - the police were finished with it as a crime scene, and Lester's car had been fished out of the creek. So long as he didn't light a fire or let himself be seen by Sullivan's son next door, he wasn't expecting anyone to visit – until *I* arrived.'

'You took a risk.'

'Not really, I think he was relieved to see me, basically he had nowhere else to go.'

If Josey hadn't been the one to bring Arthur Sheridan in, he might not have fared quite so well in convincing the authorities to give him exclusive rights to the interview. It also didn't hurt to let Arthur think that by doing so, Detective Josey, a non-copper, might be the best person to appease the police.

Brown was grinning. 'What can I say; well done.' He was about to walk away when he thought of something else. 'From what he told you, and I know it's all in the report, how do you picture what went down, leading up to Sheridan planting his blood on the Jeep?'

'It was Magrie behind the wheel of the Raptor on the highway. What happened was; he found out from Bobby Barton's father that Andy and I were asking questions. The two garages are only five kilometres apart, so they knew each other. Roger Barton had no idea why the motel owner was so interested in us.'

'And at the crash, you couldn't see who was behind the wheel, so you figured it was Arthur, because at that stage you didn't know about Magrie.'

'Not quite true, it was a little more complicated than that. Like I said, Magrie was driving the Raptor when we were following him in the jeep, but then he got out and switched to remote control. There are a couple of reasons why he did that. I assume he noticed Andrew was missing, but I think he was worried the police might show up at any minute. The fact is he was able to do just as much damage in or out of the vehicle. After the attack, as you know I woke up to a scene that didn't match what I remembered. Bobby had somehow gotten from the pond to the Jeep, which made no sense.'

'And you say Sheridan denies doing it.'

'And he didn't; let me back up a bit. Remember I said I thought Arthur might be unconscious inside the Raptor.'

'Yes.'

'Well he was; when I located him at the cabin, he was ready to talk, and I got the full story . . .'

~

Unconscious on the front seat of the stationary Raptor, Arthur regained his senses, half dead and covered in his own blood. The first thing he saw when he lifted his head to look across the bonnet was Magrie walking past the nose of the Raptor holding the remote console.

Twenty feet away, to the other side of him, was a vehicle on fire. The whole scene was like the beginning of a dream.

Keeping low and out of sight, he watched the motel owner stride across to whoever it was that was propped up in a nearby pool of water, appearing uncertain about the intentions of the man approaching him. He looked like he might be a mechanic himself. The burnt overalls the man wore seemed to explain why he was sitting in the water, and suggested he may have come from the burning car, which looked like it was one of those American Army Jeeps.

The next thing, Magrie is dragging him out of the pond and up onto dry ground. This was not some sort of bizarre rescue; he already knew what this crazy bastard was capable of from his own run-in and hadn't the strength or will to get involved, in spite of what he was now doing to the fellow.

Unbelievably, Magrie had the helpless bugger on the ground choking him.

Recalling his own experience, he became fearful of being next, but he daren't make a run for it.

Across the bottom rim of the windshield he observed the limp victim being dragged across to the jeep, he had no clue as to why it was burning. In fact he had no clear memory of anything after Magrie attacked him and took charge of the Raptor, other than being aware he'd been thrown onto the front seat where he now lay in further fear of his life, from where he had ridden out the deadly jaunt that pursued, drifting in and out of consciousness.

Magrie now stood by the burning vehicle with the victim in his arms, looking like he was ready to throw him into the flames. With no writhing or screaming from the victim, the fellow was clearly already dead from having been strangled.

A small blessing.

There was no doubt in his mind as to why the victim needed to die, and why the body needed to be burnt, Magrie didn't want witnesses, or any form of evidence that the victim had been strangled; *why make the coppers job easy for them*. Which meant, as expected, the next item on the list was to get rid of the Raptor, and the body on the front seat.

With what little strength he had, he used Magrie's assumptions to his advantage, lunging at him when he appeared in the doorway. He knew in the first few moments that this didn't even come close to giving him the gain he expected. Hands as strong as multigrips had taken hold of his throat. A lot of things flashed through his mind as he starved for air, craving to cry for mercy. Included was the thought that this is how it ends . . .

~

'He would have died at the scene if the police hadn't arrived when they did,' Josey told the inspector.

'How'd Sheridan find time to plant the blood?'

'Like Lester and Arlene, Arthur was saved by the sound of distant sirens approaching . . .'

~

Arthur felt the clamp on his throat snap away, yet he was

still in deep trouble, muscles in his throat refused to play ball. In sudden relief, and just in time, he managed to suck in an uncertain gulp of air, his second and third drawback were just as uncertain of success – eventually though; born on a train of coughs Arthur began to regain control of his breathing.

With all of this going on he hadn't seen the Raptor speed away, and the closing sound of a police siren prompted him to do the same for fear of getting the blame for the body in the jeep.

It was then that he had an epiphany, but had little time to orchestrate it . . .

~

'He planted the blood, which wasn't a problem, he was covered in it. You know the rest.'

'Not quite, where were *you* all this time?'

'I asked Arthur about that, and he claimed he never saw me. I was right in front of his eyes, buried in the mud.'

'Holding your breath?' Brown asked quizzically.

'Apparently not, I'd somehow manage to get my face clear of the mud. Even the Condobolin cops said they didn't see me at first. Mathews told me he spotted what he thought was a rock, until he noticed it had a *tongue* in it.'

Brown couldn't help a nervous laugh as he looked across at Andrew and made an assumption. 'And young Andy missed seeing the rest of it, because he was passed out in the scrub.'

'Right; when he came round, the police were already at the scene. If he'd known I was stuck in the mud he might have acted differently.'

'That's when he rang his brother.'

'He wasn't sure what to do - Lester told him not to engage and that he should leave.'

'Perkins could have saved you a lot of time if he'd told you this at the start.'

'At that stage, like me, Andrew and his brother believed the enemy was Arthur. He called me by the way.'

'Who; Andy?'

'Yeah, I think he just wanted to apologise for leaving me stranded.'

'He wasn't to know.'

'I was on the verge of calling him anyway. I know you guys tried without success. I sensed he was all right, given your boys couldn't find him, and his call gave me the chance to get he and young Stan together, another one who didn't want to talk to police. I wasn't aware they knew each other, Andy kept that from me.'

'It's another case of not trusting the police - and I include *you, Detective* if you don't mind me saying,' he reprimanded lightly.

In spite of the inspector's copper attitude, Josey felt he still had him on side, which was important given there was an official need to explain why he hadn't reported the body in the boot when he first found it.

Rebecca approached with a wine for Brown and a beer for Josey. 'Things are looking a little dry over here,' she quipped.

Grinning, they swapped their empties for the replenishments. She didn't know what to make of Brown sniffing his fresh glass of wine, *was he checking to see it was the same brew he'd been drinking*?

315

'Can I borrow my husband?' she asked amiably.

'No, I'm not finished with him yet.' He laughed at her alarmed expression, 'Just kidding, he's all yours.' Brown watched them go as his own spouse joined him.

'I hope you're not giving that fine detective a hard time,' she said wishfully.

'Who, *me*?'

She tilted her head shrewdly.

Rebecca was saying to Josey as they moved from earshot. 'Molly and I have been thinking; we wouldn't mind getting back on the road to finish our holiday.'

'The Delaware is currently a pile of sticks in case you've forgotten.'

She planted a kiss on him.

Seeing them pecking like teenagers, Mrs Brown shuddered at the thought of what could have happened at the hands of Joe Magrie if things had gone differently.

A knock at the door drew their attention away.

'He's here,' Rebecca announced to the room.

'*Who's* here?' Mrs Brown asked her husband quietly.

Molly was at the door opening up. 'Hello, come in.'

'Who's *this*?' Brown's misses was asking her stunned husband; the man they were looking at seemed totally out of place.

They watched with bemused interest as Josey and his wife moved across to take the new arrival's leather jacket and to greet him – *warmly*.

'How odd,' Mrs Brown said under her breath.

She almost visibly cringed when their hosts began to bring the visitor across in their direction. 'What the hell is this,' she whispered to her husband.'

And then he was there, standing in front of them, looking even worse up close.

Rebecca was still holding his antique jacket. 'This is an old friend of ours - Denham, meet Inspector Brown and his wife Mary.'

Mary literally couldn't speak.

Although Geoffrey had already guessed who this out-of-place person was, he managed not to give the joke away.

Rebecca ignored the discomfort and asked Denham, 'Is there anything else I can take from you?'

He looked at her, thought for a moment and put his hand to his nose. 'Would you mind holding this?'

'No of course not.'

The look on Mary's face was priceless.

Molly did her very best not to laugh, but wasn't able to refrain a moment longer.

Baumac was now removing his nose and handing it to Josey's wife, who happily took it and stuffed it into one of the jacket pockets. She accepted the ears and wig and did likewise.

Unable to hold back on the hilarity, Geoff explained, 'This is one of Detective Josey's partners, Carl Norris. As you can see he's somewhat of a disguise artist.'

Josey eased in and told Geoff, 'We knew you wanted to see Mr Bourmac for yourself – so, we hope you enjoyed the show.'

He did, and continued laughing in appreciation.

His wife wasn't sure what to make of the whole performance. Her perplexed expression fuelled the raucous laughter that arose out of Denham Bourmac's utterly over-the-top antics.

CHAPTER THIRTY ONE
The sum of it

When the Josey and the Norris families arrived back at Aunt Jude's property, the first thing they laid eyes on was a brand new Delaware replacement, along with its original owner, Mrs Myrtle Arden. She had her hand to her mouth as though the shock of what happened to the young family was still resonating from weeks ago.

'You poor darlings,' she said sympathetically. 'What a nightmare you must have had.'

Josey didn't want to go there, so he focused on the shiny new mobile home. 'What do we have here?'

'Oh, now what's it look like; you couldn't have continued your holiday with what was left of that other wreck.'

She had a way with words.

'Don't look so suspicious,' she demanded, 'your van had full insurance. And, in case you didn't notice, I haven't cashed your check; which means I still own it.'

'Wow,' Molly expressed.

Josey knew registration papers constituted ownership, and that insurance policies don't pass over to new owners, but he let the old lady have her way - for the moment.

'All right,' Aunt Jude put in. 'Inside all of you,' she insisted.

'I'll be on my way and let you folks relax,' Myrtle decided, 'You must be exhausted after driving all the way from Sydney.'

Josey looked around for any sign of a car that might have brought the old lady from Condobolin. The only vehicles in sight were the Kia rental and Carl's Toyota.

Noticing, Jude told him, 'Johnny's taking Myrtle back, she wanted to see you all for one last time, isn't that right, Myrtle.'

'Well yes of course.'

One last time is often more real-than-not for the elderly.

'On that score, you'll be staying for lunch,' Jude instructed in her usually adamant manner; 'Johnny has more time than he knows what to do with – there's no hurry, come on in.'

They all followed her inside out of the hot sun. Molly and Rebecca locked arms; first up the stairs behind their host. Josey helped Myrtle negotiate the three timber steps while Carl and Nicole took up the rear with Johnny.

Well into the evening the familiar visitors negotiated Judith's house like leaves on a pond, floating in and out of rooms like they owned the place. Myrtle took up a chair in the breeze of an open window, mesmerized by the company so often not present at her own quiet little home.

An event that was meant to be just lunch turned into an entire afternoon of stories and reflections. The centre of attention shifted from one person to the next. Curiosities tended to draw an audience, creating zero inconsequential chatter.

Carl's talent for disguises was of great interest. People wanted to know how he learnt such a skill, even to the point of fooling people who knew him well, his ruse in the so-called love room an exceptional example.

'I couldn't let you know who I was,' he told mother and daughter, 'because they were watching the whole time, even though they said they weren't. And don't worry about the media they recorded, it's been destroyed.'

Josey's girls were still a little embarrassed by the whole affair. 'You don't need to explain,' Rebecca insisted, 'we thought you handled the situation very delicately.'

'Here-here,' Josey agreed.

Carl caught his eye. 'I can only imagine what you must have been going through, mate; I know that if it was Nicole dealing with what Rebecca and Molly had to, it would have broken me.'

Josey held on him, clearly having trouble responding.

Alarmed, Molly moved in and hooked onto his arm. 'Dad, are you all right?' she asked knowing full well he wasn't.

When his wife slid to his side and drew his attention enquiringly, it got the better of him. Emotion swamped his soul, raising imaginings of what could have happened to his family.

There was one person to thank for preventing the inevitable, and he was standing right in front of him. Carl needed to be recognized for his brave selfless act, but Josey's vocal cords cramped in his throat, only breaking free when he was unable to sidestep a wave of stress.

He sobbed in the arms of those that promptly encircled him with compassion and understanding.

Other tears were drawn; even Mrs Arden began to weep, a reaction she quickly arrested with the acquisition of a handkerchief from her purse.

Myrtle's stress prompted Aunt Judith to leave Johnny's side apologetically and offer support for the old lady.

Taking in the faces of the others, Rebecca's eyes bid they release him to her. Arms freed their soothing touch, allowing his wife to lead her husband to the cool of the verandah, away from the attention, to the calming blanket of night that stretched to infinity.

Noticing the old lady being comforted by Aunt Judith, Molly approached to see if she could help. 'Can I do anything for you Mrs Arden?'

She looked up at the young girl and said casting her eyes toward the open window, 'Yes, promise me you will look after that man out there, he has been handed a blow that no father should ever have to endure.'

Molly shed tears then and struggled to say, 'I will.'

Carl's wife Nicole, stood by her husband's side to offer her support, it was clear to her that he was battling with finding a way to console his boss – his friend.

'Baby,' she pleaded, 'leave it to Rebecca, she's just what he needs.'

Carl wasn't handling Josey's breakdown too well, it was something he'd never seen before, or ever wanted to again.

'Darling,' she told him fervently, 'I couldn't be more proud of you right now; and I'm pretty sure Cam feels the same way.'

He was too stressed to see it, but loved her so much for saying so.

Rebecca walked with Josey under the dome of stars, far enough away that the lights of the house became significantly tiny. She knew it would take more than a long walk to get her husband beyond this ordeal, yet she was well aware, time would bring him back to himself; back to the wonderful detective that he remains.

The upshot was, Josey, Rebecca and Molly recommenced their holiday a few days later, while Carl and Nicole remained with Aunt Judith on her property for around the same time.

Two weeks of travelling around in the motor home brought Josey and his family to the point where they couldn't wait to get back to Sydney, back to their spacious home. They travelled via Condobolin to drop off the motor home to Mrs Arden, telling her that she could resell it whenever she was ready.

Her response was, 'It will be sitting right here for you when you come back.'

They humoured her by not arguing, but deep down none of them wanted to see Condobolin ever again.

Josey insisted they pay a visit to Jerry Sullivan, and to

keep his promise to apologise for the conduct in keeping the discovery of his father's body to himself.

Leaning all responsibility onto Joe Magrie, the true villain, young Sullivan could not have been any more gracious or accepting.

Although Josey would never forget how close his family came to meeting their end, in the otherwise beautiful Central West of New South Wales, his life, and there's, soon resumed some semblance of normality; beginning with news from his other partner—Maxine Priest—that he had a case involving a writer, a writer who believed someone was stealing his work, and asking if Josey could investigate who it was and how to bring it to a stop.

He could barely wait to get back to work, to hear what Maxine had to say about their new client, back to a case that didn't involve mayhem and murder – or so he thought.

James William Davis

To view or order this or other works by J.W. Davis
go to
davisible.com

James William Davis

Holiday Horror

www.ingramcontent.com/pod-product-compliance
Lightning Source LLC
Chambersburg PA
CBHW020327120726
47904CB00002B/306